"Nick!"

Nick was at her side in a moment. "What's wrong?"

Swiveling to face him, Maddie grabbed his hand and pressed it to her stomach.

"The baby's kicking," Maddie said, and looked up to see her own wonder reflected in Nick's eyes. This wasn't the first time she'd felt the odd sensation, but it was the first time she'd realized what it was. Maddie started laughing. "I can't believe it. Can you feel my baby moving?"

"Yeah." Nick chuckled as he laid his other hand on Maddie's stomach. "Sure is rambunctious." The baby kicked again. "Come on, sweetheart," he coaxed. "Let us know you're in there."

"Easy for you to say. You're not the one the baby's kicking."

Maddie giggled at the absurdity of having four hands pressed her belly. Nick lifted his gaze to look into her eyes and the laughter died in her throat. For a moment, the world stood still, and everything else around them faded away. Everything except Nick, with his deep blue eyes, pulling her into their depths.

Dear Reader,

As the mother of a sixteen-year-old, I've recently become preoccupied with the two extremes of childhood—babies and teenagers.

Anybody who's ever held a newborn baby knows there's nothing as sweet or loving. Babies take hold of your heart and leave you totally vulnerable. You have no choice—you love unconditionally. I remember when my daughter was born, I often wondered who needed whom more. Then she grew up. And there's nothing more frustrating than living with a teenager. But this child, who claimed you at birth, has not let go of your heart. You still love unconditionally. No matter what madness she brings to your life.

Wouldn't it be interesting, I thought, if I could somehow combine the bliss of bringing home a new baby and the whirlwind of living with a teenager. And so Maddie came to life, a woman alone, waiting for the birth of her first child. And Nick, a man trying to understand the anger within his teenage son. Maddie and Nick find in each other the missing pieces of their lives and their hearts. Together they face their demons, and together they triumph.

But I'd be remiss if I left out one important ingredient: the magic moment when Nick's son first sees Maddie's infant daughter. Because not even teenagers can resist the lure of a newborn. And Nick's son is no exception.

Patricia Keelyn

P.S. I love to hear from my readers. Please feel free to write me at:

P.O. Box 72753
Marietta, Georgia
30007

Patricia Keelyn

Where the Heart Is

Harlequin Books

TORONTO • NEW YORK • LONDON
AMSTERDAM • PARIS • SYDNEY • HAMBURG
STOCKHOLM • ATHENS • TOKYO • MILAN
MADRID • WARSAW • BUDAPEST • AUCKLAND

ISBN 0-373-70631-6

WHERE THE HEART IS

Copyright © 1995 by Patricia Van Wie.

All rights reserved. Except for use in any review, the reproduction or utilization of this work in whole or in part in any form by any electronic, mechanical or other means, now known or hereafter invented, including xerography, photocopying and recording, or in any information storage or retrieval system, is forbidden without the written permission of the publisher, Harlequin Enterprises Limited, 225 Duncan Mill Road, Don Mills, Ontario, Canada M3B 3K9.

All characters in this book have no existence outside the imagination of the author and have no relation whatsoever to anyone bearing the same name or names. They are not even distantly inspired by any individual known or unknown to the author, and all incidents are pure invention.

This edition published by arrangement with Harlequin Enterprises B.V.

® and TM are trademarks of the publisher. Trademarks indicated with ® are registered in the United States Patent and Trademark Office, the Canadian Trade Marks Office and in other countries.

Printed in U.S.A.

Dedicated to Andrea,
who will always be my baby,
and to her brother, David,
who showed me how loving
a big brother could be.

And to Brenda Chin
and the rest of the Superromance department,
without whom Maddie and Nick's story
never would have been told.

A special thanks to Sharyn Kloster,
who's been answering my medical questions
for longer than either one of us wants to admit.

Thanks also to Carol Springston,
for the quick read and insightful comments.
To Debra Dixon,
for being unafraid to share what she's learned.
And to Gin Ellis,
for hitting me over the head with Roger.

CHAPTER ONE

WHY HAD SHE COME BACK?

As Maddie Aims maneuvered her sleek red Porsche through the center of Felton, Georgia, the question ran through her head like a broken record. *Why?* She scrutinized her surroundings, taking in the details, the sights, the sounds, the smells of the place—as if the answer were written here in the streets of her hometown.

At first she noticed only those things that had remained the same—Felton Square, the hodgepodge of stores and offices clustered along Main Street, the Baptist church, perched on a slope of land that marked the rise of the mountains behind the town, and the park, with the daffodils swaying in the gentle March breeze and the trees eager to burst into an array of soft greens.

Memories—good and bad—crowded her thoughts, vying for her attention. She'd spent the first seventeen years of her life in this town. A lifetime ago.

She pulled her car into one of the angled parking spaces facing the park and switched off the ignition. Then she sat a moment, a bit overwhelmed. The Gazebo, surrounded by bright yellow tulips, caught her eye. Her thoughts drifted back to the night she and

Nick had hidden from the sheriff underneath its freshly painted floorboards. She smiled at the memory and was tempted to get out to see if a certain section of latticework was still loose.

Then her mood darkened, and she restarted the car. She didn't want to think about Nick Ryan. She had enough to deal with right now, without dwelling on the past.

As she drove away from the park, she put Nick out of her mind and began to notice the changes in the town. Small, subtle things. There was a new video store between Dell's Bakery and Collier's Grocery, and the Felton Theater had six screens, instead of one. Randles Hardware had become Randles and Son, while the motel at the edge of town had been converted into an upscale bar and grill.

Progress.

Evidently time had not forgotten Felton. Even in this small town, lost in the mountains of northern Georgia, things could change. The thought reassured Maddie as she turned into Felton's tree-lined residential area. Maybe things would be different with her mother, as well.

But when she pulled into the driveway of her mother's house on Peachtree Lane, her confidence slipped away. For here, the march of time had stopped. She shut off the engine but made no move to get out of her car. The large house loomed before her with its clean white paint and perfectly manicured yard, looking exactly as it had the last time she'd seen it.

Sixteen years ago.

Opening the car door, she stepped out into the bright March sunlight. The air was cool and crisp and filled with the pungent smell of evergreen. She took a deep breath. This was one of the few things she'd missed about home—the clear, clean mountain air.

She leaned into the car and grabbed her purse. When she'd arrived in Felton last night, she'd phoned to tell her mother that she was in town and planned on stopping over this morning. Not surprisingly, Adelia hadn't sounded particularly pleased at the prospect of seeing her long-lost daughter. It had been months since they'd spoken, and years since they'd seen each other.

Still, Adelia *was* her mother, and because Maddie was in Felton, she knew she'd have to see Adelia at least once. Besides, there were things her mother had a right to know.

Adjusting her purse strap, Maddie made it up the walkway and onto the front porch before her courage deserted her. She considered opening the door and walking in, but quickly dismissed the idea. Taking a deep breath, she knocked.

After a few moments a small dark woman opened the door. "Yes?" she said. "May I help you?"

"Hello." Maddie forced a smile. "I'm Maddie Aims. Is my mother at home?"

The woman's surprise was obvious. It made Maddie wonder if Adelia had bothered to inform her maid about her daughter's imminent arrival.

"Who is it, Frances?" came an all-too-familiar voice from the direction of the sitting room.

That voice, cold as a late-winter frost, sent a chill down Maddie's spine. She almost told Frances "never mind." She didn't need to talk to her mother in person. The phone would do, as it had in the past. She could get through the next few months without any help from the Ice Queen.

But Maddie was here, so she might as well go through with it. Pulling herself together, she brushed past the maid and headed toward her mother's sitting room.

"It's me, Mother. Maddie." She stopped on the threshold of the room and waited as Adelia rose from her chair.

"Madeleine?"

It jarred Maddie to see how little her mother had changed. She was still the tall stately widow. A little grayer and thinner, perhaps, but time had been kind to her. She still looked like the Adelia Aims Maddie remembered. "Hello, Mother."

Adelia said nothing, but stood ramrod straight, one hand braced against the back of a nearby chair, the expression in her pale blue eyes unreadable.

"May I come in?" Maddie asked. This was Adelia's room, and for as long as Maddie could remember, it had been off-limits to her except at her mother's invitation.

Adelia gave a start, as if the sound of Maddie's voice had surprised her. "Of course." She edged away from the chair, but didn't release her hold on it. "This is your home, too."

Maddie knew better than to believe that. She'd stopped thinking of this as her home around the time she'd turned twelve, when she'd gone to live with her father. Even when she was forced to come back after his death, this house had remained Adelia's.

"Come in," Adelia repeated, though she still made no move toward her daughter.

Maddie braced herself and stepped into the room slowly, absorbing the details of her mother's sanctuary. Like Adelia, the room remained unchanged. Adelia's taste had always run toward delicate expensive furniture covered in muted floral pastels. No doubt there had been some refurbishment, new wallpaper and draperies, possibly new upholstery, but basically the room looked the same as it had sixteen years ago.

Maddie preferred her Miami condominium. She loved the clean straight lines, the uncluttered surfaces and the white-on-white with just a splash of bold color. She knew her mother would hate it.

"Nothing's changed," Adelia said as if to reassure her daughter.

Maddie took a seat on the settee across from Adelia's chair. "I can see that." But it wasn't the room that Maddie referred to. It was her mother, and the coolness of her response to the daughter she hadn't seen in years.

Adelia remained standing, and Maddie noticed the way she unconsciously pulled at the seam on the top of her chair. It seemed an odd thing for her mother to do. Adelia never fidgeted.

"You look well, Madeleine," Adelia said, abruptly changing the direction of Maddie's thoughts.

"Do I?"

"Yes." Adelia lifted her free hand to rest against the collar of her ivory silk blouse, making Maddie suddenly aware of her own shoddy appearance.

Glancing down at her gray sweats and tennis shoes, she apologized before she could stop herself. "I'm sorry. I should have changed. But I..." She hated this compulsion she had to automatically offer an explanation. "I haven't unpacked yet."

Adelia nodded, her face an impassive mask, and Maddie knew her apology had fallen on deaf ears. The old resentment rose like bile in her throat, and she found herself remembering all the reasons she'd avoided her mother for the past sixteen years. All the arguments. All the tears. She had the strongest urge to get up and walk out. It would save them both a lot of anguish.

Then the sequence of events that had brought her home clambered to the surface of her thoughts, and she realized that nothing her mother might say could touch her. With the weight of Roger's indecision still heavy on her heart, nothing else mattered. Except the joy. She slid her hand to the small swell of her stomach.

Finally Adelia moved around the chair to sit. "Why the sudden visit?"

"I'm not here for a visit."

Adelia carefully folded her hands in her lap. "Oh?"

"No." She met her mother's cool blue gaze and kept her voice even. "I'm planning to stay in Felton for a while."

"Really. How long?"

Maddie shifted uncomfortably, suddenly uncertain how to break her news. "I'm not sure."

"Would you like some tea?" Adelia asked. "Or coffee, perhaps? Frances is a fine cook and she made some fresh pastries this morning."

"Yes." Maddie breathed a sigh of relief at the temporary reprieve. "Either would be fine."

"Frances," Adelia called as she stood and moved toward the hallway, where the maid appeared. "Bring us a tray, please. Coffee?" She glanced back at Maddie for confirmation. "And some of those wonderful croissants you made this morning."

Frances headed for the kitchen, and Adelia stood in the doorway for a moment, before turning to reenter the room. She smiled at Maddie, the same stiff smile Maddie had seen a thousand times over the years—the smile Adelia used whenever she had to deal with any unpleasantness.

Maddie deserted the couch and moved to the window, keeping her back to her mother as they waited for the coffee. Again, she questioned her sudden decision to return to Felton. Oh, she understood why she'd left Miami. But why come here? Why come to Felton when she could have gone anywhere? And in particular, why had she decided to visit her mother when it would have been simpler to phone?

They'd never been close. Even as a child, Maddie had always been her father's daughter. When Adelia had kicked her husband out of her house, Maddie had screamed and fought until they let her live with him. After that, Maddie and Adelia's relationship had only become worse.

Unconsciously she let her hand again stray to her stomach.

Two weeks ago she'd returned to Miami from a business trip overseas, feeling sicker than she could ever remember. Afraid that she'd picked up some exotic bug in her travels, she'd gone in to see her doctor. His diagnosis had been the last thing she'd expected. Then she and Roger had argued. Although it wasn't an argument, really. Just a discussion that had left her dreams for their future shattered into a million pieces. That was when her blood pressure had soared through the roof, and her doctor told her to stop working and get some rest. In a matter of fourteen short days, days that seemed more like a lifetime, her world had come unraveled.

Maybe that was the reason she'd returned to Felton. She'd come back to the familiar. And that included Adelia.

When Frances delivered the tray, Maddie returned to her seat. Adelia poured and handed the first cup to Maddie, whose stomach churned at the strong aroma. She should have asked for tea. Setting the cup aside, she decided she'd postponed the inevitable long enough.

"I'll be here six or seven months. Eight at the most."

"I see." Adelia returned the silver pot to its tray and picked up the plate of pastries, offering them to Maddie.

"Thank you." Maddie took one, hoping to still the queasiness in her stomach.

Adelia picked up her cup and took a sip of coffee. Then she said, "I suppose you'll be staying at the house Davis left you." She refused to refer to her deceased husband any other way than by his first name. He was never "my husband" or "your father." He was just "Davis."

Maddie hated that.

"Yes, I'll be staying at *Father's* house."

"What kind of trouble are you in?" Putting down her cup, Adelia leaned back and folded her hands in her lap. "Have you lost your job? Do you need money?"

Maddie returned the untouched pastry to the table. "What makes you think I'm in trouble?"

"Why else would you have come back?"

Why indeed?

Maddie had always made excuses for not returning home to the cold atmosphere of her mother's house. She knew it, and so did Adelia.

"I haven't lost my job. I've taken an extended leave of absence. And I have enough money to carry me through." She didn't know why she didn't just blurt it out. She'd always prided herself on her directness. But not with her mother. Never with her mother.

Adelia retrieved her coffee cup. "Of course, it will be nice to have you in town for a while."

Silence filled the room, and Maddie knew her time had run out. She couldn't put off telling her mother any longer. "Mother." This time she met Adelia's ice blue gaze and forced her voice to remain steady. "I'm going to have a baby."

Adelia froze, cup in hand. Then, after what seemed an eternity, she set down her coffee and almost missed the edge of the table, catching the fragile china just in time.

"A baby?"

Maddie nodded, her voice suddenly caught somewhere between her lungs and her lips.

"Well, I..." Adelia clenched her hands in her lap, but not before Maddie saw them tremble. "A baby," she repeated, pressing her lips together, while letting her gaze drift around the room. For a few moments, Maddie thought she saw a faint shimmer of moisture in her mother's eyes. Then Adelia focused on her daughter, and Maddie realized her mistake.

"Of all things." Adelia's words were no more than a whisper, but they were rife with disapproval. "How could you?"

The question stunned Maddie. "How could I?" Then anger replaced her surprise. "How could I what, Mother? Become pregnant? Or embarrass you?"

Maddie propelled herself off the couch and returned to the window, hugging herself tightly. She'd been wrong. Her mother's criticism still stung. And she suddenly realized with blinding clarity why she'd come home.

"That's not what I meant," her mother said.

"Isn't it?"

"No."

Maddie forced back her tears. Somewhere deep inside, she'd hoped her mother would help her deal with the sorrow and the joy this unborn child had brought her. She should have known better. Adelia had never thought of anyone but herself. Maddie turned to glare at her mother. "Then what did you mean?"

"You're not a child. How could you have allowed such a thing to happen?" Adelia lifted her chin as if to emphasize her words. "There's no excuse for it today."

"You're assuming, Mother, that it *was* an accident."

The statement stopped Adelia cold, as if she couldn't imagine planning such a thing. But it was an accident. A crazy accident that Maddie couldn't be sorry about. Even though it scared her. Even though it had made Roger turn away from her.

"What about the father?" Adelia asked.

What *about* Roger?

A fresh wave of nausea churned Maddie's stomach, and she grabbed the back of the couch to steady herself. He didn't know if he wanted her anymore. He wasn't sure he could deal with being a husband and father.

"What about the father?" Adelia asked again, more insistently this time.

Burying her fear, Maddie kept her voice steady. "We're not together right now."

"Not together. What does that mean?"

"What do you think it means?" Maddie snapped.

Silence. Again. Maddie felt locked in the hard glare of her mother's eyes.

"Have you thought this through, Madeleine?" Adelia asked. "Have you considered the consequences?"

Maddie lifted her chin, refusing to flinch under Adelia's iron scrutiny. "I'm thirty-three years old, Mother."

"And unmarried."

"This is the nineties." Maddie crossed her arms, refusing to give ground and let her mother see the turmoil within her. "I don't care what people say about me."

Adelia shook her head. "It's not that. Raising a child alone is difficult. Ask me. I know."

Maddie circled the couch and sat down on the edge. Despite her fear she held on to her joy like a lifeline. And she wasn't going to let anyone take it away.

"Mother. I want this baby."

Adelia sat without speaking for several moments, her hands still clenched in her lap. "Well," she finally said, her words falling like chipped ice, "it looks like nothing's changed. You are still your father's daughter, doing what you want no matter what the consequences."

"You're right, Mother. I haven't changed." Maddie stood, once again wrapping herself in an invisible cloak of indifference. "And neither have you."

LATER, ALONE in her father's house, Maddie let the tears flow unchecked. Wrapped in an afghan, she sat curled in the rocker she'd carried upstairs from the living room. The windows stood open, and she welcomed the feel of the cool night air against her skin. It was nearly midnight, and it seemed as if the rest of the world slept.

What had she expected from Adelia?

It was an old question, an old disappointment. But it still had the power to hurt. She knew better than to expect anything from her mother. And yet, she'd come here thinking, hoping, things might be different between them.

It was obviously too much to ask.

"So what do you think, Baby?" Maddie whispered to the child growing inside her. "Should we stay in Felton?"

Maddie closed her eyes and pictured her baby as it must look now. It would be about the size of Maddie's closed hand, with soft nails on its fingers and toes, and hair just beginning to appear on its head. A couple of weeks ago Maddie had known nothing about pregnancy. Since then, she'd devoured several books on the subject, familiarizing herself with each phase of her baby's development.

"I know it's a little scary," Maddie continued in a low voice. "Being alone right now." *Without your father.*

Again, fear and loneliness washed over her. She'd wanted so much from Roger. Maybe too much. "I'll manage," she said aloud. She had this house and enough money put aside to last awhile. "No matter what Roger decides."

She glanced at the phone by the bed. Maybe she should call, just to tell him she'd arrived safely. Then she shook her head and turned to gaze back out the bedroom window. No. He'd said he needed time. Time to decide whether he was ready to be a husband and father. Even though they'd lived together for the past three years, he'd said he wasn't sure he could deal with commitment. And she'd had no choice but to give him the time he'd asked for.

She pressed her hands against her abdomen, trying to communicate her love to her unborn child. How long before she would feel movement? The books said another two months. It seemed an eternity. Maddie smiled, thinking how miraculous it would be to hold her baby in her arms. It would make all the problems she faced worth it. And how much more wonderful if Roger came to her, ready and willing to stand by her side. But if he didn't, maybe this child would help her forget as she made a place for the two of them.

"JON!" NICK RYAN called as he stored away the last of his tools. "Are you done?"

Nick closed his toolbox while listening for his son's reply. When none came, he crossed the room and stepped outside. He glanced around the yard, but Jon was nowhere in sight. Stepping off the porch, Nick headed around to the side of the house where the boy was supposed to be working.

"Jonathan!" he called again, irritated when he saw the pile of lumber still lying in the yard. It looked untouched. "Damn it!" He'd had just about enough of the boy's laziness.

Nick walked around back where the yard abruptly ended at the edge of an evergreen woods. As he'd suspected, he found Jon sitting on a log, scribbling in that damn notebook of his. Nick would give a lot to see the contents of the thing; the boy carried it with him everywhere. For now, though, there was work left unfinished.

"I thought I told you to put that lumber in the shed," Nick said.

At the sound of his father's voice, Jon jumped to his feet and quickly closed his notebook. "I was going to do it," he said defensively.

"When?" Nick glanced at his watch before dropping his hands to the waistband of his jeans. "I told you to do it three hours ago. And now I need to get back to the office."

Jon shrugged and boldly met Nick's gaze. "Sorry," he mumbled, and started to walk past his father toward the pile of lumber.

Nick snagged his arm as he went by, and Jon turned, his eyes sparking with more than teenage rebellion. Nick's irritation melted into pain. The boy's dark eyes were so like Sarah's, while the anger Nick saw in them was so like his own.

"Jon," he said softly, wanting desperately to reach his son, this boy who'd become a stranger. "I know you're hurting. We both are."

Jon remained defiantly silent.

Nick nodded toward the house. "I thought we'd agreed that finishing the house together would help us both."

"I never agreed to anything." Jon yanked his arm from his father's grasp. "*You* decided for both of us."

Nick shook his head. "It's what your mother would have wanted."

"My mother's dead."

"You're not the only one who misses her." Nick reined in his churning emotions. "She was *my* wife, remember? That's why I thought this house—"

"Mom hated this house!"

"That's not true," Nick said.

"It *is* true. And she hated this town. She only stayed so you could feel like a big shot."

"That's enough." Nick's anger rose, replacing the helplessness he felt when dealing with Jon. "I'm your father, and I won't have you talking to me that way."

The boy was beyond caring. "It's your fault!"

Nick's anger collapsed, deflated by the agony in Jon's eyes and the fear that maybe he was right.

"If you hadn't dragged us to this hick town, she wouldn't have started drinking." Jon's agitation grew to near hysteria, and his voice cracked ominously. "You killed her!"

The accusation fell like a dark impenetrable wall between them. Sarah's death had brought them to this impasse. And Nick didn't know if there was anything he could do about it.

No! He shook his head. He wouldn't give up. On either of them.

"Jon." He reached out to touch his son, but Jon took a step out of reach, tears brimming in his eyes.

"I hate you!" he screamed, and tore off in the direction of the road.

"Jon, wait!" But the boy kept running. Nick suppressed the impulse to go after him, to try reasoning with him once again. What could he say that he hadn't already said a dozen times? How could he defend himself against an accusation that had buried itself in his soul with the sharp sting of truth? How could he help the boy when he wasn't even sure he could help himself?

Nick walked over to the pile of lumber, his thoughts on his wife. Sarah had missed Atlanta. He'd known that. But there hadn't been anything he could do about it. They'd come to Felton when her father had suffered a heart attack. Ted Sommer had needed someone to care for his medical practice while he recovered. Who better than the son-in-law to whom he'd been a mentor and put through medical school?

But even after Ted had been back on his feet for months, getting stronger every day, he wasn't ready for his daughter's family to leave. They were all he had. Nick understood. Although in truth, Nick admitted to himself now, he hadn't been ready to leave, either. He'd come back to the place of his childhood and found his home.

So he'd stalled Sarah, telling her they'd return to Atlanta soon. He hadn't known how serious the situation had become—the drinking or her hatred of Felton. He'd been blind, and she'd paid the price. And he couldn't get past the fact that he could have prevented it. If only he'd been paying attention.

But it wasn't too late for Jon.

Maybe the time had come to leave Felton. He could pack up and take Jon back to Atlanta. Ted wouldn't be happy about it. But what good would it do any of them to stay if Ted and Nick lost the boy in the process?

Fifteen minutes later, Nick climbed into his truck and picked up his cellular phone. He dialed his office, and Bette answered on the third ring. "Doctors' office. May I help you?"

"Bette," Nick said to his nurse, "I'm running about a half hour late. Can you ask Ted to cover for me?"

"Sure thing, Doctor."

"Thanks." Nick braced his head with his hand, rubbing at the headache building behind his eyes. "Where would I be without you?"

"Probably in some sewer somewhere."

It was an old joke, and Nick laughed shortly, although there was no humor in it. "See you in a while."

He clicked off the phone, started his truck and headed down the dirt road, watching for Jon. When he saw him, Nick breathed a sigh of relief, grateful for once at his son's predictability. Jon was walking along the road, heading for the highway. He'd probably convinced himself he was going to walk the three miles back to Felton.

Nick stopped the truck alongside the boy and leaned over to open the passenger door. "Get in, son."

Jon glared at him, and Nick noticed the smears on his face where he'd wiped away his tears. The sight brought a fresh ache to Nick's soul. He hadn't a clue what this boy needed. What either of them needed.

"Come on," he added, suddenly exhausted. "I took care of the lumber."

Jon hesitated a moment longer before climbing into the truck and slamming the door behind him. Nick bit back the automatic admonishment that sprang to his lips. Complaining about slamming doors wouldn't get him anywhere. So Nick took a deep breath and put the truck into gear.

Damn it, Sarah! he silently cursed. *Your son needs you. I need you!*

CHAPTER TWO

MADDIE HATED doctors' offices. They made her feel like a child again. First a nurse told you to undress and gave you a paper covering to put on. Then you sat and waited in a room a tad too chilly, on a table high enough so that your legs dangled in space.

Of course it didn't help that she'd waited in this same examining room when she was a kid. A room that looked exactly as it had twenty years ago. Dr. Ted Sommer—who must be as old as Methuselah by now—had kept everything the same. Not even the wallpaper had changed. It still displayed grinning clowns holding bunches of balloons. She smiled wryly. Today no doctor would dare put this wallpaper on his examining room walls.

Tired of sitting on the table, Maddie scooted off and moved to a chair under the window, careful to keep the paper smock tucked around her. She may have to sit in this room that reeked of her childhood, but there was no reason she couldn't do so more comfortably. Picking up a copy of *Parenting* that someone had left behind, she started thumbing through it.

Absorbed in an article on newborns, Maddie didn't hear the door open.

"Hello, Maddie."

The deep voice, a familiar echo from the past, pulled her from her reading. She looked up and met a pair of brilliant blue eyes that spoke to her of the best and worst parts of her adolescence.

For a moment she couldn't speak. The shock of finding this man standing in the doorway was too unsettling. The last time she'd seen him, he'd been on the verge of adulthood. Now, here he stood, a man who'd fulfilled all the promise of that long-ago boy.

"Nick?"

"Yeah." He smiled, but she saw the hesitation in his eyes. "How are you?"

She rose slowly from the chair as waves of memories threatened to overwhelm her. For several moments she was unable to make sense of her runaway thoughts or the emotions clamoring in her heart. Then one memory surfaced above the rest. Nick's betrayal. And the long days and weeks she'd cried over losing him.

"Good. I'm good." The voice was hers, but it sounded odd, distant, a little too automatic. "I didn't know you were in Felton."

Nick moved farther into the examining room, closing the door behind him. "I've been here for almost three years."

Her gaze dropped to his white lab coat and the stethoscope hanging around his neck. Suddenly she became all too aware of her present state of undress and quickly crossed her arms. "And you're a doctor, I see."

Nick glanced away for a moment before bringing his gaze back to rest on her. "It's been a long time, Maddie."

She thought she heard more in his words, more than the awkwardness that edged his voice. There was regret, too. And maybe some guilt. "Yes, well, I guess there wasn't much point in getting together after all these years." She tucked her trembling hands tighter under her elbows.

Once more, Nick's gaze slid away. "No, I guess not."

An awkward silence filled the room.

Maddie uncrossed her arms, only to cross them again, wishing for some real clothing. Nick didn't seem to notice. He just stood there, absorbed in his own thoughts, obviously as uncomfortable as she was. Why had he come in here? It was a question she couldn't begin to answer. So she searched for something to say, anything to end this uneasy reunion and send Nick on his way. Nothing came to mind. After all these years, she couldn't think of a single thing to say to him. Nothing safe, at least.

Finally she could no longer bear the silence. "I'm happy for you, Nick." Her voice brought his gaze back to her. "That you got through medical school, I mean. I know it's what you wanted." She tried to smile, but wasn't sure she'd succeeded. "And I always knew you'd make it."

"You were the only one who did." A tenuous smile warmed his eyes, those luminous sapphire eyes that had captured her heart when she'd been no more than a child. "You and Ted Sommer."

"Yes, well..." Heat rushed to Maddie's cheeks, and she fought the urge to turn away. "What did the low-lifes in this town know?"

Nick shrugged and slipped his hands into the pockets of his lab coat. "Not much, I guess."

Maddie realized he was as lethal a man as he had been a boy. Maybe more so. His hair was still black as sin, his skin the rich whiskey brown of temptation, while his blue eyes promised the innocence of sun-drenched summer days. It was an entrancing contrast. One she refused to fall victim to again.

Hoping her voice sounded normal, she forced herself to ask the next question. "How is Sarah?"

He shifted to lean against the examining table, and a shadow flickered across his features. "She died. About a year and a half ago."

It was a shock. The last thing she'd expected to hear. "I'm sorry," she said. And she meant it. As often as she'd cursed Sarah Sommer sixteen years ago for taking Nick away from her, Maddie had never wished the other woman harm.

Nick nodded, accepting her expression of condolence. "How about you?" he asked. Again his eyes held a tentative curiosity, as if he feared she'd refuse to speak to him. "I'm surprised to see you back in Felton."

"Yes, well, life's full of surprises."

Nick smiled tightly, thinking that surprise didn't begin to describe his reaction to seeing Maddie again. When he'd noticed her name on Ted's appointment schedule, the past had swept over him, bringing a mixture of sweet memories and regret. He'd had to see her. Then he'd walked into the room, and she'd looked up at him with those seductive gray eyes of hers, and he felt sixteen all over again. And for a moment, he'd only remembered the sweetness.

"So," he said, when she volunteered no further information, "how long have you been back?"

Maddie sat back down in the chair, placing the magazine on her lap. "About a week." She seemed calm and collected, as if they'd never been more than casual acquaintances. For reasons Nick couldn't begin to understand, that bothered him.

"Are you planning on staying?"

Maddie shrugged. "For a few months, anyway."

Nick didn't know what else to say. There were many other things he wanted to tell her. But not now. Not here. "Maybe we could get together sometime," he said. "Talk about old times."

Maddie shook her head, her eyes wide and wary. "I don't think so, Nick."

He started to object, but suddenly the door opened and Ted Sommer stepped into the room.

"Sorry, Nick," he said. "I didn't know you were in here."

"That's okay." Nick stepped aside to give Ted a clear view of Maddie. "I was just saying hello to an old friend. You remember Maddie, don't you?"

"Of course." Ted crossed the room and took Maddie's hand in his. "She used to be one of my favorite patients."

"How are you, Dr. Sommer?" Maddie gave the older man a smile, and envy tightened in Nick's stomach. She hadn't smiled for him, and it smarted.

Though he knew he had no right to expect anything from Maddie. Not even a smile.

"It's good to see you back in Felton, Madeleine." Ted leaned over and kissed her on the cheek. "And expecting a baby, too. Congratulations!"

"Thanks." Color rose to Maddie's cheeks, and she glanced at Nick. "I was just about to tell Nick about the baby."

Nick forced a smile as the thought of Maddie bringing someone—a man, the father of her baby—back to Felton with her wreaked havoc with his insides. He just barely controlled the urge to ask about the guy.

"Congratulations," he said, instead. "Are you planning on having the baby here?"

Maddie nodded and turned her attention back to Ted. "If Dr. Sommer thinks it's a good idea."

"I think it's a wonderful idea!" Ted beamed and patted her hand.

"Great," Nick said aloud, though his mind still reeled at the thought of seeing Maddie with another man, and the knowledge he had absolutely no right to feel anything but happy for her.

He needed to get out of here. He needed room to think. To breathe. "Well," he said, "I better get back to work before my boss finds me loafing."

"It was good to see you again, Nick." Maddie met his gaze, and he saw the relief that belied her words. She, too, had felt the strain of their unexpected meeting.

"Yes. You, too." He moved to the door, but stopped before closing it behind him. "I'll see you around, Maddie."

"Yes," she said. "Sure." She reached up to brush a strand of ebony hair behind her ear, and Nick saw the slight tremor in her hand. Maybe she wasn't as indifferent to him as she seemed.

Nick left the examining room and went to his office. Closing the door behind him, he lowered himself into the chair behind his desk.

Maddie.

A million memories—sweet, sweet memories—whirled through his mind. Leaning his head against the back of his chair, he closed his eyes, letting the past wash over him.

For four years, Maddie had been the only light in his life, the dream that had kept him from succumbing to the reality of his world. He'd always loved her. They were best friends—and more—for most of their teenage years. But she was a girl from the right side of town, and he... well, Maddie never belonged with a guy like him.

And he'd proved that, hadn't he? He'd taken everything she had to give—body and soul—and then thrown it away.

Regret, like a black pool, swirled about him, pushing the sweetness of the past aside. He'd made so many mistakes. Hurt too many people. Maddie and Sarah.

Now Maddie was back in Felton and expecting another man's child. It shook him to the core. And in that moment he realized he'd never really gotten over her.

MADDIE STEPPED outside the clinic and lifted her face to the sun, seeking its warmth. Dr. Sommer had given her positive news. Her high blood pressure, which had sent her running from the stress of Miami, had come down significantly since she'd returned to Felton. With the proper diet, rest and exercise, he'd told her it should be back to normal within a couple of weeks. She and her baby were going to be fine.

It looked like coming home had been a good decision, after all.

She started toward the parking lot and then changed her mind. She'd come back for her car later. She was expected for lunch at the house of her closest childhood friend, Lynn Banks. It was only a few blocks away, and since Dr. Sommer had told her to get lots of exercise, today seemed a good time to start.

As she set off for Lynn's, Maddie's thoughts returned to Nick. He looked wonderful. The teenager who'd been Felton High's leading heartthrob was nothing compared to the devastatingly handsome man he'd become. Still tall and lean, he'd broadened across the chest and shoulders, making her instantly aware he was no longer a boy. His size, and those damnable blue eyes of his, were enough to thaw any woman's heart.

She could deal with his looks.

There were other things about him that worried her more, things that weren't so easy to dismiss. The memories of their shared past, for one. His grief, for another. She'd seen his distress when she'd mentioned Sarah. And despite the heartbreak he'd once caused her, she'd wanted to reach out to him. They'd been so close once. It was hard to forget....

Maddie took another deep breath and pushed aside the disturbing memories. It was ancient history. *He* was ancient history. He'd made his choice ages ago, when they were both little more than children. There was nothing she could do for him now.

She found Lynn's house easily.

As kids, she and Lynn had passed this way every day on their way to and from school, and their conversation had often centered around "the house." It had been abandoned for years, and Maddie considered it a monstrosity. She claimed it was designed by a drunken architect—or not designed at all, just randomly pieced together by a builder who added rooms whenever the whim struck him. Lynn, on the other hand, loved it and declared that someday she'd buy it and turn it into a showplace.

Now, as Maddie stood on the sidewalk in front of Lynn's house, she acknowledged her friend's foresight. The house still wasn't one Maddie would have chosen, but there was something magical about the ivy-covered turrets, the sparkling stained-glass windows and the mishmash of architectural styles. Something that reminded her of Lynn.

A few moments later, she stood on the front porch and rang the doorbell. A scurry of paws against hardwood floors, along with a rash of barking, greeted her arrival, and Maddie laughed aloud.

"Quiet, Butch," commanded Lynn from the other side of the door, which did nothing to alleviate the animal's excitement. "Just a minute," she called, and then to the dog added, "Come on, Butch. It's out in the backyard for you." Her voice drifted away, along with the whine of the animal.

Maddie tried to imagine Lynn handling a dog that sounded like he outweighed her by a good fifty pounds. Of course, Maddie had never quite figured out how Lynn handled her husband, Jack Banks, either. He'd been Felton High's star linebacker, and at six four, he towered over Lynn's five-foot-two frame.

Just then the door swung open, and her old friend stood in the entrance.

"Don't I get to meet Butch?" Maddie asked with a grin. "He sounds like a charmer."

"Only if you like big hairy beasts," Lynn answered, her eyes full of mischief.

Maddie crossed her arms and gave an exaggerated sigh. "You were always the one with a thing for oversize males."

Lynn laughed and opened her arms. "Come here, you. Give me a hug."

Maddie stepped forward and hugged her friend fiercely.

"Just look at you," Lynn said as she pulled back, checking Maddie out from head to toe. "You look absolutely fabulous. Lord, I bet you're still a size six."

Maddie laughed and gave her another quick hug. "Not anymore."

"You can't possibly be three months pregnant." Lynn stepped back and cast an appraising eye on Maddie's middle.

"Ah, the wonders of bulky clothing." Maddie lifted her sweater and turned sideways, showing off her budding tummy.

"What's that?" Lynn leaned over to rest a hand on Maddie's stomach. "Is that supposed to be a baby in there? Or did you just drink too much beer last night?"

"Very funny!" Maddie let her sweater drop back into place. "You haven't changed a bit. In fact, I think you've gotten more irreverent with age."

"Nah." Lynn dismissed Maddie's comment with a wave of her hand. "I'm just more vocal about it now. And because of my age, I get away with it."

Maddie shook her head and smiled. "It's good to see you."

"You, too." Lynn linked an arm through Maddie's and led her toward the back of the house. "Come on. I sent the kids out for the afternoon and I've fixed us a special lunch. Chicken salad with all the trimmings. I assumed that you, like the rest of us, needed to watch your fat intake. Little did I know you could probably stand to gain a few pounds."

"On the contrary. Dr. Sommer told me to watch what I eat. Besides, I like chicken salad." Maddie gave Lynn's arm a squeeze. "How many kids?"

"Three. One in high school. And I have to tell you, I have no idea how I'm going to survive the next four years."

Maddie laughed, doubting there was anything Lynn couldn't handle.

They stepped into a large modern kitchen where sunlight streamed in from the skylights overhead. Lynn had set the table for two, with brightly colored place mats and fresh flowers.

"You shouldn't have gone to so much trouble," Maddie said as she took in the appealing setting.

"What trouble? A couple of place mats and flowers I picked up at Collier's yesterday. Go on," Lynn said, motioning toward a chair. "Sit down. Everything's ready. I just need to pull it out of the fridge."

Watching Lynn move around her kitchen, Maddie realized just how many years had passed since she'd last seen her friend. Time had worked its magic, and Lynn looked every bit the head of this old house. She hadn't grown an inch, at least not in height, but she possessed the confidence that came only with maturity.

"So, did you happen to notice that Dr. Sommer has a partner now?" Lynn asked.

"Nick? Yes. It was a bit of a surprise."

Lynn lifted her eyebrows. "Yummy, huh?"

"He always was."

"Yup. And it looks like you were right about him all along." Lynn headed for the refrigerator, pulled out two covered bowls and set them on the table. "I have to tell you, we all thought you were crazy back in high school. We were jealous as hell, but we thought you were crazy nonetheless."

"You just didn't know him." Maddie started removing the coverings from the bowls while Lynn returned to the refrigerator. In some ways, her friends had been more right than they knew. More right than Maddie would ever admit.

"Ha." Juggling a pitcher of iced tea and a plate of sliced melon, Lynn returned to the table and sat down across from Maddie. "We knew enough."

"You didn't know anything. Nick was special. Did you know he took care of his father from the time he was twelve. *Twelve,* Lynn."

Lynn interrupted Maddie with a wave of her hand. "I heard that stuff sixteen years ago. He was a great guy." Resting her elbows on the table, Lynn leaned forward. "So come on. Tell me what was really going on between you two."

Maddie reached for the iced tea and filled both their glasses. Keeping her voice steady, she said, "There's nothing to tell. We were friends."

"Come on, Maddie, we're adults now. Do tell."

Maddie did a quick cross-your-heart with two fingers and raised her hand as if taking an oath. At Lynn's look of total disbelief, Maddie burst out laughing. What could it hurt to tell Lynn the truth now? "All right," she said. "So there was more between Nick and me than friendship."

Lynn sat forward in her chair. "How much more?"

"I was in love with him."

"I know that." Lynn wiggled her eyebrows suggestively. "I want the details."

Maddie rolled her eyes skyward. "Okay. So he was my first."

"I knew it!"

"You didn't." Maddie shook her head, not believing Lynn for a minute. She and Nick had been very discreet. They hadn't even held hands in public. "You were just guessing."

"Are you kidding? All those hours you spent with him." Lynn sat back in her chair. "Those nights you snuck out of the house to meet him. The ones I covered for you. How could I not know?"

"You only thought you knew."

"So what happened?"

Maddie propped her elbow on the table and rested her chin on her hand. "Sarah happened."

"Why the little—"

"My feelings exactly," Maddie interrupted. "But really, Lynn. It was a long time ago. And the woman's dead."

Lynn looked properly contrite. "Sorry." A few moments later she asked, "Do you still love him?"

"It's been sixteen years."

"What difference does that make?"

Maddie shook her head, wanting to change the subject. Her relationship with Nick was old news. "Can we eat now? I'm starved."

"Sorry, I forgot. You're pregnant." Lynn laughed and handed Maddie the plate of melon before jumping up to grab a bag of potato chips from the counter. "And pregnant women need their nourishment."

"I thought you said this was a low-fat meal?"

"I said, with all the trimmings." Lynn popped open the bag of chips. "These are the trimmings."

Maddie laughed, and they dug into their lunch. A few moments later she asked, "How did Sarah die?"

Lynn sobered immediately. "It seems she was out driving. It was a miserable night, one of the worst storms of the year. The rumor is she was drinking. Anyway, she missed a curve north of town." Lynn shook her head and turned back to her lunch. "It was really horrible."

"Poor Nick."

"He has a teenage son. Jon. My daughter, Anna, knows him pretty well. She says he's still taking it hard. I imagine they both are." She paused for a moment, before looking up and adding, "Maddie, you haven't said anything about the father of your baby. So I assumed—"

"Lynn..." Maddie started, but stopped when her friend shook her head and held up a hand.

"I know. It's none of my business. I was just going to say that you and Nick were close once. Nick could really use a friend right now. And—" she hesitated a moment "—my guess is so could you."

Maddie's gaze shifted away. "That was a long time ago, Lynn."

"Was it?" Lynn's strange question brought Maddie's eyes back to her. "Was it really that long ago?"

Maddie nodded. "A lifetime."

After that, Lynn turned the conversation to happier topics, and the rest of the afternoon passed quickly. They talked about past escapades and old acquaintances—who was doing what, who'd married whom, who'd stayed in Felton and who had left. It was hard to believe they hadn't seen each other in sixteen years. It felt like yesterday.

Then the front door burst open, shattering the illusion. They were immediately surrounded by boisterous children and a hyperactive canine. Lynn introduced her brood, including Butch, handling the chaos with an aplomb Maddie envied and doubted she could ever achieve.

It was time for her to leave.

With a series of hugs and promises to return, Maddie let herself out the front door. She stood on the porch to catch her breath. While she'd idled away the hours with Lynn, the day had dimmed, returning to its normal state of winter gray. Behind her, she could still hear the sounds of the family inside, and for a moment she envied Lynn.

Would her own life ever bear any semblance of normalcy? Would she ever have a home and family like Lynn? She thought of Roger and the dreams she'd put on hold because he needed time. She'd thought she'd finally found her place with him. She loved him. And for the past three years she'd lived with him, believing he returned that love.

She fought back the tears that always seemed so close to the surface lately. She'd been a fool. Roger had only wanted her as long as it was convenient, as long as she fit his life-style and his vision of the future. He'd never wanted a wife. And he'd certainly never wanted a baby.

A low distant rumbling pulled Maddie's gaze to the western horizon. Massive dark clouds had gathered, promising a night of wind and rain. Maddie shivered and pulled her coat close around her. She hated storms.

She thought of Nick and smiled at the memory of all the nights he'd sat with her years ago, keeping her company during the worst of the spring rains. Once they'd been like two wounded animals drawing their strength from one another. Then she'd gone off to college, and he'd found Sarah.

Now, once again, Nick was alone and so was she. Did he feel the same sharp sting of loneliness? Did he look out the window at the approaching storm and remember those nights when they were young? Did he turn to his son as she turned to her unborn child for comfort? Was Lynn right? Did they need one another again?

No!

Maddie shook her head and left Lynn's porch. She was sorry about Nick's loss, but she had her own problems to deal with. She'd trusted Nick once, and it had been one of the biggest mistakes of her life. Right up there with believing in Roger.

She laughed bitterly at the irony of it. History really did repeat itself. She'd loved and trusted both Nick and Roger. And both men had left her alone and hurting.

Another roll of thunder brought her thoughts back to the approaching storm, and she threw a wary glance at the darkening sky. Enough mental wanderings, she told herself. She needed to hurry if she was going to beat the rain home.

CHAPTER THREE

"HEY, EINSTEIN!"

Jon kept walking, ignoring the boy who hollered at him.

"Johnnie!" whined a second voice. "Hey, Johnnie!" No one but Fatso could squeal like that.

Jon cursed under his breath. He didn't like the idea of dealing with Roc when he was alone, but when Roc had Fatso, his favorite sidekick, with him, things could get bad real fast.

Jon kept walking, resisting the urge to change his pace because of the two hicks calling out to him. The best thing to do was ignore them, and maybe they'd find someone else to torment.

Suddenly Roc darted in front of him, and Jon came up sharp to avoid a head-on collision. "Hey, Jonboy," sneered Roc, stabbing a finger at Jon's chest. "We're talking to *you.*"

"Give it a rest, Roc." Jon brushed the other boy's hand away. "I'm not interested in anything you've got to say."

Jon sidestepped and started to walk around the other boy, but he hadn't got two steps away before Roc grabbed his arm. "Did ya hear that, Fatso? Einstein's not interested."

Jon jerked his arm free and turned to face the other boy. Rick "the Roc" Moran hadn't got his nickname for no reason, but Jon was almost as tall and no weakling. "What do you want, Roc?"

Roc stepped closer, but Jon held his ground, refusing to budge before the other boy. "Hear you're acing Mr. Dobb's math class."

Jon crossed his arms and shrugged. "So what if I am?"

Roc laughed and glanced at Fatso before turning all his attention back to Jon. "So we don't like that."

"Am I supposed to care what you like?"

"Yeah, you oughtta care," Roc sneered, again stabbing a finger at Jon's chest. "'Cause we don't like no city-boy coming here trying to make us look bad."

"Hey, man. I sure am sorry." Jon kept his cool, at least on the outside. Inside, he wanted to bury his fist in the boy's ugly face. "I didn't mean to make you look bad." Fatso would be all over him from the rear, and Fatso probably outweighed him and Roc together. But, hey, it was worth the risk. Dropping his book bag on the ground, he grinned sheepishly. "But you know, I can't help it if you haven't got anything inside your skull but rocks...Roc."

The insult hit home. "Why you—"

"Hey, Jon!" Startled, all three boys turned at once as a petite blonde hurried up and joined them. "I've been looking everywhere for you."

"Not now, Anna," Jon said, exasperated that she'd picked this moment to show up. The girl was always around when he least wanted her—which was pretty much all the time.

"You heard Jon-boy," Roc growled. "Get lost, Anna."

"Why should I?" Anna crossed her arms and lifted her chin defiantly. Despite himself, Jon had to admire the way she stood up to the bully. "Just so you can goad him into a fight. Two to one. Looks like pretty uneven odds to me."

"Anna..." Jon wanted to shake her. Didn't the girl have any sense? He didn't need her standing up for him.

"Ain't no business of yours," added Fatso.

"I'm making it my business."

"You better git, girl," Roc warned. "Or you could get yourself in a whole mess of trouble."

"Are you threatening *me?*" Anna advanced on Roc, and if Jon hadn't been so angry about her interference, he would have laughed when Roc stumbled backward. "Are you forgetting who my daddy is?" Anna continued. "All I have to do is tell him you put one finger on me, just one dirty finger..." She didn't need to say more. Not only was Anna's father the sheriff in Felton, he was over six four, pushing a lean 220 pounds, and everyone knew he adored his oldest daughter. Jack Banks had to be the one man in town that even a bully like Roc wanted to avoid.

It took a moment, but Roc recovered his composure. "I ain't got no quarrel with you, Anna." Then he turned his beady eyes back to Jon and added, "But you're dead meat, city-boy. You can't hide behind her skirts forever." With that, he and Fatso took off.

"What the hell were you doing?" Jon asked, turning on Anna as soon as the other boys were out of earshot.

Again she lifted that defiant chin of hers. "I was trying to keep you from getting beat up."

"I can take care of myself." He grabbed his bag and swung it over his shoulder. "And another thing. I'm tired of you hanging around me all the time. Why don't you go find some girls and play dolls or something." The moment the words were out of his mouth, he regretted them. But it was too late. The damage was already done.

Anna's big brown eyes instantly filled with tears. "Fine with me," she said, her brave voice suddenly shaky. "Be that way. What do I care if Roc beats you senseless?" She turned and took off toward the school.

"Anna," he called, but she didn't stop. He tossed his bag back down on the ground. "Damn!" Why did he have to go and say that? What a jerk he was. A first-class jerk.

NICK FOUGHT the urge to go see Maddie for nearly a week.

Logic told him she probably wanted nothing to do with him. He'd hurt her badly once, destroying their friendship. Though he'd give anything to undo the foolishness of his youth.

No, that wasn't true.

He couldn't wish that his son had never been conceived, that he and Sarah had never crawled into the back seat of her car. He loved Jon too much. But he could wish that he hadn't hurt Maddie in the process. He'd loved her once, too.

And maybe that was why the desire to see her kept at him. If he could explain to her what had happened, tell her the truth about Sarah, maybe Maddie would forgive him.

It was his morning out of the office, and he usually spent it working on the house he was building outside of town. But the project had lost its appeal since the last time he and Jon had been out there together. So, without really thinking, he found himself heading toward the opposite side of town. To Maddie's.

Approaching her house, he spotted her out front. She stood on tiptoe, wielding a large pair of gardening shears, trying to reach the last few upper branches of an overgrown bush. Scattered around her feet and across the yard were various pieces of cut greenery, evidence she'd been pruning most of the morning.

"Here," Nick said as he walked up beside her. "Let me help you with that."

Maddie took a step away from him. "Thanks, but I can manage."

"Come on, Maddie." Nick reached for the shears. "Let me get the ones you can't reach." Maddie lifted her chin in a stubborn gesture he remembered well. He almost laughed aloud. Instead, he said, "Just the top ones, Mads."

She hesitated a moment longer, even while her expression began to soften somewhat—maybe at the use of the nickname she'd always claimed to hate—and handed him the shears. "Don't call me Mads."

Ignoring her, Nick reached up and easily snipped the last few errant branches. "There," he said, stepping back from the bush to see if he'd missed anything. "I think that's it."

"Thanks." Maddie retrieved her shears, the ghost of a smile nipping at the corners of her mouth. "There are times when I wish I were a little taller."

Nick chuckled. "I remember when you used to swear that five eight was too tall for a girl."

"I guess a lot of things have changed." She met his gaze for a moment and then turned away. "So, what are you doing here?"

"It's my morning off." He paused. "I thought I'd come over and see how you were doing."

"I'm fine." Laying the shears down on the front steps, Maddie walked across the yard to a large, plastic-lined trash can and pulled it over to where she could start filling it with debris. "How did you know I was staying here?"

"I ran into Lynn Banks." Nick followed her example, picking up handfuls of cut greenery. "Though it wouldn't have been too hard to figure out on my own. I knew you wouldn't be staying with your mother. And this place has been vacant for the past couple of years."

"I tried renting it out for a while," she said offhandedly. "But I couldn't stand the idea of strangers living in Daddy's house."

They worked together quietly for a few minutes, stuffing the can with branches and leaves, pulling out the plastic bag when it was full, replacing it with a new one, then starting the process all over again.

"Maddie," Nick said, breaking the silence, "Lynn also told me you're here by yourself."

"That's right," she said, without breaking stride. Although, he caught the momentary faltering of her hands and the slight tightening of her features. Even after sixteen years, he could still read her. And this was something she didn't want to talk about. He should let it go.

Instead, he asked, "Where's the baby's father?"

She stopped and looked at him, her brow furrowed in an expression of total disbelief. "Do you really think that you, of all people, have the right to ask me that?"

No. He had no rights at all where she was concerned. Yet it didn't stop him from thinking of her, of wanting to know more about her—what she'd done with her life these past sixteen years, who she'd become, who she'd loved.

"You're right," he said finally. "It's none of my business. I'm sorry." Without waiting for a reply, he resumed picking up the remaining branches littering her lawn.

For several moments she remained silent, watching him. Then she said, "Nick, you don't have to do my yard work for me." Her voice had lost its angry edge, and Nick stopped to look at her again.

It was almost his undoing.

He felt the pull of her, of the gentle silver in her eyes and the soft sad smile on her lips. "Maddie—" he took a step toward her, but stopped just short of touching her "—can we talk?" When she didn't say anything, he added, "We used to be good at talking."

Still, she didn't answer, her eyes reflecting thoughts dark as a winter night. When she spoke, her voice was almost a whisper. "That was a long time ago." She turned away, grabbed one of the full bags and headed toward the curb. "Besides, there's nothing to talk about."

Nick caught up to her and took the bag. "But there is."

Maddie sighed and turned to face him. "We were kids, Nick. Let's not dredge it up."

Standing there looking at her, Nick realized the fine line he walked. If she sent him away, he might never have another chance to explain. And somehow he had to make Maddie understand what happened sixteen years ago.

Then he said, "Okay, I'll leave it alone."

"Good." Maddie turned and started toward another of the bags.

"That is, if you'll agree to join me for lunch."

"I can't." Her answer was automatic. "I still need to fertilize and put down fresh mulch."

"I'll help you later. After we eat." Nick closed the distance between them, taking a plastic bag from her hands. "We'll walk down to the Bee-Bop and talk about old times."

"Nick—"

"Please, Maddie." He reached out and brushed a smudge of dirt from her cheek, liking the feel of her skin against his fingertips. It was as soft and smooth as he remembered. "I just want to talk."

She took a step back, away from his outstretched hand. "The Bee-Bop's still there?"

"Yeah." Nick grinned, recalling the hours they'd spent in the old diner. "But it's a little different now."

"Different?" Maddie arched her eyebrows.

"I'm afraid it attracts a slightly older set now."

A smile crept across her lips. "Don't tell me it's no longer the teenage hot spot."

"Someone bought out old Mr. Salle a few years back, and they've changed it somewhat. You need to see it to understand."

Maddie hesitated a moment longer and then nodded. "Okay. But just because you've got me curious." Motioning toward the bags they'd filled, she added, "If you'll carry the rest of these out to the curb for me, I'll go get cleaned up."

Nick smiled. "Deal."

He breathed a sigh of relief as Maddie disappeared into the house. On his way over, he'd told himself he just wanted to explain about Sarah and apologize to Maddie for hurting her years ago. He'd been lying to himself. And he hadn't even realized it until she'd almost refused his invitation to lunch. What he really needed was to see her smile. To be friends again. Maybe to laugh and remember old times. To be forgiven.

Maddie took only a few minutes. But when she stepped back outside, Nick nearly forgot all thoughts of friendship. She'd changed into a pair of black stirrup pants and a lightweight sweater that matched the gray of her eyes. She looked at him and smiled. The sun captured streaks of satin in her dark hair, and her eyes tempted him, daring him to think of her as anything but a woman. A very desirable woman.

Nick moved to the edge of the steps. "You look nice."

For a moment Maddie stood on the porch, fighting the urge to turn around and run back into the house. While she'd been inside, she'd told herself she was crazy to accept Nick's invitation. She was asking for trouble. She'd put him behind her a long time ago and didn't want anything more to do with him.

Still, she'd rationalized, she'd been stuck working on the house all week. Except for a few excursions downtown to pick up groceries and a couple of conversations with Lynn, Maddie hadn't spoken to another soul. Not even Adelia had bothered to call—of course, that wasn't exactly surprising. Maddie was going stir-crazy. She was used to being around people, and this solitary life-style was a shock to her system.

Then she'd stepped back outside and realized her mistake.

Nick stood smiling at her from the porch steps, and she felt a familiar tightening in her chest. He was too handsome for his own good. No man with such wickedly dark hair and skin should have eyes the color of a summer sky. And though it had been a fascinating contrast on the boy, it was utterly dangerous on the man. Pulling her gaze away, she moved down the steps. After so many years, he shouldn't affect her this way. He shouldn't affect her at all.

They set off walking toward town, and even without looking at him, Maddie felt the strain of being close to him. Too much history lay between them, too many things that had been left unsaid years ago. The next time she felt lonely, Maddie decided, she'd stay home and give Lynn a call. She certainly wouldn't make the mistake of going off with Nick Ryan again.

Searching for something to break the awkward silence, Maddie said, "I heard about your father, Nick. I'm sorry."

Nick glanced at her. "Thank you. But it was ten years ago, and he did it to himself."

"Lynn said you'd managed to put him into a nursing home."

"When I went away to school. There was no other way. He couldn't take care of himself." Nick shook his head. "Not that it did any good. He still managed to drink himself to death." He paused and then casually draped an arm around her shoulders. "Enough about my old man. How's the Ice Queen?"

Maddie laughed lightly. "Talk about people who never change."

"I don't know. Adelia's not that bad."

"Ha! You don't know her."

Nick shot Maddie a look but didn't say anything more. They'd just passed the old Baptist church, separating the residential area of town from the business district, when Maddie spotted the newspaper office where she'd worked after school years ago. She'd been meaning to stop in for days.

"Does Carl Katz still run the *Felton Finder?*" she asked, nodding toward the one-story building across the street.

Nick glanced in the direction she indicated. "Who else would have the job?"

"Come on." Maddie started off across the street, motioning for him to follow. "I want to say hello."

Maddie had worked at the *Felton Finder* during her last two years of high school. It had started off as an occasional afternoon or Saturday spent helping Mr. Katz. After a while though, her attitude toward the job changed. She grew to love everything about it—the smell of print, Carl Katz's gruff manner, the stain of ink on her fingers and especially the writing.

Eventually she spent most of her free afternoons at the paper and half days on Saturday. Stepping inside the door felt more like coming home than anything else since her return to Felton.

Carl Katz sat at a desk behind the counter, pecking away on an old manual typewriter. "Just leave the mail on the counter, Jeb," he said without raising his head. "I'll look at it later."

Maddie shot Nick a conspiratorial smile before leaning against the ink-stained counter. "I would think you'd have figured out how to use a word processor by now."

Carl looked up, squinting through his bifocals. "Well, I'll be. Can it really be Maddie Aims?"

Maddie grinned. "In the flesh."

Carl's gaze shifted to Nick and then settled back on Maddie. "I see you're still hanging around with that no-account boy from across the river."

Maddie suppressed her laughter. It had been one of their favorite arguments. "He's still the best-looking guy in town."

"So you keep saying." Carl shook his head, though his eyes gleamed with delight. "Heard he wants to be a doctor. It'll never happen."

Maddie turned and smiled at Nick, who looked at her and Carl as if they'd lost it. "Oh, I don't know about that," Maddie said, not taking her eyes off Nick. "I think he has potential."

"Humph!" Carl glared at her for a moment longer and then broke into a huge smile. Leaving his desk, he came around the counter and gave her a fierce hug before taking her hands in his. "So what took you so long to come back, girlie?"

Maddie shrugged and returned his smile. "I've been busy."

"Too busy to come back and see old friends?"

Maddie shifted uneasily, a sliver of guilt worming its way beneath her skin. He was right. She'd let her problems with her mother keep her away from Felton and the people in it.

"I haven't seen your byline anywhere," Carl went on, interrupting her thoughts. "And I've been looking."

She shook her head a little sadly. What was done was done. "I never finished my degree in journalism."

"Never finished?" Carl tightened his hold on her hands, a look of concern on his face. "I thought your mama told me you graduated top of your class."

"Mother told you that?" Maddie would've laid odds that Adelia never spoke of her to anybody—especially not someone like Carl Katz.

The old newspaperman nodded. "Sure did."

"Well, I did graduate in the top five of my class, but both my degrees are in business." She glanced at Nick, who had moved up next to her.

"Degrees?" Carl's voice pulled her attention back to him.

"I have an MBA from Northwestern," she said. Carl didn't look impressed, so she added, "I work for an international consulting firm in Miami. I'm their marketing expert."

"Well, I'm sorry to hear that, girl." Carl released her hands and moved back behind his counter. "You had a lot of potential as a writer."

Maddie forced a smile. She wasn't used to someone dismissing her job. Most people were impressed by what she did. Evidently Carl Katz was the exception. He acted like she'd settled for second best. She glanced at Nick, who stood silently watching her, but she couldn't read the expression on his face.

"I'm good at what I do," she said, turning back to Carl. "I travel all over the world." Almost as an afterthought, she said, "And I really like it."

"Good." Carl nodded, but his expression didn't change. "That's good, at least."

Suddenly Maddie felt very uncomfortable, not knowing what else to say. She'd come in here to say hello to an old friend and ended up feeling as if she'd let him down.

"Well," Nick said, stepping in to fill the silence. "We need to be going."

"It was good seeing you, girlie." Carl nodded and returned to his typewriter. Then he added, "Don't be a stranger."

"I won't," Maddie managed, but she wasn't sure she wanted to come back. The memory of the dreams she'd let go were too strong here. Nick took her arm and they started to leave.

"Doc."

Carl's voice stopped them, and Nick turned, his hand on the door. "Yes?"

The old man pursed his lips and nodded. "I was real sorry to hear about Sarah."

For a moment Nick didn't respond, though Maddie could feel the tension in the hand that held her arm. Then he nodded, acknowledging the other man's condolences. "Thank you, Mr. Katz." Opening the door, he let Maddie go first before following her outside.

Walking beside him, Maddie felt the weight of Nick's grief. She could see his misery in the grim set of his features, sense his sorrow in the air surrounding him. She didn't want to be aware of it, but the bond they'd formed as children still existed—whether she wanted it to or not. And his suffering chipped away at the barrier she'd built around her heart.

"Nick," she began, unable to look at him. "I'm really sorry about Sarah, too."

He nodded but remained silent.

She wanted to let it go. She didn't want to offer more than any other concerned acquaintance might offer. But she couldn't. He'd been her best friend once, and his pain touched her in a way she couldn't explain or dismiss.

"Are you okay?" she asked. "I don't mean just now. I mean, in general. Are you all right?"

For several moments, she thought he wouldn't speak—and that would have been her answer. Then he said, "Yeah, I'm okay."

Maddie chewed her bottom lip, tormented by the strong desire to offer something of herself to him. "If you want to talk about it," she said, "I'm here."

Again Nick hesitated before answering, and Maddie knew he was considering her offer. "Maybe sometime," he finally said. "But not today." He lifted his face to the sun, then turned to her and smiled, though it didn't extend to his eyes. "It's too nice out. And I just want to enjoy spending a little time with you. It's been too long."

Maddie nodded and smiled, too, feeling as though she'd just made a narrow escape. But from what, she couldn't say.

A few minutes later Nick escorted her through the door of their favorite teenage haunt, and Maddie couldn't believe the change. The only thing the same about the Bee-Bop was its name.

When they were kids, the Bee-Bop had been a popular soda-and-sandwich shop, complete with blaring jukebox, torn vinyl booths and squeaky counter stools. During the day the place had served a decent breakfast and lunch, and local adults patronized the premises. But by unspoken consensus, at three o'clock every afternoon, the kids took over.

The new owners had attempted to redecorate in a style reminiscent of the past, but the result was an overly bright restaurant that looked exactly like what it was—a nineties' version of a fifties' diner. Everything was new, from the shiny black-and-white tiles to the crisp, fifties-style uniforms on the staff. The effect was startling and a bit garish.

"Despite the decor," Nick said, obviously reading Maddie's thoughts, "the food's pretty good."

Maddie let out a short laugh. "It better be."

A girl in her late teens approached them with menus in hand. "Hi, Dr. Ryan," she said, giving him a smile that offered more than food. "Table for two?"

"Thanks, Bridgette." Nick answered her smile with one of his own, and Maddie thought the girl was going to collapse on the spot. Rolling her eyes, Maddie followed Bridgette to their table. But once they were seated, she couldn't hold back any longer. "I guess some things never change."

Nick looked at her, an expression of innocence on his face. "What?"

Maddie shook her head, not buying his act. "You're still turning every female head for a dozen miles. And loving every minute of it."

"Who? Bridgette?" Nick glanced in the direction of the hostess. "She's a kid."

"A kid who's old enough to be out of school and working." Maddie crossed her arms and rested them on the table. "I bet she's almost—" she flicked her wrist "—nineteen."

"That's what I said. A kid."

It was Maddie's turn to don an innocent look. "Why are you so defensive? All I said was that you're still knocking them dead."

Nick gave her a speculative grin. "You're jealous."

"Ha!" Maddie leaned back in the booth, keeping her arms crossed. "Of what? A mere child with perfect teeth and twenty-year-old thighs? Not me."

Nick laughed and shook his head. The sunshine was back in his eyes and Maddie let the warmth flow over her. Nothing was quite as exhilarating as being with Nick. Time hadn't changed that. And it scared her.

"Shall we order?" she asked, thinking she understood Bridgette's dilemma perfectly.

To Maddie's surprise, the food really was good. They ordered fajita salads that turned out to be every bit as fancy as the ones she got in Miami. While they ate, their conversation revolved around the baby.

Nick turned out to be a surprisingly good listener, even as she rattled on about things only an expectant mother would care about. Subjects like baby furniture and which formula to use, whether cloth or paper diapers were better and whether to breast- or bottle-feed. She'd just about wound down as the waitress cleared their plates and freshened their beverages.

"You've been amazingly patient, Dr. Ryan," she said, taking a sip of her tea.

"I like hearing your plans for the baby." Nick's expression softened. "I enjoy listening to you." For a moment he held her gaze, his eyes a deeper blue than usual.

Maddie felt the pull of him—there was something incredibly seductive about this man, something compelling. But that was the danger, wasn't it? Falling for Nick again. Letting him sweep her away with his charm and devastating looks. Letting him make her feel special. Believing in him.

With an effort, she lowered her gaze and studied the cup in her hand. She wouldn't let herself want something from Nick—not even the close friendship they'd once shared.

"Have you thought of any names?" he asked, breaking into her thoughts.

Maddie looked up, relieved that he seemed unaware of her thoughts. "I haven't thought of a boy's name yet. But if it's a girl, I'm going to call her Lily."

"Lily." He seemed to test the name, rolling it around on his tongue as if to get a feel for it. "I like it. A bit old-fashioned, but I like it."

"Me, too."

Just then, Nick's beeper sounded, and he reached down to shut it off and check the number on the display. "Sorry," he said a moment later. "I need to call my office." With a shrug, he slipped out of the booth. "Comes with the territory."

Maddie watched him cross the restaurant to the hostess station. He still wore a pair of jeans better than any man she'd ever known. The denim molded itself sinfully to his long legs and bottom, and there was something achingly masculine in his movements. Something almost...decadent.

He kept his back to the room as he picked up the phone, and Maddie let her gaze drift upward, over his trim waist to the dark hair teasing the collar of his shirt. He needed a haircut. But then, he'd always needed a haircut, she remembered. The shoulders, however, were definitely broader, stronger. But even as she admired the expanse of muscle pulling at the seams of his shirt, she saw the sudden tension in them, and she knew something was wrong.

When he returned, his face was set in grim lines. "I'm sorry, Maddie. I need to go."

"Emergency?"

"It's my son, Jon." Nick shook his head, a look of helplessness on his face. "He got in a fight at school. The other kid had a knife."

Fear for Nick and his son coiled in her stomach. "How bad is he hurt?" She started to rise, but Nick stopped her with a hand on her shoulder.

"I don't know." He pulled his wallet out of his back pocket and dropped a couple of bills on the table. "They've taken him to the office. Ted's with him, but Bette wouldn't have called if it wasn't serious. I've got to go."

Maddie slipped out of the booth. "I'll come with you."

"No, that's not necessary." His eyes were haunted. "Stay." He motioned toward the table. "Enjoy your tea."

Maddie grabbed his arm, forcing him to look at her. Whether either of them wanted it or not, he needed someone right now, and she was going to be there for him. "I'm going with you," she said.

CHAPTER FOUR

FORTUNATELY NICK'S OFFICE was only a short distance from the Bee-Bop. Nick half ran, half walked the few blocks in silence, and Maddie had to struggle to keep up with him. His thoughts were obviously on his son.

Maddie couldn't blame him. In fact, almost immediately on leaving the restaurant she began questioning her resolve to accompany him. And by the time they entered his office building, she knew she should have gone home. She'd just told herself an hour ago that she couldn't afford even a casual relationship with Nick, and here she was, traipsing after him as he rushed to take care of his son. At the moment it seemed the height of stupidity. There was absolutely nothing she could do. So why had she insisted on coming with him?

She was still searching for an answer as she followed Nick into the waiting room of his office.

"Room four," Bette said without preamble. "Dr. Sommer is with him."

Nick crossed the room in a few quick strides, pushed through the door leading to the examining rooms and stopped short, as if suddenly remembering Maddie was with him. Turning toward her, he said, "Maddie." The bright sapphire of his eyes softened for just a moment. "Maddie, I—"

"Go on, Nick," she interrupted, not wanting to hear what he planned on saying or feel the tug of emotion his words might generate within her. "Your son is waiting."

Nick stood there for a moment longer, his eyes searching her face, while Maddie steeled herself against him. Then he nodded and turned away, closing the door behind him.

Maddie felt as if she'd barely escaped. How could she have allowed herself to get caught up with Nick again? He wasn't the needy teenager she'd known sixteen years ago, the boy who had little more than dreams in his future. This Nick Ryan was a man who'd fulfilled his ambitions and become a doctor. And he'd done it without her. He could manage now on his own, as well.

"Sorry to interrupt your lunch," Bette said, pulling Maddie from her thoughts.

Maddie shrugged and crossed to the reception window. "What else could you have done?"

"Not much. Jon's got a pretty nasty cut above his right eyebrow." Maddie winced. "It's going to need stitches," Bette continued. "But it looks worse than it is. Head wounds bleed heavily." She paused for a moment before adding, "The scary thing is that it happened at all."

"Yes." *Progress.* Not only had Felton moved into the nineties with the Bee-Bop and a video store, but now it had teenagers carrying knives. "Who did it?"

"Don't know. But I suspect Sheriff Banks will be here pretty darn quick asking that same question."

"Didn't Jon say anything?"

"Are you kidding?" Bette snorted. "Obviously you haven't been around a teenager lately."

"But if another boy came at him with a knife..."

"It doesn't matter. He's fifteen," Bette said, as if that explained everything. "Just remember to enjoy that baby of yours while it's still small. And while *you* still know a thing or two."

Maddie slid her hand to her stomach, her thoughts turning to her unborn baby. Would her child one day cause her to pull her hair out, cursing adolescence with its capricious mood swings and hormonal imbalances? Maddie laughed lightly at the question. And the answer. No doubt her child's behavior would be as baffling as that of any teenager.

Smiling at Bette, she said, "I swear I'll enjoy every stage of this baby's life. Fortunately the best ages come first."

Bette laughed, but before she could say anything else, the phone rang. Maddie drifted away from the reception window, wondering what she'd gotten herself into. When she'd been seventeen, she'd been a little unpredictable herself. She'd thought herself alone in the world.

Except for Nick.

He'd always been there for her, holding her up.

There it was again. The pull of their old bond that she and Nick had formed twenty years ago. She couldn't seem to get away from it. She remembered the day they'd became friends as if it were yesterday.

She'd taken second place in the school's annual essay contest. It had been quite an accomplishment for a ninth grader. But on the day of the award ceremony, she'd been depressed. She'd made it through the afternoon of speeches and presentations. But afterward, waiting outside in the icy January wind for her mother to pick her up, Maddie had been overwhelmed by loneliness.

Shivering, she'd pulled her coat closer around her and wished she'd worn pants, instead of the new dress she'd gotten for Christmas. She'd reminded herself that she'd picked her clothes for a reason. She'd wanted to look good for the ceremony in case her mother found time to attend. It had been a stupid idea. Her mother hadn't shown up.

She'll be here, Maddie told herself. Any minute now.

Other kids and their parents came and went, emptying the school, calling their congratulations to Maddie as they passed. Still, she waited, the cold penetrating her thick winter coat as the minutes ticked by.

Come on, mother.

If her father were alive, *he* would be here. Maddie fought the tightening in her throat and the flush of tears filling her eyes. Wrapped in her thoughts, she didn't notice the lone boy leaving the school until she heard him call, "Hey, Maddie!"

She turned toward the vaguely familiar voice as he bound down the last few steps and headed toward her. She recognized him immediately. Nick Ryan. She didn't really know him, but she knew of his reputation—actually, every girl in Felton High knew all about him. He was absolutely gorgeous and as dangerous as boys came.

"Hey," she said, echoing his greeting. "What are you doing here?" He hadn't entered the essay contest, and she couldn't think of any other reason he'd be at school on a Sunday afternoon.

"Just hanging around. I hear you did real good today."

"I did okay." Maddie shrugged and turned back to check the street. Still no sign of her mother. *She wasn't coming.*

"You waiting for someone?"

Maddie kept her eyes on the street. "My mother is supposed to pick me up."

"She's late, huh?"

"She probably got tied up or something."

"Yeah, probably."

Something in his voice made Maddie turn around. She'd never been this close to him before, so it wasn't surprising that she'd never noticed the perceptiveness in those infamous blue eyes of his. His gaze told her he understood. Her mother wasn't going to show, and he knew how she felt.

"I'm going your way," he said, breaking the spell with his voice. "I'll walk you."

Heat rushed to Maddie's cheeks as she realized she'd been staring. Trying to hide her embarrassment, she turned back to look down the nearly empty street. How could someone like Nick Ryan possibly understand about her mother?

"If she comes looking for me..." Maddie shouldn't even be talking to him but she was tired of standing in the cold. And he really was the most gorgeous boy in the whole school. What could it hurt to let him walk her home?

"Okay," she said, and turned to give him a tentative smile. "Let's go."

Nick grinned and turned to cut across the empty parking lot. Maddie took one last look down the street.

"You coming?" he asked.

Turning her back to the empty street, she smiled at Nick and closed the distance between them. "Yeah."

"Great." Nick casually draped an arm over her shoulders and grinned. "Who knows? This could be the start of a beautiful friendship."

That had been the beginning. For four years, Maddie and Nick had been inseparable. Then she'd gone away to college, and he'd married Sarah Sommer. It had shattered Maddie's heart and destroyed their friendship. At least, that was what she'd always believed. Evidently it had only been her heart that had been broken.

"I should be going," she said softly, thinking that distance was her best defense against the connection she felt with Nick. "There's nothing I can do here."

"Why not hang around awhile," Bette said, startling Maddie. She hadn't realized that Bette had hung up the phone. "Nick may need a friend when he gets done."

Nick's needs. Wasn't that what this was all about? The reason she'd come with him to the office? As much as she wanted to keep her distance, she'd come here to offer him her support. Years ago, Nick had been there for her when she needed him. She couldn't turn her back on him now.

All she could do was try to protect herself in the process. "Okay," she said. "I'll stay awhile."

She settled on the waiting room couch and picked up one of the magazines from a nearby table. It would keep her from dwelling on the past. And the present.

It seemed like she waited for hours.

Then the door open, and Jack Banks stepped inside. Maddie hadn't seen him since she'd been back in town, and although she wouldn't have believed it possible, he was bigger than she remembered. Maybe it was just the shock of seeing him in a uniform. But she didn't think so. It looked to her like he'd grown another inch or two since the days when he'd relentlessly pursued her best friend.

"Maddie," he said with a broad smile that pleasantly transformed his plain features. "Lynn told me you were in town, but I wasn't expecting to find you here."

"Hi, Jack." Maddie rose to meet him, trying not to be intimidated by his sheer size. "It's good to see you."

Jack gave her a hug before setting her away from him. "You look as good as Lynn said. Are you here to see the doc?"

"No." Maddie retreated a step so she wouldn't have to strain her neck to look up at him. "I was with Nick when he got the call about Jon. I suppose that's why you're here, too."

Jack removed his hat and ran a hand through his short crop of blond hair. "Bad business when kids start using knives on each other. How is he?"

"I don't know." Maddie nodded toward the reception window. "Maybe Bette's heard something."

Jack walked over to the window, but Bette had evidently stepped into the back.

"Do you know what happened?" Maddie asked, moving up beside him.

Jack sighed. "From what I can tell, Jon and two other boys got into a fight after school. One of them had a knife.

"The problem," Jack continued after a moment, "is that I only have one kid who even admits to being there. And he isn't saying much. Nobody else was anywhere around. At least that's what they want me to believe."

"But you think there were other kids there?"

"I'd bet my badge on it. I also have my suspicions about who pulled the knife. That's why I need to see Jon."

Parenthood suddenly seemed like a frightening prospect to Maddie. Especially alone. She thought of Roger and wondered if she'd misjudged his reluctance to become a father. Maybe he'd been the more realistic of the two of them. Maybe his reluctance had more to do with fear than anything else.

"Makes you wonder, doesn't it," Jack said. "Fortunately someone had enough sense to call for help. My deputy found Jon heading home, holding a blood-soaked rag against his forehead." He shook his head.

"Guess we should be grateful for that much, anyway."

"Sheriff." Both Maddie and Jack turned at the sound of Ted Sommer's voice. "I figured you'd find your way over here sooner or later."

"Doc," Jack said, nodding toward the older man, "how's the boy?"

"Oh, he'll live. He's too damn ornery to do otherwise. Come on back. Maybe you can get something out of him."

Jack gave Maddie's arm a reassuring squeeze before shoving his hat under his arm and stepping through the doorway. Before following the sheriff into the back, Ted shifted his gaze to Maddie. "Do you need to see me?"

"No. I'm fine, Dr. Sommer." Maddie felt the heat rise to her cheeks. "I was with Nick when Bette called."

Ted arched his eyebrows quizzically.

"I just..." She started to explain but changed her mind. How could she explain her relationship with Nick to Sarah's father? Especially when she didn't understand it herself? "I'm glad Jon's all right."

Dr. Sommer shook his head. "Well, I wouldn't exactly say he's all right." He smiled wryly, suddenly looking old and tired. "He's just not in any physical danger."

FOR THE PAST HOUR Nick had held a tight rein on his emotions. When he'd gotten the call from Bette, fear had been his first reaction, with anger coming close on its heels. She'd told him on the phone that Jon wasn't seriously hurt, but those weren't the words that registered in his mind. All Nick kept hearing was that Jon had been in a fight—a knife fight for God's sake—and that he needed stitches above one eye.

The fear and anger had warred within him as he'd headed for the clinic. He'd almost forgotten that Maddie was with him. Almost, but not quite. Somewhere inside he knew. And was grateful.

Once he saw Jon, his fear and anger took second place to more practical considerations. Ted had prepped the boy for stitches, cleaning the ugly slash and applying a topical anesthetic to deaden the area around the cut. He'd been just about to start the actual stitching when Nick walked in and took over. Nick managed to put ten sutures in his son's head without thinking about how the wound had gotten there. But as he tied the last stitch, his anger resurfaced. Someone had taken a knife to his son—and had just missed the boy's eye.

It shouldn't have happened. Not to Jon.

Nick had made sure his son had all the advantages he'd never known as a boy. Money. Clothes. A nice home in a decent neighborhood. Nick had grown up across the river in an area cluttered with wooden shacks. There, parents lived in dread of seeing their children come home with knife or bullet wounds. But in the foothills that rose behind the north end of town, the place where Nick had brought his family to live, this shouldn't have happened.

As if sensing his mood, Ted left the room to get Bette to help Nick finish up. Maybe the older man had guessed that Nick couldn't trust his hands to clean away the last of the dried blood on Jon's head and apply the dressing. Neither he nor Jon spoke as Bette went about her work. She clucked over Jon like a mother hen while the boy tolerated her ministrations in rigid silence.

After she left, Nick asked the question uppermost in his mind. "Who did it?"

Silence.

It didn't surprise him. Actually nothing about Jon surprised him anymore. Not since Sarah's death, anyway. Nick saw the stubborn set of the boy's jaw and knew his son would refuse to answer. Jon's expression reminded Nick of Sarah. She, too, could be obstinate.

"Jon," he said sternly, "I want to know what happened."

"Nothing." The boy looked him straight in the eye and lied. "I cut myself." His eyes sparked with a defiance that had become all too familiar to Nick. He fought the urge to shake the boy.

"Nick." Ted's voice snapped Nick out of his silent turmoil. "Sheriff Banks wants to talk to Jon."

Ted moved aside, and Jack Banks stepped into the small examining room. He nodded at Nick, an expression of concern in his eyes. One father to another.

Nick appreciated the silent show of support, but it didn't help. It was *his* son sitting here with a gash in his head, refusing to shed any light on how it got there.

"How are you doing?" Jack asked Jon, all his attention now focused on the boy.

Jon shrugged. "Okay, I guess."

Jack dropped his hat and a small bag onto a nearby chair and sat on the edge of the examining table. "Do you want to tell me what happened?"

"There's not much to tell." Jon's gaze shifted to Nick and then back to Jack. "I cut myself with a fishing knife."

Nick let out a snort of disgust.

"Is that so?" Jack's voice reflected his own disbelief. "Seems a pretty strange place to cut yourself." He reached up and tilted the boy's head back, trying to get a better look at the position of the knife wound. "Been doing a lot of fishing lately?"

Nick saw the flicker of indecision in the boy's eyes before he answered. "Some."

Jack kept his gaze on Jon, and Nick could see his son squirming under the other man's scrutiny.

"Are you sure that's what happened?" Jack asked again.

Jon hesitated. Evidently lying to a law officer was a bit harder than lying to his father. Nick held his breath, hoping his son had the sense to tell the truth.

"I'm sure," Jon said finally. "I wasn't paying attention to what I was doing."

"Pretty careless of you," Jack said.

Jon shrugged. "It was stupid."

Jack nodded in agreement, though Nick figured Jack wasn't referring to Jon's "fishing" accident. "Well, these things happen," Jack continued. "Where's the knife?"

"I..." Jon hesitated, stumbling over his words. "I guess I must've lost it."

Jack slid off the table and picked up the bag he'd dropped on the chair earlier. From inside the bag, he pulled out a plastic bag containing a switchblade. "Is this it?"

Again, Nick saw the wariness in Jon's eyes. "Uh, yeah, I guess. Where'd you find it?"

"Around." Jack raised the bag to the light as if to get a better look at its contents. "Doesn't look like much of a fishing knife to me." Using a handkerchief from his pocket, he reached into the bag and pulled out the knife. Then he pressed a hidden button and a four-inch blade sprang into view. "In fact, I do believe this particular model is illegal."

Jon paled.

"Looks more like something a kid might pick up in the *city* somewhere," Jack added. "Say, in Atlanta."

"No way!" Jon blurted out, then flushed brightly as he realized his mistake.

"No way what?" Jack asked.

"No way you're going to pin that on me."

"I thought this was your knife."

Jon started to speak, but ended up mumbling something incoherent.

"What's that?" Jack prodded.

"I said," Jon emphasized the first two words before softening his voice to finish the sentence, "maybe that's not my knife, after all."

A heavy silence fell over the room as Jon's distress hung in the air like a palpable thing. Jack had backed the boy neatly into a corner, and Nick's paternal instincts urged him to step forward and stop the other man. It took all his willpower to stay out of it.

Jon was no longer a child.

He was a young man. And he was in trouble. The knowledge weighed on Nick. Jon was his son. Nick longed to put his arms around the boy and assure him that everything would be okay. But he couldn't. Trying to shield Jon would only make matters worse.

Jack finally broke the silence, and his voice took on an edge of steel. "I know you were fighting." He'd finished humoring Jon and his lies. "Whoever pulled this knife was carrying an illegal weapon. And he could have done a lot worse than tickle your forehead." He paused, letting his words sink in. "I'm only going to ask you one more time. Whose knife is this?"

Jon stared at Jack for a moment, and Nick thought he detected a slight tremble around the boy's mouth. Then Jon shook his head, his features acquiring a familiar stubborn set. After a few moments Jack sighed and dropped the knife back into the bag.

"Jon..." Nick stepped forward, leveling a warning glare at his son.

Jon pressed his lips together, his gaze darting from one man to the other. For a moment Nick thought he'd broken through. Then Jon lied once more. "I told you. I cut myself."

"Well—" Jack picked up his hat and moved to the doorway "—I can't help you if you won't tell me the truth. But believe me, boy, I will find out." With a silent nod at Nick, he left the room.

Frustrated beyond words, Nick stared at his son. It was like looking at a stranger. This was not the boy he knew, the baby he'd bounced on his shoulders, the child he'd wrestled with on the living room floor.

Sometime since the night Sarah had driven her car off that cliff, Nick had lost his son.

Not trusting himself to speak, Nick left the room, seeking the solitude of his office. Then he remembered Maddie and abruptly changed direction, hoping for reasons he couldn't have defined that she was still in the waiting room. As he opened the door, she came to him, and he saw the question in her eyes.

"Jon's okay," he said, and then realized that Bette or Ted had probably already told her. "I guess you knew that."

"Yes." She smiled softly and eased the frustration and turmoil he'd been experiencing from the moment of Bette's call.

It would be easy to lose himself in her smile, he thought. She'd always been able to make him feel good about himself, believing in him when no one else had. He was tempted to give in to that now, to pull her into his life, to have her help him get over the pain of Sarah's death.

"I was going to introduce you to Jon," he said, "but..."

"Some other time." She rested a hand on his arm, and the temptation to take the comfort she offered was almost more than he could stand. "He's been through enough today." She paused, then asked, "And you? How are you holding up?"

Her concern touched something deep inside him. He wondered how long it had been since someone had worried about him. Then he dismissed the thought as self-pitying. Still, he felt better just looking at her, knowing that beneath her cool exterior she still cared about him.

At the same time, a nagging thought crept into his mind. He had no right to Maddie's comfort. He'd chosen Sarah over Maddie sixteen years ago. How could he ask anything of her now? How could he pull her into the mess he'd made of his life?

"I'm fine," he finally answered. "Thanks." Just these few brief minutes with her had eased the tension in him. It was all he could take, all he could ask of her.

"Can I go now?"

Nick turned at the sound of Jon's voice. The boy stood in the doorway, his hands shoved into the pockets of his jeans. "Sure," Nick answered. "I'll take you home in your grandfather's car." To Maddie he said, "Maddie, this is my son, Jon."

She took a step forward, holding out her hand. "It's nice to meet you, Jon." The boy took her outstretched hand and then quickly let it go.

"Maddie is an old friend of your mother's and mine," Nick continued, hoping Maddie wouldn't call him on the outright lie. She and Sarah had never been friends.

Maddie didn't disappoint him. "I've heard a lot about you," she said to Jon.

The boy shrugged, his attitude bordering on rude, and once again Nick wanted to shake him. Where were the manners he'd drilled into the boy? Evidently Jon had lost them, along with his common sense.

The awkward silence stretched for a moment or two longer before Maddie said, "Well, I need to get going." She backed away from them, and Nick resisted the urge to stop her. *Let her go,* that niggling voice said inside his head.

"Thanks again for waiting," he said aloud.

"Sure." She gave them one last tight smile and turned, heading for the door.

"Maddie," Nick said, almost as an afterthought. "Would you like a ride?"

She didn't turn around, but raised a hand and waved over her shoulder. "I can use the exercise."

Then she left, and the room seemed unbearably empty. Suddenly Nick remembered that he'd promised to help her finish her yard work. He started after her, but Jon's voice stopped him.

"Can we go home now?"

Nick shoved his hands into his pockets and took a deep breath. *Let her go.* Sighing, he turned to Jon. "Yeah. Let's get out of here."

As SHE MADE HER WAY HOME, Maddie tried to put things in perspective.

Jon wasn't what she'd expected. Although she couldn't have said exactly what she *had* expected—maybe a younger version of Nick. Except for his eyes, he *did* look like his father. He had Nick's coloring, the coal black hair and the skin that would turn deep brown in the summer. Like his father, Jon was tall with long legs and a lean physique. But his eyes were Sarah's—dark brown and fringed with midnight lashes. Every woman he'd ever meet would envy him those eyes.

And the attitude?

That, too, must have come from Sarah. Because the
Nick Ryan Maddie remembered hadn't been so full of
anger. He'd been cocky and arrogant, but he hadn't
looked at the world with eyes brimming with resentment. But then she remembered that Jon had lost his
mother a short time ago. She recalled her own grief
when her father had died, and her heart softened toward the boy. Who was she to judge Jon? After all,
she'd been through the same pain. She wondered if
outsiders had looked at her and seen the same defiance in her eyes.

Then Maddie spotted an unfamiliar white car
parked in front of her house, and her thoughts skid-
ded away from Jon. She picked up her pace, her heart
beating wildly at the sudden surge of hope. Was the
car a rental? Was it Roger's? Surely he would have
called if he'd made a decision about her and the baby.

CHAPTER FIVE

MADDIE GLANCED AROUND her yard, looking for the
driver of the car. At first she didn't see anyone, but
then a wave of disappointment washed over her as
Adelia walked toward her from behind the house.

"Oh, there you are, Madeleine. I was just checking
to see if your car was around back."

"Mother, what are you doing here?"

Adelia stiffened. "I came over to see you, of
course."

Maddie sighed. "I'm sorry. I didn't mean anything
by that. It's just that I wasn't expecting you. If I'd
known you were coming..."

Adelia brushed away the last of Maddie's sentence
with a wave of her hand. "I was out and thought I'd
stop by."

"How nice." Disappointment settled like a weight
in Maddie's stomach. And the thought of dealing with
her mother on top of it seemed more than she could
manage.

Then the reality of Adelia actually dropping in hit
home. It wasn't like her to go anywhere unan-
nounced. Motioning toward the house, Maddie asked,
"Do you want to come in for a minute?"

"Yes. If you don't mind." As she followed Maddie up the front walkway, Adelia added, "I've never been inside this house, you know."

"Really." Maddie climbed the steps and unlocked the front door before preceding her mother inside. "It's not much. But it's comfortable."

Adelia stepped into the foyer and slowly perused her surroundings. Maddie tried to view the room as her mother might see it and suppressed a moan. The entryway was little more than a small hallway with hardwood floors and thirty-year-old wallpaper. A staircase and double doors to the front parlor filled the left side of the room, while openings to the living room, dining room and kitchen were off to the right. Compared to Adelia's house, with its large open foyer, sweeping staircase and crystal chandelier, Maddie's father's house seemed like a hovel.

"Would you like some tea?" Maddie closed the front door and motioned toward the parlor. She would've preferred to sit in the kitchen, but she didn't need to be reminded that her mother had raised her better than to invite a guest into the kitchen.

"No, thank you."

"Come in and sit down for a moment." Maddie moved into the other room without waiting to see if her mother would follow.

At least she'd cleaned yesterday, Maddie thought as she opened the curtains to the afternoon sun. "I've been gone since this morning," she explained, even as she questioned the impulse to justify herself to her mother. "So the house has been closed up all day."

She pushed up a window, letting the late-spring air filter into the room.

Adelia remained silent, and Maddie turned to find the older woman standing awkwardly in the middle of the room.

"Have a seat, Mother." Maddie knew her words sounded stiff.

Adelia nodded and lowered herself onto the corner of the sofa. "You know, Madeleine, you're welcome to stay with me if you'd like."

Maddie bit back a sharp retort. Her father had never had much money. And when Adelia had kicked him out of *her* house, this place had been all he could afford. "No, thank you," she said with what she thought was remarkable restraint. "I like it here."

Adelia glanced around the room and sighed. "Well, I guess it *is* quaint."

"It's the house my father left me," Maddie said, defending her father, not the house.

Adelia met her gaze, and for the briefest moment Maddie thought she saw something akin to pain in the older woman's eyes. Maddie dismissed the notion as ridiculous. After all, this was Adelia she was dealing with.

"You didn't come here to criticize the house, Mother," Maddie said as she took a seat in an armchair. "So why are you here?"

"I came over to find out where you've been."

It was about the last thing Maddie had expected Adelia to say. "What do you mean? This afternoon?"

"No, Madeleine." Adelia folded her hands in her lap and spoke slowly. "I mean that it has been more than two weeks since you've been to the house."

Maddie blinked, trying to discern the meaning behind her mother's words. Finally she said, "So?" And immediately regretted it.

Adelia's face showed her displeasure.

"I mean, I've been here." Maddie felt like a rat in a maze trying to find the trick door. "And without intending any disrespect, the last time we spoke I got the distinct impression that you wanted nothing to do with me or my baby."

"Don't be childish, Madeleine." In one fluid motion Adelia rose from the couch to pace the room. "Just because I disapprove of your decision to have this child out of wedlock doesn't mean I'm oblivious to what you are going through." She stopped and turned to face Maddie. "And the possible dangers. I carried a child myself once. In case you have forgotten."

"I'm afraid you've lost me, Mother." This was too much. A concerned Adelia was something Maddie had no idea how to deal with. "What are you trying to say?"

Adelia took a step in Maddie's direction. "I ran into Dr. Sommer yesterday. He told me he is concerned about your blood pressure."

Maddie's face heated. She'd have to talk to Ted Sommer. She wasn't a child, and the results of her medical checkups were no longer her mother's business. "My blood pressure is fine."

"Don't try to deny it." Adelia crossed her arms as if talking to a naughty child. "High blood pressure is not something to fool around with. Especially during pregnancy."

"I know that, Mother. And when my doctor in Miami suggested I slow down and take a leave of absence from my job, that's exactly what I did. I came here."

"These things must be watched carefully."

Maddie wondered if her mother was even listening to her. "I *am* watching it carefully. And so is Dr. Sommer."

"But how am I supposed to know that?"

"Mother." Maddie's patience was slipping away quickly. "I still don't see—"

"You're carrying my grandchild. And considering your age and marital status, it may be the only one I'll ever have. I expect you to take care of him or her. And I expect to be kept informed of your progress." Adelia walked to the door and then turned to face Maddie. "So I'll expect you for dinner every Sunday night from now on. For as long as you're living in Felton. No excuses. Is that understood?"

Too numb to do anything else, Maddie nodded. Without another word, Adelia turned on her heel and let herself out the front door.

For several moments, Maddie just sat there, the sound of her mother's car starting up and pulling away the only noise to break the silence. Then there wasn't even that. Shaking her head, Maddie thought, Adelia concerned for her?

No. Her concern had been for the baby. Still, it was more than Maddie had expected, more than she'd ever hoped for when she'd first told her mother about her pregnancy. Suddenly bursting into laughter, Maddie pressed her hands to her stomach.

"Did you hear that, Baby? Grandma wants to make sure you're all right."

As THE AFTERNOON faded into evening, Maddie's initial amusement at Adelia's dictate to join her once a week for dinner wore off, leaving confusion in its place. Maddie didn't know what to think. Or feel. The day had been filled with tumultuous events and emotions, leaving her more aware than ever of her solitary state.

Her thoughts flew from one thing to another. Amazement at her mother soon gave way to concern for Nick and his son, which only reminded her that she, too, seemed destined to be a single parent. Unless Roger came to his senses.

While waiting for Nick to tend Jon, she'd considered the possibility that Roger's reluctance had more to do with fear than anything else. Now, alone in her house, with the weight of the day lying heavily on her shoulders, she wanted desperately to believe that was the case.

She had to talk to him.

At first she told herself to wait until the weekend to call. After work, he'd be tired. But by nine o'clock, the temptation was too great.

She reached over and picked up the receiver, dialing the Miami number before she could change her mind. The phone rang four times before Roger picked it up. Maddie could barely hear him above the voices and music in the background.

"Roger, what's going on?"

"What timing, Maddie. I was just talking about you."

"Do you have guests?"

"Just a minute. I'll go into the other room so I can hear you better." In the background she heard him ask someone to hang up when he got in the bedroom.

Maddie waited, extremely conscious of the stranger in her apartment holding the receiver. Then Roger returned, and the noise faded into the background as the person on the other end hung up the receiver.

"There," said Roger, sounding just the slightest bit tipsy now that she could hear him clearly. "That's better. Now we can talk."

"It sounds like you're having a party." Maddie fought down a surge of anger. Here she'd hesitated to call him because it was a weekday.

"Just a few friends. So, how's Fenton?"

"Felton."

"You arrived safely, then?"

"If you were worried, why didn't you call?"

"Don't get testy, Maddie. I knew if there was a problem I'd hear from you."

Maddie curbed her sharp retort. He was right. She was being unreasonable. So he had a few people in. There was no point in starting an argument over the phone. That wasn't why she'd called. "Who are your guests? Anyone I know?"

"Just people from the office. I can't talk long, Maddie. I really need to get back."

But Maddie couldn't let him go yet. Taking a calming breath she posed the question she'd called to ask. "Have you thought any more about the baby?"

"It's only been a couple of weeks."

"Almost three." With a sigh, she wrapped the phone cord around her index finger. "I miss you."

"I told you I need time." He sounded irritated. "You have to be patient."

"Time isn't something I have a lot of right now, Roger. This child is yours, too."

"You promised not to rush me."

Maddie took another deep breath, trying to still her rising temper. "Okay. I won't rush you."

"Good girl. Oh, by the way, I got an offer on the condo today."

Her stomach muscles coiled in a knot. "I thought we'd decided to wait before listing it."

"It's a good offer, Maddie. I think we should take it."

She couldn't answer at first. She hadn't been expecting this. If she hadn't called him tonight, how long would it have taken him to let her know about the offer?

"I don't know," she said finally. "Let me think about it."

"Well, don't take too long. They're not going to wait forever."

He didn't sound to Maddie like a man who was afraid of raising children—just one who didn't want to be bothered. "Good night, Roger."

IT WAS STILL an hour before dawn when Nick finally gave up trying to sleep. He'd lain in bed all night, tossing and turning, his mind and heart burdened with thoughts of Jon. Disentangling himself from the sheets, he climbed out of bed and headed for the shower.

He'd failed his son.

The thought had hounded him through the long restless night. Nick thought of their life together—his and Jon's and Sarah's—going over the details, the things he should have done differently. He'd left raising Jon to Sarah. He was *her* son. Not that Nick didn't love the boy, it was just that he'd always been busy, first with getting through college and medical school, and later trying to establish his practice. He'd rationalized that he was doing it for them—for Sarah and Jon.

Now he wasn't so sure.

Maybe he'd been working for himself all along. Maybe the only thing that had ever really mattered to him was his dream. His goal. To become a doctor. Then, once he'd succeeded, he'd dragged Jon and Sarah back to Felton. A place they both hated.

Stepping into the shower, he turned on the faucet, forcing himself to remain under the sudden onslaught of icy water. It was so cold it almost hurt. And yet in a way it felt good. Jarring. Eye-opening. Numbing.

He thought of Jon's accusations the last time they'd been out to the building site together, and the guilt that had been chipping away at him for the past eighteen months buried itself a little deeper in his heart. With a groan, he pushed Sarah from his thoughts. Moving out from under the water, he grabbed the soap and rubbed it against his chilled skin, bringing it to a lather. He'd failed Sarah, but there was nothing he could do about that now. But their son was a different matter.

He must find a way to get through to Jon.

A shiver ran down his spine, and he stepped back under the showerhead to rinse off. A few moments later, he turned off the water and got out of the shower, suddenly very aware of the sharp early-morning chill on his wet skin.

Fifteen minutes later, Nick was dressed and heading down the hall. As he passed Jon's room, he couldn't fight the urge to look in on his son. As quietly as possible, he pushed open the door. Jon lay sprawled across his bed wearing only a pair of oversize, knee-length shorts. He looked so young and innocent. Like the child Nick remembered.

Nick stepped into the room and moved closer to his son's bed. His fingers itched to brush the mop of dark hair away from Jon's forehead, to touch him while he slept and wouldn't recoil. But he couldn't do it. Touching Jon in his sleep seemed an invasion of the boy's privacy. If Nick couldn't touch him while he was awake, he wouldn't touch him now.

As he started to back away, he spotted a corner of Jon's spiral-bound notebook poking out from under the bed. For a moment he considered picking it up and slipping out of the room. It would be so easy. Jon would never know. And just maybe it would give Nick some insight as to how to deal with his son. He was just about to grab the book when he stopped himself.

What was he doing?

He'd always respected Jon's privacy. It was something Nick had never had as a boy. He could hardly violate his own son's privacy now. Somehow they'd work things out.

Reluctantly Nick backed out of the room and headed downstairs. He'd leave a note for Selba, their housekeeper, telling her to let Jon sleep in today. It wouldn't hurt the boy to miss a day of school. Especially with everything that had happened the day before.

Leaving his truck in the garage, Nick set off on foot for the clinic. It was still early, and he hoped the exercise would clear his head. A few minutes later, he found himself on Maddie's street, a good three blocks out of his way. When he saw her house, he realized that he'd planned on swinging by here all along. Several times during the night, his thoughts had strayed to her.

He stopped in front of her house, thinking how homey it looked in the early-morning light, with the sun peeking beneath the low branches of the surrounding trees, casting speckled patterns of light on the white siding. By some standards, it wasn't much of a house, just a small two-story bungalow with a wide wraparound porch. Sarah would have scoffed at living here. But Nick liked it. There was something about this house that spoke of home, and it made him long to walk through its rooms.

He'd been so tempted by her yesterday. He'd been ready to push his way back into her life. Now he knew he couldn't do that to her. His motives had all been selfish. He'd wanted the comfort she could give him, the forgiveness he'd waited sixteen years to ask for. But he didn't deserve either. And Maddie didn't deserve to be dragged into the tumult of his life.

He wondered if Maddie had started work on the inside of her house. Had she set aside a room for a nursery? He could picture her painting it a soft yellow with white trim. He longed to see it and wished that their lives had played out differently so he could have helped her fix her baby's room.

He glanced around the yard at the work they'd left unfinished yesterday. Again he ached for things that couldn't be, for a life and love he'd given up. With one last sigh of regret, he turned his back on Maddie's house and headed toward town. He'd made his choices sixteen years ago. And now he'd just have to live with them. He'd send someone else to help Maddie with her yard. And he'd do what she'd asked him to do in the beginning. He'd leave the past alone.

AN ANNOYING BUZZING pulled Maddie from her sleep.

She scooted down under a blanket, hoping the sound would go away. But it came again, and she opened her eyes. It took a moment for her to figure out where she was and how she'd gotten there. Then she remembered. She'd been unable to sleep last night and had ended up on the couch, huddled beneath an afghan, reading a book that hadn't held her interest.

The doorbell rang again, and Maddie moaned.

Who in the world? She struggled to her feet and stretched to ease the kinks in her neck and shoulders.

She was too old for this. Her body just couldn't handle it.

The doorbell buzzed again.

"Hold on," she called, and glanced at the clock on the mantel to see what godawful time someone was showing up on her doorstep. Ten forty-five. Okay, so it wasn't that early. She'd just had a very long night with not enough sleep. Draping the afghan over her shoulders, she headed toward the front door and peeked out the window.

Lynn stood grinning at her from the porch.

Throwing back the latch, Maddie opened the door and Lynn stepped inside. "Good morning," she said, taking in Maddie's disheveled appearance. "I guess I woke you."

"Mmm." Maddie closed the door and ran a hand through her hair. "I was asleep on the couch."

"I could go away and come back later."

"No," Maddie said, stifling a yawn. "It's okay."

"Well, I have just the thing to wake you up." Lynn lifted her eyebrows suggestively and waved a white bakery bag in front of Maddie's face. "I brought breakfast."

Maddie eyed the bag suspiciously before taking a guess at what it contained. "Is that what I think it is?"

"Maybe."

Maddie took the bag from Lynn and opened the flap just enough to check out the contents. "Gooey-butter cake! I just may forgive you for waking me."

"Apology accepted," Lynn said smugly.

Maddie, fully awake now, grinned from ear to ear. "Do you know how long it's been since I've had one of these?"

"Sixteen years?"

"Exactly. No one else in the entire world makes these things." She took a deep whiff of the buttery confection and moaned in anticipation. "I've looked everywhere."

"It's been a while since I've had one, too." Lynn patted her hips. "It's not exactly diet food."

Maddie laughed. "So you brought it so *I* could gain a few pounds."

"Hey," Lynn said with a grin. "You're pregnant, anyway."

"Uh-huh."

"And I know you've always loved sweets."

"And if Jack caught me tempting you to go off your diet, he'd have both our heads."

"What are friends for?" Smiling, Lynn took the cake from Maddie and nodded toward the kitchen. "Are you going to make the coffee, or should I?"

Maddie winced. "I don't expect I could talk you into tea."

"With coffee cake?"

Maddie grinned sheepishly and pressed her hand to her stomach. "The smell of coffee really doesn't sit too well with me right now."

Lynn laughed and took Maddie's arm. "Personally," she said, as they headed toward the kitchen, "I always thought pregnancy was a bit overrated. We'll drink tea."

While Maddie heated the water, Lynn found cups, small plates and napkins. A few minutes later, they were both seated at the kitchen table digging into the sinfully rich treat. To Maddie it tasted like sunshine and late-Sunday-morning breakfasts when her father would pull her onto his lap and read the comics aloud. She hadn't thought about those times with her father for years.

"Earth to Maddie," Lynn said. "Are you there?"

"Sorry." Maddie smiled, while images of her father still floated on the fringes of her thoughts. "I was just remembering how Daddy used to go down to the bakery every Sunday morning and bring back gooey-butter cake for breakfast."

"You still miss him, don't you." It was a statement not a question. And there was no point denying it.

"Yes." Maddie nodded and held on to her smile. "But I have a lot of good memories." She sighed. "Well, enough of that. What did you say while I was tripping down memory lane?"

Lynn laughed lightly, acknowledging the shift in the conversation. "I just wanted to know why you were sleeping on the couch."

"Insomnia." Maddie smiled and took a sip of tea. "I came downstairs to read and must have fallen asleep."

"Are you okay? Problems with the baby?"

"No, nothing like that." Lynn's concern touched her, and Maddie sought to reassure her. "I got some news last night. And I guess I couldn't get it off my mind."

"Good or bad?"

Maddie hesitated, knowing that if she started talking to Lynn, she wouldn't be able to stop. "Well, it's not really bad news."

Lynn lifted an eyebrow without saying anything, but Maddie saw the question in her friend's eyes. She also saw the patience. Lynn was willing to listen if Maddie wanted to talk.

"In one sense, it's good news. But in another..." Maddie wrapped her hands around her mug of tea. "Oh, what the hell. I may as well tell you. Roger, the baby's father, and I own a condominium in Miami. When I came up here, we talked about putting it on the market, but decided to wait." She kept her gaze locked on her hands and tried to keep the disappointment out of her voice. "He got an offer from a buyer yesterday."

"But you said you were going to wait before listing it."

Maddie lifted her gaze to Lynn's and nodded. "That's right."

"He went ahead and listed it, anyway?"

Maddie shrugged and looked away. Releasing her mug, she picked up her fork and began toying with the remainder of her cake. "I could use the money." She dropped her fork back on the plate, her appetite long gone. "I was hoping that with a little time Roger would..." She shrugged again.

"Maddie—" Lynn leaned forward and lay a hand on Maddie's arm "—it's okay if you don't want to talk about this."

Maddie shook her head and wiped at the tears gathering in her eyes. Lately it seemed as if she spent half her time either crying or on the verge of crying. "No. It's okay. Maybe talking about it will help."

Lynn nodded and gave Maddie's arm a squeeze before releasing it. "It's got to be better than keeping it inside."

Maddie forced a smile, grateful for Lynn's understanding.

"How long have you and Roger been together?" Lynn asked.

"Three years. We work for the same firm. He's an expert on entering new foreign markets." Maddie leaned back in her chair and sighed. "I thought I'd found Mr. Right."

Lynn listened silently.

"We were supposed to get married. Only we were never able to agree on a date." A sliver of anger broke through Maddie's pain. It felt surprisingly good. "I kept telling myself it was as much my fault as his. We both traveled and we just couldn't find a time when we were both in town long enough to even plan a wedding."

"Why didn't you just go down to the county courthouse?"

"Good question." Maddie's anger grew stronger. "But I think I know the answer. Roger never really wanted to get married."

"And the baby?"

"When I told him about the baby, he couldn't deal with it." She hesitated a moment, unable to continue. Just thinking about her conversation with Roger last night infuriated her. "He said he needed time to think things over. And last night when I talked to him, he told me not to rush him.''

Lynn shook her head and took Maddie's hand in hers. ''I'm so sorry, Maddie.''

Maddie squeezed her friend's hand and smiled, letting the tears, hot scalding tears of anger, flow unchecked down her cheeks. ''Hey, I'm fine,'' she said. ''I always land on my feet.'' Grabbing a napkin, she dried her face and rose from the table. ''How about some fresh tea?''

Without waiting for an answer she grabbed the kettle and refilled it with water. As she set it on the stove she said, ''So he's evidently listed the condo without my permission, and now we have an offer.'' With a caustic smile Maddie returned to the table and sat. ''So much for thinking he's going to come to his senses and come rushing up here looking for me. He didn't even ask how I was doing.''

''What did you tell him about the offer?''

Maddie grinned. ''I told him I needed some time.''

Lynn laughed abruptly. ''The hell with him,'' she said. ''If you weren't pregnant we could go out, get drunk and bad-mouth men all night long.''

Maddie met her friend's gaze and started laughing. Lynn joined her, and Maddie's melancholy mood evaporated.

The kettle whistled on the stove and Maddie jumped up to freshen their tea. ''Well I *am* pregnant,'' she said as she poured hot water into their cups. ''And your husband is the sheriff. So, I think we'll have to be satisfied with tea and gooey-butter cake.''

For the first time since she'd told Roger about the baby Maddie actually felt good. She'd been telling herself all along that she could do this—endure her pregnancy and raise this child alone if necessary. She was a strong woman. Now, she knew she'd been right. And looking into Lynn's eyes, she knew she wasn't alone.

Lynn broke into her thoughts. "Jack said you were with Nick yesterday when he got the call about Jon."

"We were at the Bee-Bop eating lunch."

Lynn picked up her cup and rested her elbows on the table. "Did you meet Jon?"

"Yes."

"What did you think?"

"Yesterday wasn't exactly the right day to form an opinion of him." Maddie shook her head, recalling her brief meeting with Nick's son. "Did Jack ever find out who pulled the knife?"

"He has his suspicions. But nothing definite yet."

Maddie sighed, wondering again about this condition called parenthood. "I thought a lot about Jon last night. And his father." That was an understatement. When her thoughts hadn't been on Roger or the baby, they'd been on Nick and his son. "There was a lot of tension between them."

"Losing Sarah was hard on both of them."

"Yes, but—" Maddie folded her arms on the table "—it was more than that." She paused, searching for the right word to describe her first impression of the boy. "Jon was so angry."

"Remind you of anyone you know?"

"Yeah." Maddie let out a short laugh. "Me. I looked into his eyes and knew exactly how he felt. It was scary. And Nick..." She shook her head. "He seemed—" Before Maddie could finish her sentence, the front doorbell rang.

"Who on earth...?" Maddie rose and headed toward the front of the house. "Back in a minute." Pulling her robe around her, she looked out the window, then opened the door. A young man in his late teens stood there.

"Miss Aims?"

"Yes." Maddie realized she must really look a mess. She hadn't even run a brush through her hair. "I'm Maddie Aims."

"I'm Bobby Fieldman, from Fieldman Nursery."

She recognized the name. Fieldman Nursery had been around since before she was born, and she'd gone to school with several of the Fieldman brood. But she'd never met this particular member of the family before. "What can I do for you?" she asked, thinking he must be collecting for something.

"I have a delivery for you."

"You must be mistaken." She felt Lynn walk up behind her. "I didn't order anything."

"No, ma'am. There's no mistake. Doc Ryan sent these over."

The boy stepped aside so Maddie could see behind him. On the porch sat a half-dozen flats of multicolored flowers and two bushes in black plastic pots.

"Six dozen impatiens and two azalea bushes," the boy stated while handing her a small envelope with

"Maddie" scrolled in sharp masculine letters across the front. "Courtesy of the doc."

Maddie stared dumbfounded at the handwriting she would have recognized anywhere.

"Read the card," Lynn urged from behind her.

Maddie opened the flap on the envelope, but glanced again at the array of blooming color on her front porch before pulling out the card. A quick survey of the note left her more confused than ever. Nick had sent the plants and the young man from the nursery to help her finish her yard work. He was tied up in the clinic and couldn't get away.

"I can't accept these," she said when she'd finished reading the note for the second time.

The boy's smile broadened. "The doc said that's what you'd say. And he made me promise not to take 'em back."

Maddie frowned, knowing she wasn't going to get anywhere with this young man. "Okay. I'll take this up with Dr. Ryan."

"Yes, ma'am. Doc also paid for a half day of my time. He said your yard needed some fertilizing and mulching. When would you like me to come over? I'm free either today or tomorrow afternoon."

"Uh, neither for now." She shook her head, not really sure of the best way to handle this. "Let me talk to Nick—I mean, Dr. Ryan, and I'll get back to you."

"Okay." The boy pulled out a card from his shirt pocket and handed it to her. "Here's my number. Just give me a call. The most I need is a day's advance notice."

"Thanks." Maddie closed the door and turned to face Lynn, whose expression reflected her curiosity. Maddie sighed, knowing she wasn't going to get off easy.

"I was doing yard work yesterday," she explained, because she knew Lynn would get the story out of her one way or another. "Nick came by and talked me into lunch, promising he'd help me finish the yard afterward. Then he got the call about Jon, and we never got back here." Maddie shrugged and headed toward the kitchen. "He probably feels guilty."

Lynn followed. "Men never feel guilty. They don't even know what the word means."

Maddie laughed silently and shook her head. Lynn was probably right. Women seemed to have the market on guilt. So why *had* Nick sent the plants?

"Maddie," Lynn said as she returned to her place at the kitchen table, "this all sounds a little suspicious to me. First you have lunch with Nick and then you rush off to the clinic when Jon gets hurt. Now these flowers..."

"Plants."

"Whatever." Lynn waved a hand dismissively. "What's going on between the two of you?"

Maddie avoided meeting her friend's eyes as she grabbed the teapot and refilled their cups. "You said yourself that Nick needs a friend right now."

"True." Lynn rested her elbow on the table and pointed a finger at Maddie. "But you said—"

"I know what I said." Maddie returned the teapot to the stove top and leaned against the counter. "And it's still true. I don't want to become involved with Nick again."

"But?"

Maddie sighed and moved across the room to sit at the table, facing her friend. "I'm worried about him. He's hurting." Lynn nodded but didn't say anything. "And I can't shake the feeling I owe him something."

"Like what?"

Maddie shrugged. "Friendship. Support."

"So what's the problem with either of those things?"

"I don't want to risk getting involved with him again. Not now, not with the baby—"

"We're only talking about friendship here, Maddie."

"I still don't trust him."

"It sounds more like you haven't forgiven him."

Maddie met Lynn's gaze and considered her words. "Maybe you're right." But the question bothering Maddie was whether she could turn her back on him. Could she forget the pain in his eyes when he'd spoken about Sarah, or his frustration when he'd introduced her to Jon? It was a question she was afraid to answer.

CHAPTER SIX

FROM HIS BEDROOM doorway, Jon heard the front door close behind Sheriff Banks. He scooted back to his bed and grabbed a Stephen King novel off the nightstand. The low rumble of the police cruiser starting up outside filtered through the windows, followed by the squeal of tires on wet pavement as the sheriff swung the car around and headed toward town. His dad remained downstairs. Jon wondered how long it would take him to deliver the bad news.

When he heard his dad's footsteps on the stairs, he buried his head in his book. His dad knocked once on his door and then pushed it open. "We need to talk."

Jon looked up, trying to hide his apprehension.

His dad hesitated at the door before crossing the room to sit on the corner of the bed. "What are you reading?" he asked.

Jon shrugged. "Just a book."

His dad nodded and glanced around the room, leaving Jon to worry about just how much trouble he was in. He knew Sheriff Banks had been upset with him Thursday for lying. But what else could he have done? If he'd told the sheriff who pulled the knife, he'd be dead meat.

"Sheriff Banks was just here," his dad said finally. He looked Jon square in the eye—his dad always did that—and it took all Jon's willpower not to glance away. "He knows who you were fighting with. And who owned the knife."

Relief washed through Jon, followed almost immediately by a flicker of fear. Who'd told? It could have been any number of kids. There had to have been a dozen guys watching the fight the other day. Who could have been dumb enough to give Roc away? Then Jon realized that whoever had, wasn't so stupid after all—Roc would believe it had been Jon.

His dad rose from the bed, drawing Jon's attention back to the moment. "You've been suspended from school for fighting on school property."

Jon blinked, unsure of what to say or how to react to being suspended. It seemed like a pretty minor problem compared to dealing with Roc.

"For two weeks." His dad just stood there, his eyes full of disappointment. "Don't you have anything to say for yourself?"

For a brief second Jon wished he could tell his dad everything—the way he used to. He quickly suppressed the urge. His dad wouldn't understand. He didn't understand anything anymore. Instead, Jon shrugged and shook his head.

"Under the circumstances, consider yourself grounded, as well. You're not to leave the house." His dad stood for a moment longer, then turned away, heading for the door. Just before leaving he stopped, his back still to Jon. "I'll run over to the school tomorrow and pick up your work for the week.'' Without another word, he left the room.

Jon tossed down the book and fell back on his bed. What the hell was he going to do now? Missing a couple weeks of school was no big deal. He was acing all his classes, anyway.

But dealing with Roc had just become a whole lot tougher.

Jon had never been as scared as when Roc pulled out that knife the other day. Up until that point, Jon had thought he'd had things under control. Sure, Roc was older and bigger, but Jon thought he could take him. And if not, he got a few cuts and bruises. So what?

But he hadn't counted on a knife.

And just because Sheriff Banks had confiscated Roc's switchblade didn't mean there wasn't another around somewhere. And now that Roc thought Jon had turned him in, there was going to be hell to pay.

Again Jon considered talking to his dad. He'd grown up in this dumb town. Maybe he could come up with some way out of this mess. But again Jon dismissed the idea. His dad just didn't get it about this town. He actually liked it here. The only solution Jon could see was to get out of Felton all together. And his dad wasn't about to agree to that.

MADDIE TRIED to reach Nick several times during the next couple of weeks. She left several messages with Bette and even one on his answering machine at home. He never returned her calls. She tried not to let it bother her, but it did. For someone who'd been intent on renewing their old friendship, he'd certainly become scarce all of a sudden.

At first she thought it was because he knew she'd try to pay him for the plants. But after several days that idea didn't hold up. Nick was never one to shy away from a friendly argument. So why was he suddenly avoiding her?

Finally she decided that if she didn't hear from him soon, she'd corner him at the clinic. Her next appointment with Ted Sommer was on a Thursday. But when she got to the clinic that morning, Bette told her it was Nick's day out of the office. Maddie shook her head. To hell with him! She had better things to worry about than Nick Ryan and his vanishing act.

Fifteen minutes later, she sat once again wrapped in an oversize paper towel as Ted Sommer checked her blood pressure.

"Fine. Fine." Ted nodded and removed the blood-pressure cuff from Maddie's arm. "Everything's back to where it should be."

Maddie breathed a sigh of relief. "Thank God."

"Seems coming back to Felton has been good for you."

"Things *were* getting a little hectic in Miami."

Ted smiled and patted her hand before turning around to write on her chart. "How are things with your mother?" he asked without looking at her.

"She's the same." Maddie hesitated. Before coming here today, she'd planned on telling him what she thought of his revealing her medical problems to Adelia. But Maddie hadn't been able to work up the nerve. It wasn't easy being an adult with the man who'd doctored you since birth. "Dr. Sommer, I don't mean to criticize, but I wish you wouldn't speak to my mother about my condition."

He lifted his head and met her gaze. "I see."

"I know you meant well, but..."

"You're right, of course." Nodding, Ted swiveled on his stool to face her and slipped his hands into the pockets of his lab coat. "Sometimes it's hard for us old-timers to remember that our patients have grown up. And as a parent myself..." He paused, pressing his lips together as if deciding whether to continue. Then he said, "I just didn't want you and your mother to miss this time together."

"I appreciate the thought, Dr. Sommer. Really..."

"No, no. My fault. I apologize." He turned back to his charts. "Being an old man is no excuse."

Maddie lowered her gaze, feeling about two inches tall for even bringing up the subject. He'd meant well. She knew that he'd always treated his patients like family. And now that his only daughter was gone...

"I never told you how sorry I was to hear about Sarah," she said.

He smiled tightly and continued making notes on her chart. "Thank you."

"I know it must be hard. On all of you."

Ted closed her file and spent a few seconds arranging things neatly on the counter. "Especially on Jon."

"I know what he's going through. I see a little of myself in him."

"I suppose you do." Ted turned to look at her, and now his smile was sad. "Too bad Sarah wasn't more like you."

Maddie didn't know what to say. Sarah had been everything Maddie wasn't in high school—pretty and popular. And she'd ended up with Nick.

"Don't get me wrong," he added. "I loved my daughter. Maybe too much." He pursed his lips and looked away. "But she always was a bit spoiled. My fault, I guess. I made sure she had everything she ever wanted."

Maddie remained silent, distinctly uncomfortable with Ted's words. He continued almost as if he'd forgotten her presence. "I'd just like to see her husband and son have a chance at happiness." He lifted his gaze back to Maddie. "They deserve that, don't they?"

Maddie nodded, unable to do anything else.

Ted smiled sheepishly. "Well, listen to me. I'm going on like an old man again. You're doing fine. Keep up with the diet and exercise and I'll see you again in two weeks."

After Ted left the examining room, Maddie considered his words. His comment about Nick and Jon deserving happiness particularly stuck in her mind. He'd confirmed her earlier suspicions that the two were having serious difficulties. As she dressed, the thought continued to tug at her, pulling out her old feelings for Nick. Maybe by being his friend again, she could help him through this difficult time. After all, she knew what it was like to lose a parent. Maybe she could help Nick understand his son.

"Bette, got any clues where I can find Nick today?" she asked when she was back out in the reception area.

Bette smiled. "I've got more than a clue. I can give you directions."

According to Bette, Nick was building a house in the hills north of town. Maddie had no problem following the other woman's unconventional instructions. Of course it helped that she was familiar with all the local landmarks. Otherwise she might have become hopelessly lost.

It was about three miles outside of town, and for most of that distance Maddie considered turning around and going back. Part of her, the rational part, knew seeking out Nick was a mistake. He was in pain, and she herself was not in the best shape emotionally, either. Roger's behavior still weighed heavily on her heart, and she had the baby to think about.

But the other side of her, the side that had once loved a troubled boy from the wrong side of the river, wasn't listening to reason. She wanted to help Nick if she could. He'd meant everything in the world to her once, and she couldn't forget that.

As she pulled into the yard of the building site, the beauty of the surroundings struck her. The skeleton of a house sat on the edge of the clearing with the mountains rising at its back, overlooking layers of tree-covered valleys. It reminded her of the spot she and Nick had frequented when they were kids.

A truck sat in the yard, but there was no sign of Nick. Getting out of her car, she heard the sound of hammering echoing among the tall evergreens.

"Nick!" she called, following the sound. "Nick! It's Maddie."

The hammering stopped, and the mountain stillness almost unnerved her. Then Nick strode out onto the front porch wearing only dust-covered jeans. Something quickened within her. When had he developed a physique that looked like he belonged here, building a house, rather than closed up in a clinic all day? As she remembered, he'd been a well-put-together young man. But this was something else again. Something very adult male.

"Maddie?" His voice snapped her out of her thoughts and pulled her eyes upward to meet his cool gaze. He didn't look exactly pleased to see her. "What are you doing here?"

Sarcasm seemed her only defense. "It's good to see you, too, Nick." She crossed her arms and gave him what she hoped was a disquieting glare. "I was beginning to wonder if you'd left town."

He frowned and shifted uncomfortably. "I've been busy."

"Too busy to return a phone call?" She didn't even attempt to keep the irritation from her voice. "Actually it was several phone calls. In fact, Bette and I have gotten to know each other very well."

"Sorry. As I said, I've been busy."

She considered letting it go. After all, she hadn't come out here to rake Nick over the coals for not returning her phone calls. But she did want to know why he'd sent her plants and then decided to avoid her. "I thought at least you'd come by to see how the flowers and bushes looked once they were planted."

Nick folded his arms and for a moment remained stubbornly silent. When he finally spoke, she heard an unexpected edge of emotion in his voice. "I saw them the other day. On my way to the office."

That surprised her. Her house wasn't on the route between Nick's place and town. He'd obviously gone out of his way to pass by. The realization reinforced her resolve to make him tell her why he'd decided to ignore her. "And?"

He met her gaze again, his eyes a slightly warmer shade than they'd been a few moments earlier. "They're beautiful."

"I want to pay you for them. And for Bobby Fieldman's time."

Nick shook his head. "Forget it."

"Really, Nick."

"I said, forget it."

Maddie knew she wasn't going to win this battle. And it didn't really matter. She hadn't sought Nick out to discuss the plants.

"So what is it, Nick?" she asked, remembering the direct approach had always worked best with him. "Why have you been avoiding me?"

He sighed. "Let it be, Maddie."

She opened her mouth to protest, but then thought better of it. What now? She considered getting back into her car and driving away, consoling herself with the knowledge that she'd at least tried to be his friend. Instead, she motioned toward the panoramic view. "You've picked a beautiful site for your house."

Nick scanned the surroundings. "Yeah, it's nice."

She let a moment slip by and then said, "I thought you might argue about the plants, so I thought I'd even the score by bringing you lunch." She lifted the bags she'd brought from the car. "That is, unless you don't like Dell's subs anymore."

For a moment he just stood there, apparently struggling with some internal battle.

"Come on, Nick," she said. "Even muscle-bound carpenters need to eat."

Another moment passed, and then he smiled, not easily, but enough to acknowledge her effort. "Muscle-bound?"

Maddie shrugged and grinned.

His smile grew. "What kind of subs?"

"The big ones, with double everything."

"What a memory." This time his smile reached his eyes, and she breathed a sigh of gratitude. "Let me go clean up."

"Okay." Maddie set the bags containing the sandwiches on the front steps. "I have sodas in the car." She went to retrieve the small cooler, and by the time she had everything spread out on the porch, Nick had returned to sit next to her on the steps.

He'd found a shirt and put it on without bothering to button it. At first she was grateful for the removal of that distracting male chest from her line of vision. But the brief glimpses she caught every time he moved tantalized her even more. She wondered what was wrong with her that she should be so distracted by the sight of a well-developed set of male pecs. It must be hormones, she decided. Maybe pregnant women were more susceptible to gorgeous men.

She handed him a sandwich and soda, and for a few minutes they ate in silence. Finally she couldn't stand the quiet any longer. "So tell me about this place you're building."

"It's a house."

"Very good, Nick. I never could've figured that out."

Nick sighed. "What do you want to know?"

Maddie ignored his obvious reluctance to discuss the subject. "Oh, I guess first of all, where did you learn to build houses?"

"I worked in construction when I was in college." Nick kept his eyes focused on his sandwich. "I like working with wood. I enjoy the feeling of creating something."

"Very admirable."

"It's an outlet. And when Sarah died..." His voice seemed to catch, and Maddie felt a twinge of jealousy she didn't dare explore. "I thought this would be a good way for Jon and me to spend time together."

She considered following that line of thought, but decided against it. Something in Nick's expression told her they were treading on dangerous ground. "Are you planning to live out here when it's done?"

"No." He paused, then added, "Actually I don't know. It started out as a vacation house. Look, Maddie—" Nick scrunched the sandwich wrapper and shoved it back into the bag "—I'm afraid I'm not very good company today."

"I've noticed." She handed him her wrapper, and he stuffed it into the bag with his. "Do you want to talk about it?"

"Talk about what?" He kept his eyes focused straight ahead while his hands worked the paper bag into a rough ball.

"Whatever's got you in such a snit."

He shifted to look at her. "A snit?"

"Yeah."

"I'm not in a snit."

"Believe me, Nick—" she looked him straight in the eye and dared him to tell her she was wrong "—I know a snit when I see one."

Nick scowled at her for a moment and then broke down and smiled, shaking his head. Only Maddie. He'd never had any defense against her. Sarah would have begged and pleaded or used some roundabout way to get what she wanted. She never confronted him directly the way Maddie always had. He hadn't realized how much he'd missed that until this moment.

"Tell me about Jon."

Her voice brought him out of his reverie. "Jon." Nick ran a hand through his hair. Just thinking about the boy frustrated him. "He hates living in Felton. Just like his mother did." *And he blames me for her death.*

Maddie turned sideways on the porch, resting her back against the railing. "Sarah didn't like Felton?"

"She always hated it. She wanted out as badly as *we* did when we were young."

"So why did you come back?"

"Ted had a heart attack."

Maddie shook her head. "I didn't know."

"He's better now. But he was laid up for months. He needed me to take care of his practice for him." Nick sighed. "It was supposed to be temporary."

"So what happened?"

"Even after he got better, Ted didn't want us to leave. Sarah and Jon were his only family."

He sighed again and decided to tell her something he hadn't admitted to anyone else. Even Sarah. "I guess I wasn't in a hurry to move back to Atlanta, either. It's funny. After all those years I couldn't wait to get out of Felton, now I've grown to love it here."

"And Sarah?"

"She got depressed and started drinking. And I..." *I hardly noticed.* "I guess I didn't realize how serious it had become." He hesitated, afraid to say more, yet needing to talk to somebody who'd understand. This thing about Sarah had been festering inside him for nearly two years, and he needed to get it out in the open. "The night of her accident I was delivering a baby. She wasn't too happy about being left by herself so she hit the bottle."

"Nick, she knew what she was getting into when she married you. She was a doctor's daughter."

"Oh, she had no trouble being a doctor's wife." Nick let out a short laugh and shook his head. "Not in Atlanta, anyway, where she had her friends and the club. But here in Felton? That was a different story."

"I'm sorry, Nick."

"Yes, so am I."

"Nick..." He heard the hesitation in her voice. "Nick, you can't blame yourself for her death."

"Why not?" *Jon does.* "Who else is to blame?"

"It was an accident."

He met Maddie's gaze, wishing he could believe her. "Was it?"

"Yes." Maddie leaned forward, her eyes flashing like silver in the afternoon light. She'd always stood up to him. And for him. He was grateful that some things hadn't changed. "If you must blame somebody," she continued, "blame Sarah."

"Sarah?"

"You didn't force her to drink that night."

"I might as well have."

Maddie seemed out of words. He could see the frustration in her eyes. But this time he couldn't let her defend him. This time she couldn't make things better.

"So why didn't you return my calls?"

"I thought it best." Resting his elbows on his knees, Nick clasped his hands in front of him. "We should leave the past alone."

"That's what I thought. But as I remember, you were the one who wanted to talk about old times." There was no accusation in her voice, only bewilderment.

"I was wrong."

"Does this have something to do with Jon?"

He glanced sideways at her, surprised at her perception. Although he shouldn't have been. Maddie had always been able to see right through him. She'd always known what he was thinking, sometimes before he knew it himself.

"Well, things are a little touchy between us right now."

"The way I look at it," she said, "we could both use a friend. I'm expecting a baby without a husband. And you—" she reached across the distance between them and took his hand "—you've lost your wife. And you have a son who is hurt and angry. What harm could it do to spend a little time together, talk about old times, maybe even groan a little about the current sorry state of our affairs?"

"Maddie—" he turned his hand and wove his fingers through hers "—I wish..."

There was so much he wanted to say, so much he wanted to tell her. But he couldn't. He'd hurt her enough already. Shaking his head, he separated their fingers and set her hand back on her knee.

"Okay." She pressed her lips together and stood, the sting of his rejection visible in her eyes. Her strength reminded him of that night sixteen years ago when he'd told her that he and Sarah were married. She'd been silent then, too. Silent. And angry. Proud. And hurt.

Nick knew he couldn't let her leave like this. Not again. "Hey, Mads."

She stopped and turned around.

"Did you ever learn to cook?"

"Me?" She shook her head. "Never. You?"

"Nope." He rose from the porch step and took a stab at brushing the dust from his jeans. "But I grill a mean steak."

"Yeah?" A slow smile spread across her face, bringing the light back into her eyes. And into his heart.

Nick returned her smile and tucked his hands into the waistband of his jeans. He felt like a teenager again, asking for a date. "How about Friday night?"

"I don't know." Her eyes sparkled with mischief. "I might be busy."

"Jon and I could use a little feminine company."

She hesitated a moment longer and then said, "Okay. But on one condition."

"Name it."

"I supply dessert."

Nick groaned aloud. "Not gooey-butter cake."

"Hey, is it a deal or what?"

Nick laughed and crossed his arms. "Okay. It's a deal."

The silence spread between them, slow and easy. The way it used to when they were young.

"About seven?" Nick asked, suddenly unsure of his own voice.

"Yeah. That's fine." Maddie wiggled her fingers at him and turned to leave. "See you."

"Yeah. See you."

ON THE WAY BACK to town, Maddie's mood brightened considerably. The sun shone in the clear blue sky and the air coming through her open window brushed against her face, fresh and clean. All around her winter had given way to spring. She threw back her head, loving the feel of the air whipping through her hair, and joined the singer on the radio as he sang about eternal love.

Despite all her earlier reservations, she was looking forward to having dinner with Nick and Jon. Felton had been good for her health, but she'd been lonely. Her decision to reestablish her friendship with Nick was looking better and better all the time.

Once in town, she decided to make one last stop before heading home. The *Felton Finder*. She'd been thinking about it since the day she and Nick had stopped in last week. She needed something to do, and from the looks of things at the newspaper, Carl Katz could use an extra set of hands.

When she walked through the door, Carl sat at his desk, pecking away at his antiquated typewriter. "I knew you'd be back," he said without looking up.

"Then you knew more than I did."

"Once the paper gets in your blood, it doesn't go away."

"I managed for sixteen years."

"But you're back." He looked at her then, a wicked smile on his face. "And I could use a good writer."

Maddie sighed and walked around the counter to prop herself on the edge of his desk. "It's been a long time since I've done any writing, Carl."

"No problem, girlie. With a little help, it'll come back. It's like riding a bicycle."

"Well, I don't know about that." Maddie grinned and crossed her arms. "But I'll make you a deal. I'll take a stab at it, if you let me help out in other ways, too."

"I don't need any other help."

"Look, Carl, I've got an MBA from one of the best business schools in the country." Maddie pointedly glanced around at the sorry-looking office. "I'm sure I could find some way to help out around here."

Carl obviously caught her unspoken message. "There's nothing wrong with this place."

"Nothing that a little modernization wouldn't cure."

"I can't afford to modernize."

"You can't afford not to. If you give me a hand with my writing, I'll show you how to bring this place into the nineties."

Carl seemed to consider her offer. "Can't pay much."

"I don't need much. In fact, for the next five months or so, we'll consider it an even trade. Your skills for mine."

"And after that?"

"Let's just take this one step at a time, shall we?" Smiling, Maddie got off the desk and started to leave. Carl's voice stopped her before she reached the door.

"What happened, Maddie?"

Maddie stopped and turned. "What happened?"

Carl rose from his desk and removed his glasses. "Why did you quit writing?"

Maddie sighed and let her gaze wander around the familiar office. "I'm not sure, Carl. I gave up on a lot of my dreams all at the same time. Working for a newspaper, writing." *Nick.*

After a moment Carl said, "Well, maybe things worked out for the best then."

"What do you mean?"

"Maybe you needed to come home to rediscover your dreams."

Her conversation with Carl played through her mind as Maddie made her way home. When she got there, she headed for the stairs that led to the attic, where she'd stored the last of her father's papers, along with her own memorabilia.

Fifteen minutes later, under a stack of dusty old boxes, Maddie found the trunk filled with her things. Opening the lid, she stared at her collection of odd keepsakes, mementos of her high school years. On top lay a framed photograph of her and Nick at the senior prom. Her hand trembled as she reached down to pick it up. Sitting on the edge of the trunk, she smiled at the memory of that night.

Nick had been so handsome, despite his ill-fitting rented tux. He'd gone to please her, and Maddie had been proud to be with him. Some of the other boys had snickered at him behind his back—very few of the kids from across the river ever attended school functions. But none of the girls had laughed. Maddie had been the envy of every female there.

How things had changed for Nick.

Setting the picture carefully on the floor, Maddie turned back to the trunk and spotted a stack of notebooks. She pulled them out, grateful now that she'd carefully marked each with the date and contents. There were five journals covering her high school years, plus several notebooks filled with her attempts at fiction.

Maybe Carl had been right.

She put the photo back in the trunk but kept the notebooks out. Standing, she closed the lid. Maybe it *was* time for her to rediscover some of her old dreams.

CHAPTER SEVEN

ANNA FIGURED she had to be the biggest idiot in Felton. Going to see Jon after the way he'd treated her had to qualify her for some kind of lunacy award. She still couldn't believe he'd told her to go play with her dolls, of all things. Just who did he think he was?

Heck, he'd been the one mature enough to get into a knife fight with Roc and Fatso. Shaking her head at macho-male stupidity, she decided she was only the second-biggest fool in Felton. Jon Ryan was definitely the first.

Ever since he'd come to town she'd tried to be nice to him. Not that it mattered. He had an attitude the size of a mountain, acting as if he was too good for everyone else. Nobody could stand him.

So why did she bother?

She couldn't say for sure, but there was something about him. He reminded her of the stray puppy she'd found out by Fieldman Creek when she'd been a kid. Jon had the same big brown eyes, and every now and then, he looked just about as lost as that puppy. She'd tried to make friends with him. She'd even warned him about Roc and Fatso, but he'd been too stupid to listen. So why should she care if he'd gone and got himself cut? Served him right.

She was a glutton for punishment, she realized. Because here she was, standing on his front porch.

"Hi, Selba," she said to the housekeeper when she opened the door. "Jon around?"

"Why, come on in, Anna." Selba stepped aside to allow Anna to enter. "He's been out of sorts for the past couple of weeks. Stuck in the house and all. But maybe your pretty face will brighten his mood."

Anna smiled, though she doubted seeing her would do anything other than make Jon crankier. "I hope so," she said.

"Go on up." Selba motioned toward the stairs. "His room is the last one on the right."

"Thanks." Anna steeled herself and headed up the stairs. At the door to Jon's room she stopped and took a deep breath before knocking. "Jon. It's me. Anna." When she didn't get an answer, she pushed the door open slowly. He lay across the bed on his side, his head propped on one hand, totally absorbed in a book.

"Jon?" she said again, and he looked up, clearly surprised to see her. "Hi," she said shyly, suddenly wishing she hadn't come.

Jon closed his book and sat up quickly, swinging his legs over the side of the bed. "Hi." He didn't immediately tell her to leave. She figured that was something at least.

"How's your head?"

He reached up and absently touched the white bandage above his eye. "Fine."

Anna forced a smile, feeling more awkward than she'd ever felt in her life. What was she doing here? "Nice room," she said as she glanced around.

His room was a lot neater than any she'd ever seen. Nothing like the disaster areas her brothers lived in. There were no posters on the walls, no collections of strange items cluttering the dressers and desk. His bed was made, and there wasn't a stray shirt or pair of jeans anywhere to be seen. The only thing indicating that anyone really lived in this room was a set of shelves overburdened with books. She wondered if it always looked like this, or if Selba had just cleaned.

"Uh, have a seat," Jon said.

"Thanks." She crossed to his desk and pulled out the chair. "We all heard you got suspended."

"Yeah. Tough punishment."

"Roc, too. For a month."

"Lucky him."

For several uncomfortable moments neither of them spoke. Once again Anna regretted the impulse that had brought her over here. Jon had never shown the least bit of interest in her attempts to be his friend. So whatever gave her the crazy idea he'd be happy to see her now?

"Since you're stuck in the house," she said as heat rose in her cheeks, "I brought you something to read." Anna bit her bottom lip and held out the paperback she'd brought for him. As Jon reached for the book, she quickly added, "I noticed the other day you were reading Stephen King."

"Yeah. He's cool."

"This is his latest. My brother said it was pretty good." Then, as an afterthought, "I hope you haven't already read it."

Jon studied the book in his hand, and Anna held her breath, waiting for him to hand it back to her.

"No, I haven't," he finally said. Then he looked at her, and her heart skipped a beat. "I've been meaning to pick it up the next time I got to the bookstore."

Again there was silence. The room seemed suddenly warmer. Jon looked at her with those soft brown eyes of his, reminding her of that stray puppy again. She thought she'd die of embarrassment if he didn't look away soon, because she could no more move than fly.

"Thanks." That one word, spoken into the tense stillness, broke the spell and nearly sent her running for the door. She just barely held on to her nerve and kept her feet rooted to the floor.

"Well," she said, trying to sound normal, "I guess I should be going." She rose from the chair, hoping to escape with what little pride she had left. Then she remembered one of the most important reasons she'd come over here. "I wasn't the one who told my dad," she blurted out."

"What do you mean?"

"My dad asked if I knew anything about your fight." Anna bit her bottom lip as she recalled her conversation with her father. She hadn't lied. Exactly. She hadn't been around there to see the fight. So at the time she hadn't known anything for sure. "I didn't tell him about the argument you had with Roc and Fatso. Or about the fight, either."

"Anna." She looked up at him. Again the room seemed too warm, and she wasn't sure where her next breath was coming from. Then he said, "Why don't you stay for a while." A small smile appeared on his face, and Anna's heart melted. "We could watch a movie or something."

Anna took a step toward the door, suddenly very unnerved by the boy in front of her. "I can't," she said. "I've got an algebra test on Monday. I need to study."

"Hey, I'm good at math."

Anna blinked, not sure what to say. She'd grown used to an unfriendly Jon Ryan, a gruff unappreciative boy who wasn't worth her trouble. She could resist him. Almost. But this new Jon, with soft puppy-dog eyes and a smile that sent her heart racing, was another matter. She wasn't at all sure she knew how to deal with him.

"I mean, maybe I could help you. Now. Or over the weekend, maybe. That is, if you want."

"You'd do that?"

He shrugged. "Sure."

She hesitated a moment longer before saying, "Okay."

Jon returned to his bed and grabbed a math book off his desk. "So let's get started."

NICK LIVED in the section of town that Maddie had spent the first seventeen years of her life trying to get out of. Just two blocks from her mother's home, his street featured ancient oaks and half-acre yards, with houses large enough to fit a dozen one-room shacks like the one he'd grown up in. It felt strange to be going to see Nick in these surroundings. Even a little eerie.

Maddie rang the doorbell and was surprised when Jon, not Nick, opened the door. "Hi," she said, smiling brightly. "Remember me? Maddie."

"Sure." Jon backed away from the door. "Come on in."

Maddie stepped inside. "Did your dad tell you I was coming?"

"Yeah." Jon shut the door and shoved his hands into the pockets of his jeans. "He got home late and went upstairs to take a shower. He'll be down in a few minutes."

"Okay." Maddie glanced around the impressive foyer and then remembered the package in her hand. "Here," she said to Jon, handing him a white bakery box. "I brought dessert."

He took it hesitantly. "Uh, cool." He didn't seem to know how to act now that his hands were out of his pockets. "What is it?"

"Apple cobbler from Dell's." Maddie took a step toward the boy and lowered her voice. "But don't tell your father. He thinks it's gooey-butter cake."

"Okay. Sure." Jon obviously didn't get the joke. With a gesture toward the back of the house, he asked, "Do you want to go into the family room?"

"Sounds good."

Jon led her into a spacious great room that served as both kitchen and living area.

"Nice," Maddie said.

Jon shrugged, moved over to the refrigerator and set down the bakery box. "You want something to drink?"

"Not just yet, thanks."

The room radiated comfort, despite its ultramodern decor. It was a look Maddie had tried to accomplish in her Miami apartment. Sarah had done it better.

White-on-white dominated: white tile floors, white cabinets and appliances in the kitchen area, and white furniture in the family room area. But Sarah had used soft and livable fabrics in off-white to cover her furniture, and handwoven throw rugs in the same color as the furniture. Pillows in muted pastels lay scattered about the room, and there was greenery everywhere. A large ficus tree stood in one corner, while hanging baskets of blooming impatiens filled another. An assortment of plants lined the top of the kitchen cabinets, and in a hothouse window, which ran from floor to ceiling next to the kitchen table, multicolored African violets added their own touch of color.

The effect was further enhanced by a large marble fireplace on one side of the living area and sliding glass doors leading out to a large deck, that seemed to run the entire length of the back of the house. It was a far cry from the interior of most of the houses in Felton. Sarah must have gutted and remodeled the entire place.

Maddie gravitated toward a display of family pictures on the mantel over the fireplace. There were several photos of all three of them—Nick, Jon and Sarah—as Jon was growing up. Also, there were a couple of wedding shots that Maddie skimmed over, and one just of Sarah. Maddie picked up the picture and studied it.

Sarah was beautiful.

Maddie didn't remember that about her. She did recall that Sarah had been popular with the boys in school. But at the time, Maddie hadn't paid much attention. As Lynn had said, Maddie had been too concerned with her own world. And Nick. How ironic that it had been Sarah who'd married him and carried his son.

Studying the dark-eyed beauty in the picture, Maddie understood how Nick had fallen in love with Sarah. She glanced from the picture in her hand to one of the wedding pictures on the mantel. They were a handsome couple.

"You look like your mother," she said to Jon as she brought her gaze back to the photograph in her hand.

"That's what my dad says. Everyone else thinks I look like him."

"I did, too, at first." She turned to study Jon, comparing him to the picture of his mother. "It's the coloring that makes people think you look like your dad. But they're wrong. You look like Sarah."

Jon crossed the room to stand behind her and peer over her shoulder. "Yeah?"

"Look, you've got her eyes."

"Yeah, well, Dad's are blue."

"It's more than the color. It's the shape. And look at her mouth. It could be yours."

Jon gazed at his reflection in the mirror above the mantel. "I see what you mean."

"And those cheekbones." Maddie shook her head. It was almost too obvious. "If you were a girl, you'd be the spitting image of her."

Jon seemed to consider that for a moment and then asked, "Is what my dad said the other day true?"

Puzzled, Maddie met his gaze in the mirror. "About what?"

"About you and my mom being friends?"

Maddie glanced down at Sarah's picture and considered stretching the truth. Evidently Nick wanted Jon to think that she and Sarah had been friends in high school. But she couldn't lie. Something in the boy's eyes begged for honesty.

"I knew your mom," she said finally, as she placed the picture back on the mantel. "We were in the same class all through school. But no, we weren't good friends."

"I didn't think so." Jon straightened the picture Maddie had just set down and moved back across the room to stand once again behind the kitchen counter.

Maddie followed him with her eyes. "Why not?"

"She hated this town. She said she didn't have any friends here."

"I don't know about the last couple of years." Maddie chose her words carefully. "But your mother was very popular in high school. She was a cheerleader and the prom queen in our senior year. She had a lot of friends."

It was as if he hadn't heard her. "She used to say that she always hated living here. Even when she was a kid."

Maddie sighed inwardly and lowered herself onto the couch. She was treading on dangerous territory here—talking about Sarah to the woman's son. A boy who obviously loved and missed her fiercely. Maddie tried to remember how she'd felt after her father died, what she'd wanted from the adults around her. All she could remember was the anger.

"I wanted out of Felton when I was younger, too. We all did." Jon didn't look like he believed her. "It's true," she went on. "Your father and I were always making plans to leave here and never come back."

"So why did you? Come back, I mean."

Maddie shrugged. "I asked myself the same question when I first got here. Then I realized that *I* came back because I needed a quiet place to wait for my baby. And because there are people here for me."

"Where's your husband?"

"I don't have one."

Jon blushed. "I'm sorry. I didn't—"

"Don't worry about it, Jon." Maddie smiled and brushed his apology aside with a wave of her hand. "It was a natural mistake. Most pregnant women have husbands. But there are other people here for me. My mother. And friends. Like your father."

Jon looked away, evidently still embarrassed. Maddie wished she knew a way to make things easier for him. She didn't have much experience with teenagers, and she doubted that what she'd learned about losing a parent would help him very much. Because she'd discovered that the pain never totally went away. It just dulled with the passage of time.

"Sorry I'm late." Nick's voice brought Maddie out of her reverie, and she noticed Jon stiffen the moment his father stepped into the room. "I got held up at the clinic."

Maddie smiled warmly at Nick, while still very much aware of the suddenly rigid teenager across the room. "No problem. Jon and I were just getting acquainted."

Nick's gaze slid to his son, the wariness in his eyes belying his smile. "Great." He clapped his hands together and headed for the refrigerator. "Well, I guess I need to get going on those steaks." He went to open the door, spied the bakery box on the counter and looked up at Maddie. "You didn't? Gooey-butter cake?"

Maddie rose and crossed her arms. "I told you I'd bring the dessert. My choice. Remember?"

Nick shook his head and walked over to the counter. Just as he reached for the box, however, Jon grabbed it. "That's for dessert," he said, and carried the box into the large walk-in pantry.

Nick blinked twice before focusing on Maddie, who shook her head and shrugged. She couldn't help him. Evidently this was a departure from Jon's normal behavior. When the boy returned, Nick asked, "Jon, how about starting the fire?"

"I already did." Jon didn't look at him as he grabbed a soda from the refrigerator. "I'm going upstairs now."

"Sure." Nick still looked stunned. "Thanks."

Once he left the room, Nick turned to Maddie. "Looks like my son is watching out for your interests."

Maddie grinned and closed the distance between them. "I've always had a way with the Ryan men," she said, although she really thought Jon's actions had more to do with defying his father than keeping her secret.

The rest of the evening went more smoothly than Maddie expected. She helped Nick put dinner together, tossing the salad and zapping potatoes in the microwave while he grilled the steaks. As always, being with Nick was relaxing. They joked and laughed, as if they'd been doing this together for the past sixteen years, instead of living separate lives.

When dinner was ready, Nick called Jon and the boy joined them out on the deck. She had to admit, things got a little tense at that point. Nick did his best to keep the conversation flowing and the atmosphere light, but Jon wasn't buying it. Around her, Jon had been just another awkward teenager. But with his father he'd become an angry young man, whose eyes sparked with defiance.

It reminded her of meals shared with her mother years ago, and her heart ached for both Nick and Jon. She had no idea what kind of relationship Nick had had with his son before Sarah's death, but she doubted it was the silent battlefield it was now. She wished she could do something to help them, but she hadn't the faintest idea where to start. After all, she hadn't done very well with her own relationships.

After dinner Jon retreated once again to his room without waiting for dessert. Maddie, too, claimed she was too full to eat another bite. Nick said he felt the same, and for a few minutes they cleared the table without speaking.

"I'm sorry," Nick said as he carried the last of the dishes into the kitchen.

"For what?" Maddie closed the glass doors behind him.

"For the way Jon behaved."

"Hey. You forget who you're talking to." Maddie moved up beside him and set the dishes in the sink before turning to smile at him. "Remember, I was the world's surliest teenager."

Nick crossed his arms and leaned against the counter. "Yeah. You were pretty rotten, weren't you?"

"To the core."

Nick grinned, and heat coiled slowly within her. Damn, she didn't want to be attracted to Nick Ryan again. She wanted to be his friend, nothing more. But the years had not weakened the effect of those eyes on her. Or that smile. She'd never known another man as handsome as Nick, a man who could turn her inside out with nothing more than a cocky grin and the flash of his deep blue eyes. Not even Roger.

The thought jarred her, and suddenly Maddie wanted to go home. "It's getting late," she said. "Let me help you with these dishes and then I should get going."

"Leave them," Nick said, gently taking Maddie's hand and leading her away from the sink. "I'll do them later. Did you walk or drive?"

"Walk." Her gaze drifted to their joined hands, fighting the familiarity of his touch.

"Good. I'll drive you home."

"That's okay." Maddie pulled her hands from Nick's and crossed the room to grab her purse. "It's only a few blocks."

"I *want* to take you," Nick insisted. "Besides, I have something to show you. Come on."

Maddie knew better than to argue with him. Nick had it in his head to take her home, and she couldn't object further without looking foolish. And it was just a short ride, no more than a few blocks. A few minutes later, after calling goodbye to Jon, Nick helped her climb into his truck. At a little over four months pregnant, she wasn't very big yet, but it was still a long way up for someone whose balance was already off kilter.

"I guess I'm not as limber as I used to be," Maddie said, referring to her growing stomach.

"Just wait. It's going to get a lot worse." Nick closed her door and went around to climb into the driver's side.

"I forgot," Maddie said with a smile. "You've been through this before."

Nick turned in his seat and grinned. "Yep. And Sarah wasn't exactly one to suffer in silence. She made sure we were *both* pregnant."

Maddie laughed, thinking that at least she and Sarah would have agreed on something. "Sounds reasonable to me."

"Looking back, maybe it wasn't so bad. But at the time, going out in the middle of the night for Mexican food seemed a bit much."

"Mexican food?"

Nick started the engine. "Sarah ate beef burritos for the entire nine months."

Maddie laughed. "Pizza."

"Excuse me?"

"I've never really been crazy about it before."

"But now?"

"I can't get enough of it."

Nick laughed, too, and backed the truck out of the driveway. "I'll remember that."

Of course, Maddie didn't have anyone to send out in the middle of the night. Not that it really mattered—the two places in town that made pizza only stayed opened until ten.

As Nick pulled onto the street, he said, "If you're not too tired, there's something I'd like to show you."

Maddie hesitated. She was tired, wasn't she?

"Come on, Mads," Nick prodded. "It'll only take a few minutes."

"Okay." Maddie rested her head against the back of the seat, giving in to that part of herself that wasn't quite ready to end the evening. "But stop calling me Mads."

They rode in silence as Nick headed toward the outskirts of town and turned onto a gravel road leading into the foothills. The road hadn't been there when Maddie lived in Felton, but before they'd gone far, she had a fair idea where they were going. Eventually Nick drove the truck into a clearing at the top of a hill and killed the engine.

Silence stretched out around them, dark and soft as the night itself. Below, Felton nestled into the fold of the hill, its lights nothing more than distant pinpoints in the valley below. Above, a blanket of stars covered the heavens.

"Do you know where we are?" Nick's whispered question rippled through the stillness.

Maddie opened the truck door and climbed out, circling to the front of the truck. Nick followed her. "Our place," she said as a rush of warm tears and memories swelled within her.

Nick leaned against the hood next to her. "I was afraid you'd forgotten."

"Forgotten." Maddie glanced at him and then quickly turned away. "How could I forget? I lost my virginity on this hill." Then she turned to him again because she had no choice. "And I fell in love."

Nick sighed and reached down to take her hand. "Me, too."

Then what happened? she wanted to ask. *Why did you turn to someone else the moment I left town? Why did you let Sarah come between us?* But she couldn't ask those questions. No more than she could have asked them sixteen years ago. Instead, she turned back to stare into the darkness.

After a while she said, "When did they put in the road?"

"About a year ago." He paused, then, "I had it done."

"You?" Maddie shifted sideways to study him. "Why?"

"This is my land." He turned to meet her gaze, and it was all she could do to keep from backing up. There was an intensity in his expression that unnerved her. "I bought it years ago, before I could even afford the payments."

Maddie shook her head. "Why?"

Nick shrugged and looked away. "Who knows? For the memories maybe. To keep somebody else from buying it and putting up condos or something. Who knows?'' After a few moments he added, ''I come here whenever I need to get away.''

Confusion lodged in Maddie's heart. Nick's words implied so much while saying so little. Could she trust her instincts? Or should she ask him to explain? Their sixteen years apart won out.

''Nick, why aren't you building your house on this hill?''

At first she thought he wouldn't answer. When he finally spoke, she could barely hear him. ''Because Sarah never belonged here.''

Maddie fell into a stunned silence. To hear Nick say the words she'd asked for, to know that she'd held a place in his heart all these years, left her puzzled and saddened. She turned away because she couldn't look at him any longer without throwing herself at him and demanding an explanation.

''Maybe we should go,'' Nick said.

Maddie nodded and moved toward the door of the truck, but stopped with her hand on the handle. She'd almost missed it, the small flutter in her stomach, almost like a gas bubble. Then it came again, harder, and she pressed her hands to her stomach. ''Nick.''

Her alarm must have shown on her face, because Nick was at her side in a moment. ''What's wrong?''

Swiveling to face him, Maddie grabbed his hand and pressed it to her stomach. Then they both felt it.

''The baby's kicking,'' Maddie said, and looked up to see her own wonder reflected in Nick's eyes. It wasn't the first time she'd felt the odd sensation, but it was the first time she'd realized what it was. It came again and Maddie started laughing. "I can't believe it. Can you feel her?"

"Yeah." Nick broke into a smile of his own. "What makes you think it's not a 'he'?"

"I just have a feeling." Then she clutched her stomach again. It was harder this time. "Oh, she's getting rambunctious."

Nick laughed and lay another hand on Maddie's belly. "Come on, sweetheart," he coaxed. "Let us know you're in there."

Maddie giggled. "Easy for you to say. You're not the one she's kicking."

The baby kicked again. "That's right, sweetheart. We're out here waiting for you."

Maddie laughed at the absurdity of having four hands pressed to her belly. Nick lifted his gaze to look into her eyes, and the laughter died in her throat. For a moment, the world stood still, and everything else faded away around them. Everything except Nick, with his deep blue eyes, pulling her into their depths.

He lowered his head, brushing her lips with his. His touch stirred her heart, searching for an ember of the love that had once lived within her. It lasted only a moment. Then panic seized her and she nearly bolted. But he shifted his hands to cradle her face, and she lost all desire to flee. The warmth in his eyes held her, calmed her, rendered her beyond thought. Then he kissed her again. Only this time he pulled her close, sliding his hands down her back as he coaxed her lips to open beneath his.

It seemed an eternity before he released her. "Oh, Maddie," he murmured as he rested his forehead against hers. "It's been so long."

She melted into his embrace. No one had ever felt quite as right as Nick. The familiarity of his embrace nearly overwhelmed her. Along with the differences. The width of his shoulders and the strength in his arms told her it was no longer a boy who held her. But his warmth was the same, as was the gentle way he held her, as if she were a piece of fine porcelain that might shatter if he held her too tight. Had he held Sarah, his wife, this way? The question brought her back to her senses and she pulled away.

"Maddie?" He tried to draw her back into the circle of his arms, but she shook her head and pushed against him.

"This shouldn't have happened, Nick," she said, and took another step backward, coming up against the door of the truck. "Take me home now."

"Maddie, please."

She wouldn't look at him. She couldn't. So she turned and reached for the door handle. "Just take me home, please."

"Look at me." Snagging her arm, Nick turned her to face him, holding on to her upper arms. "I'm sorry," he said, his voice a soft whisper. Her panic receded and she lifted her eyes to meet his gaze. "I don't know what got into me."

Maddie cut off his words by pressing her fingers to his lips. "It's okay, Nick. We were caught up in the moment. The moonlight. Old memories. The baby.

That's all." She hesitated. "Let's just forget it happened."

Nick wanted to argue with her. He couldn't forget how it felt to kiss her not even if he'd wanted to. It was as if he'd been asleep for the past sixteen years and had suddenly awakened in her arms. But he knew Maddie didn't want to hear any of that. Not now. Maybe not ever. So he nodded, and opening the door to his truck, he helped her into the cab.

When they pulled up in front of her house, they sat quietly for a few moments. Finally Nick broke the silence. "Maddie, I'm sorry."

"I was wrong," she said.

He studied her profile, his heart filled with a sudden hope that crashed around him with her next words.

"I think it's best if we don't spend any more time together."

"Don't, Maddie." He reached over and tried to take her hand, but she pulled it away and turned to look at him.

"We're both too vulnerable right now. You miss your wife."

"Maddie, don't do this."

"And me." She sighed. "I'm in love with someone else."

Her words tightened around his heart. Yet he'd known there was someone else, someone she cared enough about to have his child. Well, where was the bastard?

Maddie opened her door, and Nick snapped back to the moment. He started to open his own door, but she stopped him. "Don't." She climbed out of the cab and turned back to him before heading into the house. "This is for the best, Nick. Goodbye."

He watched her walk away until she disappeared into the house. He sat there for several minutes fighting the urge to go after her, to ask the questions ricocheting through his mind. "Where was this man who'd won Maddie's love and loyalty? Why the hell wasn't he here with her?

Finally he started the truck and headed north into the mountains. Going home was out of the question. He wouldn't be able to sleep. He'd only toss and turn until his thoughts drove him from his bed. He couldn't even go back up to his hill. The place no longer belonged solely to him. Maddie had once again staked her claim on it. And he knew he'd never be able to go there again without remembering the bittersweet torture of the past hour.

For a few brief moments things were as they should have been between them. They were happy. He'd felt Maddie's baby kick within her. But he'd forgotten that the child belonged to another man. That Maddie belonged to another man. Then he'd kissed her, and nothing had ever felt more right. He loved her. He'd never stopped.

And now it was too late.

With his thoughts whirling through his mind, there was nowhere left for him but the mountains, the night and hours of mindless driving that would push him to the edge of exhaustion.

CHAPTER EIGHT

MADDIE SAT CURLED beneath an afghan in the bedroom that had been hers for the two short years she'd lived with her father. There was comfort here. More than any place she'd ever lived, this room belonged to her. But even here, she couldn't hide from the truths the evening had revealed.

Nick still had the power to hurt her.

Sitting here in the dark, she could still taste his lips on hers, feel the long-dead feelings his touch had awakened. It would have been so easy to let herself go with him, to forget the past and everything that had happened between them. To forget Roger.

But for how long? And at what price?

Right now Nick needed her as much as she needed him. The two of them together had always been stronger than apart. They were drawn to each other by the missing pieces in their lives. But what would happen when those missing pieces no longer yawned like gaping holes in their souls?

She couldn't risk it.

Once she'd believed that Nick would always love her. She'd paid for that mistake dearly. Nor could she trust her own emotions while she was so vulnerable. What if she gave Nick her heart, only to discover that she'd used him to run from the pain of losing Roger? She couldn't pretend, by leaning on Nick, that Roger hadn't hurt her.

The phone rang. A quick glance at the clock told her it was just before midnight. A little late for a call, she thought irritably.

The phone rang again, but she hesitated to answer it. On the third ring, she unfolded herself from the rocker and slowly crossed the room. On the fourth ring, she picked up the receiver.

"Hello."

"Maddie?" The familiar male voice spoke to her across miles of space and months of loneliness. Although she knew who it was on the line, she couldn't bring herself to respond. They hadn't spoken since the night Maddie had called him. "Maddie, are you there?"

She found her voice. "Yes, Roger. I'm here."

"I know it's late." His voice held no apology. "Did I wake you?"

"No. I wasn't sleeping."

"You don't sound like yourself. Is everything okay?"

"I'm fine." Maddie sank onto the edge of the bed, her hand going automatically to her rounded stomach. "We're *both* fine. What do you want?"

She heard his momentary hesitation, something totally out of character. But then again, so had been the tone of her voice. "I accepted the offer on the condo today. I hope you're not going to cause any problems about it." When she didn't say anything, he prodded, "Maddie, are you there?"

"Yes."

"Do you want me to call back in the morning?" There was no mistaking his irritation now. He'd allocated this time to talk to her about the sale of their condominium, and he expected her to comply with his timetable.

"No. Now is fine."

"Did you hear what I told you?"

"Yes, Roger." Impatience and irritation crept into her voice, as well. "You said you accepted the offer on the condo."

"And we set a closing date." Again, there was a split-second pause before he added, "There's no need for you to come down. If you sign a limited power of attorney, I can manage the closing without you."

He didn't even want to see her. Bitterness washed through her, souring her words. "Since that's the way you want it, send me the paperwork."

"Wouldn't you like to know how much we got?"

"It doesn't matter."

"Oh, really." His voice took on a patronizing tone that sent ribbons of resentment down Maddie's spine. "That's a rather irresponsible attitude, don't you think?"

Maddie choked back a surge of hysterical laughter. "I'm being irresponsible? That's rich, Roger."

"And what is that supposed to mean?" He did righteous indignation so well!

"You figure it out."

"If you're referring to your child..."

"I'm referring to *our* child, Roger."

She heard his long-suffering sigh across the telephone line. "Don't start, Maddie. We've already been over this. I need time."

"Time and space. Yes, I know." Anger washed through her—hot cleansing anger. "And no, I don't care what you got for the condo. Just send me my half." She slammed down the phone, then lifted the receiver and lay it on the nightstand.

It took a moment for the rush of adrenaline to subside, for the anger churning within her to ease. Suddenly she began to shiver. Pushing herself back onto the bed, she leaned against the headboard and pulled a comforter around her.

Damn him. "Damn him," she said aloud.

She thought of Nick. Her hand strayed to the phone. One call and he'd be at her side. Quickly she pulled her hand back. It would be too easy to go to Nick, too easy to forget her pain in his arms.

She couldn't do it.

She wouldn't rely on anyone else to get her through this. It was her problem and she'd face it alone.

Hours later she fell into an exhausted sleep. But when she awoke late Saturday morning, she felt surprisingly clearheaded. Sometime during the night the truth had become so obvious that she couldn't believe it had taken her this long to see it.

Her relationship with Roger was over.

Actually it had been over the day he'd told her he wasn't sure he wanted their child. She was through waiting for him, through loving a man who couldn't love her in return. Climbing out of bed, she felt strangely energetic, as if just making the decision had given her a new outlook.

Looking back, she realized that her feelings for Roger had been dying ever since she'd come back to Felton—maybe even before that. But she'd had to get away from him to see it. Not that it really mattered. What mattered was that she now realized that marrying him would have been a mistake. She would have doomed herself and her child to a loveless home. Better she raise her child alone.

She glanced at the table next to her bed where she'd left the notebooks she'd found in the attic. She'd been going through them slowly since she'd brought them downstairs. She picked up the top one and flipped it open to the last entry. It had been written the day before she'd left for college. Turning the page over, she put today's date at the top. She was tired of reading about the life she'd once lived and the dreams she'd once held. It was time to start writing again. Time to start living.

WHEN NICK FINALLY rolled out of bed the next morning, he thanked God it was Saturday. He'd driven for hours last night, getting home well past four. Then he'd thrown himself across his bed and fallen into an exhausted slumber. Going to the clinic this morning would have been impossible.

Downstairs, he found Jon standing at the kitchen counter, eating a bowl of cereal while The X-Men graced the television set with their exploits. Nick wondered when the boy would outgrow cartoons. Then he remembered how he used to like watching them with Jon when he was small, before the pressures of medical school had made it impossible.

Actually he and Jon used to enjoy doing a lot of things together: baseball, hiking, even an occasional wrestling class at the club. Where had all that gone? It was too easy to blame everything on Sarah's death when in truth, he and his son had started drifting apart long before that. About the time they moved to Felton.

Grabbing a bowl and the cereal box, Nick headed for the kitchen table. "You shouldn't eat standing up," he said.

Jon glanced at him as if just noticing he'd entered the room. "I like standing."

Nick frowned but let it go. A few minutes later, Jon carried his bowl over to the table and sat, turning the chair so he could still see the television. Nick nodded his approval, while thinking to himself that he'd have preferred a childish outburst to the infernal silence and grudging compliance.

"What did you think of Maddie?" Nick asked, keeping the tone of his voice nonchalant.

Jon shrugged and kept his eyes on the television. "She's okay."

"What were the two of you talking about before I came down?"

Jon looked up, his defenses momentarily crumbling. "She said I looked like Mom."

"Really?"

"Yeah." Jon turned back to his cartoons. "Something about the shape of my eyes and my cheekbones."

Though his heart ached for his son, Nick struggled to keep the conversation light. "At least someone agrees with me. Maddie always did have an eye for detail."

"I guess."

The cartoon faded into a commercial, and Jon picked up his bowl and carried it to the sink. "Are you dating her or something?" he asked, surprising Nick.

"Would that bother you?"

Jon shrugged, keeping his back to Nick as he rinsed out his dish and put it in the dishwasher.

Studying the rigid set of Jon's shoulders, Nick tried to decide what to say about his relationship with Maddie. He couldn't lie. Too many people in Felton knew about the friendship he and Maddie had shared. But he couldn't tell Jon everything, either. Their relationship was already too tenuous. Nick didn't think the boy could deal with his father having feelings for any woman other than his mother at the moment.

"We dated in high school," Nick said finally. "Before I started seeing your mother. But that was a long time ago. Now Maddie and I are just friends."

Jon nodded and turned back to the television. On the surface at least, he seemed to accept Nick at his word. But who could tell with the boy anymore? Nick searched for something else to say that would keep Jon talking.

"Selba told me you were helping Anna Banks with algebra yesterday afternoon."

"Yeah," Jon answered, without looking at his father. "She's not very good at math."

"It's nice of you to work with her."

"It's nothing." Again Jon shrugged, and Nick wondered if the boy's shoulders ever got tired of the motion. "Easy stuff."

"Maybe for you. But not everybody has your talent with numbers."

"I guess."

Nick sighed with frustration. Talking to Jon was like pulling teeth. The boy's vocabulary had been reduced to a dozen noncommittal words and phrases. Nick wondered what had ever happened to the bright kid who used to chatter nonstop. Glancing at the TV, Nick considered turning it off. But then what would they say to each other? The last time Jon had said more then a few sentences, he'd blamed his father for Sarah's death. Nick didn't think he was ready to listen to that again.

Rising from his chair, Nick put his dishes in the sink and wandered outside. Sarah had insisted on the deck. It was one of the few things she'd added to this house that he'd agreed with. He often came out here when he didn't have a lot of time and needed a few minutes alone. Looking out at the mountains to the north, he could almost pick out the spot where he'd kissed Maddie last night.

Lowering himself into one of the deck chairs, he let his thoughts shift from Jon to Maddie. In all his hours of driving last night, he'd come to one conclusion. Despite Maddie's request that he leave her alone, he couldn't let their relationship stand as they'd left it last night.

If nothing else, he owed her an apology.

She'd offered friendship, a shoulder to lean on, and he'd pushed for more. Once again he'd taken advantage of her vulnerability. Only this time he wasn't a hormone-driven teenager. He was a grown man who'd already hurt too many people.

But more than an apology, he owed her the truth.

It was past time he told Maddie what had happened all those years ago. He knew it wouldn't make any difference to her now. It was too late for the two of them. She'd given her heart to someone else. But she deserved to know why he'd married the wrong woman.

MADDIE'S GOOD MOOD remained with her even when she arrived at her mother's house on Sunday afternoon. Usually she dreaded these dinners with Adelia. This was the third Sunday in a row she'd spent at her mother's house, and she still couldn't figure out why her mother insisted Maddie come every week. Or why she went along with the charade.

She'd have liked to believe her mother was sincerely interested in her health, but she didn't buy it. More likely Adelia wanted to see Maddie for propriety's sake. After all, how would it look if people knew Adelia never saw her pregnant daughter who only lived across town? Yet even as Maddie decided her mother hadn't changed in the past sixteen years, something else told her she was being too hard on Adelia.

As always, Frances answered the door, smiling and greeting Maddie warmly before showing her into her mother's sitting room.

"Ah, Madeleine, there you are." Adelia closed the book on her lap and set it on the table next to her chair. "And how are you feeling?"

"Fine, Mother."

"And your blood pressure?"

"It's still normal."

"Good." Adelia nodded. "Good."

Maddie figured she could record this conversation and just replay it every Sunday. It would save them the effort of repeating the same words each week.

"Frances has prepared a special meal for you."

"That's not necessary."

"Of course it is. You need to keep your blood pressure under control. If you were staying here, Frances could tend to your diet."

Maddie started to respond, then stopped herself. She didn't want to argue with Adelia tonight. They'd have dinner, and talk about whatever mundane topics her mother brought up and then she'd go home. Back to her journal.

As always, dinner proved delicious, despite the cool atmosphere of her mother's dining room. They'd finished eating and were headed once again toward the parlor when Maddie heard the first rumblings of thunder in the distance. Moving to the windows, she noticed the line of dark clouds moving in quickly from the west.

"It's that time of year," her mother said from behind her. "Seems that there's a storm almost every evening."

Maddie wrapped her arms around herself, rubbing at the goose bumps that had suddenly appeared on her upper arms. "Maybe I should get going before it hits."

"Why, we haven't even had our dessert yet. And Frances has gone to such trouble."

"But the weather . . ."

"Don't tell me you're still afraid of storms, Madeleine."

Maddie stiffened at her mother's words but didn't answer. Instead, she kept her back to the room, her eyes scanning the darkening sky.

"I'd have thought you'd gotten over that years ago."

Maddie turned from the windows. "No, I guess I haven't."

"Well, don't blame it on me." Adelia settled into her chair. "I told Davis to stop coddling you. If he'd listened to me, you would have gotten over it long ago."

"I was only five, Mother." Maddie moved to the edge of the drapes and pulled them closed.

"You're not a child anymore. And look, you're still afraid of a little thunder and lightning. Ridiculous, if you ask me."

Maddie turned back to face her mother. "I didn't."

Adelia frowned, but Frances entered the room carrying a tray before she could respond. "See, here is your dessert and tea. You can't disappoint Frances by not trying it."

Maddie hesitated, wanting to go, yet not sure she was up to outwardly defying her mother's wishes.

"You could wait it out here, Madeleine."

Maddie met her mother's gaze, surprised at the touch of warmth in her mother's usually cool voice. Was Adelia actually asking her to stay? After a few moments, she nodded and moved across the room to sit opposite her mother.

As Adelia fixed her tea, she said, "Of course, if your father had been paying more attention, you never would have gotten lost that day."

"It wasn't Daddy's fault."

"No?"

"I'd wandered away from the picnic grounds." Maddie shivered just thinking of that day and how she'd run through the woods, lost, in the middle of a thunderstorm. "The storm came in so quickly. I got frightened and ran. I never would've gotten lost otherwise."

Adelia didn't say anything, just sipped her tea.

"I was hysterical when Daddy found me."

Adelia shook her head and put down her cup. "Your father didn't find you, Madeleine."

"Yes, he did. I remember him holding me for hours."

"That was later." Her mother's eyes sparked with unreadable emotion. "I found you that day. Down near the river, huddled beneath some trees."

Maddie started to deny it and then stopped herself. Had it been her mother who'd found her? She couldn't remember. All she could remember was the thunder and lightning all around her. And she'd wanted her father.

"It doesn't matter," Adelia said. "Here, drink your tea. When the weather clears up you can go home."

Maddie stayed at her mother's for another couple of hours. They finished their tea and dessert, and then Maddie wandered into the library to browse through her mother's books. Neither of them broached the subject of Maddie's fear again, but Maddie couldn't stop thinking about it. She wondered if it had really been Adelia who'd found her that day. She'd grown up believing her father had found her, crediting him in daughterlike fashion for saving her from the elements. Had it really been her mother? And why did it seem so important that she know?

EVENING HAD SETTLED IN by the time Nick arrived at Maddie's house on Sunday evening, only to find her out. Exhausted from two nights with very little sleep, he stretched out on her porch swing to wait. There were only so many places she could be in Felton. And on a Sunday night, none of them stayed open later than nine.

He must have dozed off, because the next thing he knew someone was standing over him, shaking him awake. "Nick. Wake up."

Nick blinked and caught hold of the hand nudging his shoulder. "What are you doing here, Mads?"

Maddie shook her head. "I live here, Doc."

Nick glanced around him. "Yeah, I guess you do."

"Do you always fall asleep on other people's porches?"

"No." Nick yawned and swung his feet down to the floorboards. "This is a first."

Maddie sat down next to him. "Good thing. Someone else might have had you arrested."

"In Felton?"

Maddie laughed lightly and leaned back in the swing, pushing gently against the floor. "I guess not. So, what are you doing here?"

"Waiting to talk to you."

"I thought we'd decided 'we' weren't a good idea."

Nick hesitated and then asked, "Can I come in?"

She turned to look at him in the dim light, her expression unreadable. Nick held his breath. He didn't want to tell her about Sarah out on the front porch.

Finally Maddie shrugged. "I don't see that I have much choice in the matter. I can't very well send you out into the night in your present condition. You might fall asleep at the wheel and run into a fire hydrant or something. Come on." Maddie stood and offered him her hand. "I'll make you some coffee."

Nick took her hand and let her pull him to his feet. "Sounds like a plan."

"I've got some gooey-butter cake inside if you're hungry."

Nick smiled at her lightened mood. "Don't push it, Mads."

Maddie laughed softly and opened the front door. Dropping her purse on the hall table, she motioned toward the living room. "Go make yourself comfortable. I'll be with you in a minute." She disappeared toward the back of the house, and Nick could hear her rummaging around in the kitchen.

He didn't immediately go into the living room, but stood a moment in the front hallway. The room was as he'd expected, small and cozy, with a worn hardwood floor and braided rug. The staircase rose to his left, its ornate banister worn smooth from generations of hands sliding down its surface. A dozen times in the past few weeks he'd passed this house, wondering what it was like inside, wanting nothing more than to explore every room and absorb the feeling of family.

A few minutes later Maddie joined him in the living room, juggling two mugs and a bag of cookies.

"Sorry," she said. "I happen to be fresh out of gooey-butter cake. We'll have to make do with Oreos."

"Too bad." Nick stood and took one of the mugs from her hand. "I was really counting on that sickeningly sweet taste to wake me up."

Maddie grinned as he tasted the coffee. "I hope I got it right. Cream and no sugar?"

"You got it."

Maddie settled into an armchair, and Nick relaxed on the couch. For a few minutes neither spoke. Finally Maddie broke the silence.

"So, what did you want to talk about?"

Nick took a sip of coffee, reluctant to speak now that the time had come. Sitting here with Maddie these past few minutes had felt so good, so right. He wondered how long he'd be welcome in her home after he said what he'd come to say.

"Maddie—" he leaned forward and rested his elbows on his knees "—we need to talk about Friday night."

"Please, Nick. We've already been over that. It was nothing. We were both feeling nostalgic. The moonlight—"

"No." The force of Nick's denial startled even him. Sighing, he lowered his voice. "It wasn't nostalgia. And it wasn't the moonlight, either." He paused again. "Not for me, anyway."

Maddie went rigid. "What are you saying?"

"I'm saying that I knew what I was doing. I meant to kiss you. I would have kissed you again and Lord knows what else, if you'd have let me."

"You planned it?"

"No." Nick shook his head and rested his forehead on the palm of one hand. "I didn't plan it. But I'm not surprised it happened, either." *Not with the way I feel about you, the way I've always felt about you.*

"Nick, please. Let's just—"

"Maddie, there's something I need to tell you." He lifted his head to look at her. She was so lovely, with her dark hair and soft gray eyes. In the dim light she still looked like the girl he'd known and loved. He found it hard to believe that sixteen years had passed. "Something I should have told you a long time ago."

"There's already more going on in my life right now than I can deal with." She abandoned her chair and started to walk away, then stopped and turned back toward him. "I don't want to wrestle with the past as well."

Nick stood and closed the distance between them. "Maddie, please. Hear me out." He reached out and ran his hands over her upper arms. She stiffened but made no attempt to move away. "Please," he repeated, and shifted to wrap an arm around her shoulders and lead her back toward the chair.

Maddie sat, her reluctance obvious.

Nick returned to his place on the couch but reached over to take her hands in his. "Do you remember the night I came to see you at the university?" he asked. "The last time we saw each other?"

Maddie nodded, the painful memory of that night brimming in her gray eyes. "You came to tell me that you and Sarah had gotten married."

"Yes." It still hurt to think about that night. He'd left Maddie without a backward glance, but the pain had been almost more than he could endure. He'd spent the next two days camped out in the woods with a case of bourbon, not caring whether he lived or died. "But you never asked me why."

"It was none of my business."

"You and I loved each other," Nick said. "We'd planned to spend the rest of our lives together. Didn't you think that made it your business?"

"I assumed..." Maddie's voice broke, but she took a deep breath and continued. "I assumed it was because you'd fallen in love with Sarah. That's usually why people get married."

"Sarah was pregnant." For the first time since he'd made her sit and listen to him, Maddie looked up to meet his gaze. The shock in her eyes sent a shaft of fresh pain straight to his heart. "I married Sarah because she was pregnant with my child."

Maddie searched his face as if looking for the truth there. He fought the urge to turn away, hating the confusion he saw in her eyes, knowing he'd caused it.

"Why didn't you tell me?" she finally asked.

Nick sighed and wove his fingers through hers. "I'd promised Sarah I wouldn't tell anyone. She couldn't deal with anybody in town knowing about her pregnancy. Her father was the only one who knew. He pulled some strings and got me into Emory. The next thing I knew, Sarah and I were married and living in Atlanta."

Nick paused and dropped his gaze to their joined hands. "Sarah never knew that I'd come to see you. She would have been furious if she'd found out."

An interminable silence filled the room, widening the gap between them more surely than all the years they'd spent apart.

"I'm sorry," Nick said finally. "I thought you should know. And despite Sarah's wishes, I should have told you sooner."

"How convenient for you." Maddie pulled her hands from his and abandoned her chair, moving to stand with her back to him. "All these years," she said as if to herself. She shook her head and wrapped her arms around herself. "All these years I thought you'd stopped loving me."

"Never."

She didn't seem to hear him. "Do you know how long I grieved for you? How many tears I shed?"

"I hurt too, Maddie." He wanted to take her into his arms and comfort her, but he didn't dare. Something told him she wouldn't abide his touch. "For years I thought of you every single day."

Suddenly she turned on him, her eyes flashing like a million shards of ice. "How dare you! How dare you talk to me about how you suffered. You had Sarah and a son. You had a ticket to becoming a doctor. *I* had nothing. Not even the knowledge of what had happened!''

Her accusation hit home. There was truth in her words. Too much truth. "Maddie..." This time he couldn't stop himself from going to her.

"No." She raised her hands in a defensive gesture and took a step away. "Don't come near me."

Nick stopped in his tracks. "Maddie..."

She met his gaze with eyes gone steely gray. "I want to be alone now."

"I can't leave you like this. We need to talk."

Hugging herself tightly, she turned her back to him. "You've done enough talking. Just go, Nick."

Sixteen years ago he would have ignored her wishes. He would have reached out and pulled her into his arms until she stopped struggling. But staring at the stiff back of the woman standing in front of him now, he knew this wasn't the seventeen-year-old girl he'd once loved. This woman wouldn't be so easily placated. And he was no longer the brash young man who would've tried.

"Okay," he said. "I'll go. For now."

Maddie merely nodded.

"Call me," he said. "When you're ready to talk."

Maddie remained still until she heard the front door close behind him. Then she rushed into the foyer and threw the dead bolt. She didn't want him coming back.

She'd never in her life been so angry.

Returning to the living room, she gathered up the mugs and the remains of the cookies and carried them into the kitchen. How dared he tell her this after what he'd put her through! He made it sound like marrying Sarah had been some noble sacrifice on his part.

Please!

And how the hell had Sarah gotten pregnant in the first place? She certainly hadn't done it on her own. A few months without Maddie, and he'd jumped into bed with the first willing female. Noble sacrifice indeed! How naive did he think she was?

Then he had the nerve to tell her how he'd suffered. She fought the urge to throw something across the room. He'd always wanted to be a doctor. Had he married Maddie, it would have been an uphill battle. They would have faced years of struggle. And he never would have been able to get into Emory as an undergraduate student. But as Ted Sommer's son-in-law, Nick had walked right into the best premed program in the state.

It made her blood boil.

CHAPTER NINE

FOR THE NEXT WEEK Maddie ran on pure adrenaline. Giving in to the urge to fix up her house, she threw herself into the work with a vengeance. She talked to carpenters and painters, carpet layers and paper hangers. She planned her baby's nursery and redesigned her outdated kitchen to make it more spacious.

When she wasn't busy with her house, she tormented Carl Katz. She took him computer shopping and helped him pick out a system that would replace his antiquated typewriter and pay for itself in a matter of months. Then she set about studying the business aspects of putting out a newspaper like the *Felton Finder,* gaining an understanding of its problems so she could present some reasonable solutions.

By Saturday she'd begun to calm down. Much of her anger had been washed away by long hardworking days and restless nights. She'd gone over the conversation between herself and Nick a hundred times in her mind, changing her responses, stabbing him with words she wished she'd said.

Then in her last few waking moments on Saturday night, her thoughts shifted. Not once during the week had she thought about any of this from Nick's perspective. Not once had she reminded herself that Nick's marriage to Sarah had taken place sixteen years ago, and that at the time, all three of them had been little more than children—just a couple years older than Nick's son, Jon. The thought disturbed her. Almost as much as the erratic anger she'd lived with this past week.

After seeing things in a different light, Maddie thought about calling Nick at least half a dozen times a day. It wasn't that she'd forgiven him, she told herself. She just wanted to talk to him. So much had been left unsaid, and she was tired of secrets. She wanted everything out in the open. She wanted to understand what had happened.

Still, she didn't call him. She couldn't have said exactly why, but something kept her from picking up the phone. Maybe it was as simple as not knowing what to say or as complicated as not wanting to hear any more truths. Maybe there really wasn't anything left for the two of them to discuss. Maybe they'd already said too much.

On a Sunday morning two weeks after she'd last talked to Nick, Maddie woke to warm sunshine streaming through her windows. Sitting up in bed, she stretched, feeling better than she had in days. Last night she'd finally had a good night's sleep. She suspected it was because she'd been too exhausted to do anything else.

Slipping from bed, she walked over to the full-length mirror and turned sideways, smoothing her nightgown over her growing stomach.

"Good morning, Baby." She rubbed her tummy and smiled. Another week and she'd be five months along—past the halfway mark. "I guess I've been a little negligent these last weeks. Well, today we'll take it easy."

For the first time in days, she didn't rush. She took a long hot shower and then dressed, donning a new maternity outfit she'd been saving for a special occasion. She had nothing planned for the day, but she felt good and wanted to look good, as well.

When she was ready, she looked at herself in the mirror one more time. The voluminous top and stretch maternity leggings still hid her expanding middle, but she knew that would soon change. The woman in the maternity shop had told Maddie that this particular set might not be large enough for the later months of her pregnancy. But the cobalt blue top brought out her coloring, so she'd bought it anyway.

As she made her way downstairs, she remembered how she'd always loved Sundays as a girl. It had been Adelia's day out of the house, visiting her friends and making the rounds of Felton's social circuit. That meant it was Maddie's day with her father.

For most of the day, she and her father had been free to pursue one adventure after another. They'd read together in the backyard under the old elm tree or explore the woods outside town. It had never mattered to Maddie what they did as long as she was with her father.

It had been on one of their Sundays together that she'd gotten separated from her father and ended up lost in the middle of a thunderstorm. She recalled her recent conversation with her mother about that episode, but quickly pushed the thought aside. It was too nice a day to fret about something that happened a long time ago.

Suddenly she knew how she wanted to spend her day. Since coming home to Felton she'd avoided visiting her father's grave. Before she'd gone away to college, when his death had been like a open wound in her heart, she'd spent every Sunday there. She couldn't believe she hadn't thought to go out there since coming home.

She ate a quick breakfast and then headed out, stopping only to pick up a large bouquet of bright yellow daisies.

The cemetery occupied five acres on the outskirts of town. As a child, Maddie had feared it as a place of ghouls and goblins and unspeakable horrors. But when her father had been laid to rest there, it had become a place of unbearable grief. Now time and distance allowed her to see it differently. In the bright spring sunshine, it was a place of peace. The quiet rolling hills seemed to harmonize with the massive trees standing guard.

She parked near her father's family plot and got out of the car. Slowly she made her way along a dirt path, stopping to read a headstone here or there. At last she came to her father's grave and lay the handful of daisies on the grassy mound, waiting for the tears.

Instead, a sense of calm stole over her. Closing her eyes, she felt her father's presence in the depths of her soul. She'd buried him years ago but had never let him go. The time had come. Her eyes moistened and her throat constricted, but not from grief. Peace had crept into her heart.

Later, perhaps hours or mere minutes Maddie didn't know, she turned to leave. But she was in no rush to get home. She walked among the graves, relishing the tranquillity she'd found here. When she finally returned to her car, she noticed that she wasn't alone. Across the road and up the hill, Jon Ryan sat in the grass by a small headstone.

She didn't know whether to stay or leave. For a moment she stood watching him, her thoughts returning to her own adolescence, to the hours she'd spent sitting beside her father's grave. How many times had she ached for someone to ease her grief? How many times had she longed, deep in her heart, for a comforting word, for someone to hold her while she wept?

In the end, the lone figure drew her, and she found herself heading up the hill. Jon glanced at her as she approached and closed the notebook in his lap. Without speaking, Maddie sat down on the grass next to him.

"What do you want?" he asked. His voice held no rancor, only a quiet desperation.

"You looked like you could use some company."

Jon met her gaze for a brief moment and then stared at the ground. "I'd rather be alone."

Maddie knew it wasn't true. "I came to visit my father." When Jon didn't say anything, she added, "I used to come every Sunday when I lived in Felton."

For several moments, Jon didn't respond. Then he asked, "When did he die?"

"A long time ago." Maddie sat cross-legged and rested her elbows on her knees. "I was twelve."

"My mom died when I was thirteen."

"Yes. I know."

"It was so stupid." Jon pulled at the grass in front of him, tossing the torn blades aside. "She shouldn't have died."

"I know."

Maddie didn't know what else to say. She'd felt the same way about her father's death, though the circumstances had been different. Davis Aims had died of a brain embolism that no one could have seen coming. How much harder it must be for Jon, whose mother had died needlessly in a car accident.

"I loved my father more than anyone in the world," she said, wanting to reach through this boy's grief. "After he died I used to spend every Sunday here, talking to him, telling him all my problems."

"Do you think he heard you?"

Maddie smiled. "I think he heard every word."

"Do you still miss him?"

"Terribly." Maddie hesitated. "But it doesn't hurt as much as it used to."

"I miss my mom a lot." She heard Jon sigh. "Somehow I feel closer to her here."

"You'll always miss her." Maddie reached out a hand, but at the last moment stopped herself from brushing her fingers against the boy's cheek. "It won't ever stop hurting, Jon. But it *will* get easier. I promise."

He shifted his head to look at her, his eyes bright with unshed tears. She wanted to take him in her arms and tell him it was okay to cry, and if he'd been a girl, she might have tried it. But this stoic young man, so much like his father, wouldn't allow her to comfort him. Maybe Sarah would have been able to get away with it, but Maddie was still a stranger.

She struggled to her feet. "Can I give you a ride home?"

Jon took a moment to answer. "Okay." Standing, he threw one last look at his mother's tombstone before following Maddie down the hill to her car.

Maddie smiled at the resiliency of youth when Jon caught sight of her bright red Porsche. "Wow!" he said. "Awesome car."

"Thanks." Maddie smiled and unlocked the door. "Get in."

Jon climbed in, obviously taken with the plush leather seats. "When we lived in Atlanta, one of my friends' dad had a black Porsche."

"Oh, yeah? Did you like it?"

"He never let any of the kids ride in it."

"How old are you?" Maddie asked as she started the engine.

"Fifteen. I'll be sixteen in the fall."

Maddie turned the car around and headed toward the cemetery gates. "If I'm still around when you get your license, you can drive this one."

"Really?"

"Sure. Why not? It's just a car."

"Yeah, about seventy-five thousand dollars' worth of car," he said, awe in his voice.

Maddie smiled at his enthusiasm. "It's insured. And I know your father wouldn't let you drive unless you were insured, too. So what's the big deal?"

Jon didn't have an answer for that. Maddie glanced at him again and saw the huge grin on his face. Evidently she'd just blown him away. It was a start. But a start at what she couldn't say.

"So where do you live?" Jon asked. "I mean, when you're not in Felton."

"I've lived all over. But for the past three years I've been in Miami."

"Mom and I went to Miami Beach once."

"Did you like it?"

Jon hesitated as if considering his answer carefully. "The beach was pretty cool. But there were a lot of old people. I mean, like Gramps' age."

Maddie laughed. "Yep, that sounds like south Florida."

"Where else have you lived?" Jon asked, turning sideways in his seat.

"Well," Maddie thought back to all the places she'd lived, "I started off at the University of Georgia in Athens. But I left there to go to Northwestern after my first year."

"That's in Chicago, right?"

"Evanston, really. Which is a suburb north of Chicago. After I got out of school I lived in San Francisco for a few years. Then Seattle. And finally Miami."

"How come you moved so much?"

"The company I work for has offices on both coasts. I went wherever the next promotion took me."

"So, what do you do?"

Maddie couldn't believe this stuff interested him. "I'm a consultant for a firm specializing in international business."

"Do you like it?"

That was a good question. She'd never thought about it before coming back to Felton. But meeting and talking to Carl Katz had made her question the occupation she'd chosen.

"Yeah," she said. "I guess I like it." Actually she figured her true feelings about her job were pretty neutral. She didn't love her work, but she didn't hate it, either. It was just what she did. "It pays well, anyway."

"Yeah! Look at this car."

Maddie laughed. The car had been an extravagance. One she'd often wondered about herself.

"So, have you been all over the world?" Jon asked.

"Well, not exactly." Maddie pulled up in front of Jon's house, but he seemed almost reluctant to get out. "But I have traveled overseas quite a bit."

"Like where?"

Maddie had no idea Jon could be this talkative, but she decided she liked it. "London, Paris, Tokyo, Berlin. I've spent time in all the major industrial cities."

He seemed to consider this information for a moment and then asked, "So, how are you going to do all that after your baby comes?"

"You really know how to cut right to the core of things, don't you?"

Jon blushed. "Sorry. Mom always said I asked too many questions."

Maddie laughed lightly, again fighting off the urge to reach over and touch him. "I don't mind. Tell you what, why don't you stop by my house after school one day and I'll show you all the stuff I brought home from overseas? I'll answer more of your questions then."

"Okay." Jon grinned and climbed out of the car. "Hey, thanks, Maddie. You're okay."

She smiled as she watched him walk away. She liked Nick's son. He was bright and inquisitive, attributes he'd hidden the night she'd had dinner with him and his father. Thoughts of Nick brought a wave of guilt, and she glanced toward the house. She should call him. What was she waiting for?

But then she thought about the kiss they'd shared the night she'd first felt the baby kick. Just the memory sent her heart racing. What would have happened if she hadn't backed away that night?

The thought made her reconsider her reasons for not calling him. And maybe those reasons had nothing to do with finding out the truth. Maybe she was just afraid of losing her heart again.

FROM AN UPSTAIRS WINDOW Nick watched Maddie's car disappear around the bend at the end of his street.

When she'd first pulled up outside, he thought she'd come over to talk. Then Jon had climbed out of her car, smiling and waving goodbye, and a rush of jealousy washed over him. The worst part was, he couldn't say of whom he was more jealous, Jon for spending time with Maddie, or Maddie for being able to pull a smile from his son.

For the past couple of weeks he'd expected to hear from her. He'd figured that once she calmed down, she'd want to talk. But the days had gone by, and she hadn't called.

Nick turned away from the window and headed for the stairs. He was curious to know where Jon had been all day and why he'd come home with Maddie. He heard the front door slam as the boy entered the house. But as Nick approached the top of the stairs, he thought he heard his son whistling. Stopping, he listened carefully. After a few minutes, he decided he'd been wrong. Still, he changed his mind about going downstairs and returned to his office.

But the question plagued him for the rest of the day. Had it actually been whistling he'd heard from Jon, the same boy who'd hardly even smiled in the past eighteen months?

THE FIRST FLOWERS arrived on Monday. Yellow daisies. Even without a note, Maddie knew who'd sent them. Nick knew her weaknesses. And yellow daisies were one of her worst. On Tuesday it was gooey-butter cake. She moaned as she opened the gift-wrapped box, which she'd found sitting on her front porch under her morning newspaper.

By Wednesday she wasn't surprised to find a huge yellow-and-white teddy bear sitting on her front porch swing when she got home from Collier's grocery. She smiled as she carried the stuffed toy into the house and wondered what Nick would think of next.

Thursday morning and afternoon went by without any surprises, and Maddie figured Nick had given up.

Or run out of ideas. It was for the best she told herself, even as she fought her disappointment. Then at seven forty-five the doorbell rang, and Maddie's heart leapt. Suppressing the joy that threatened to burst forth, she headed for the door. It was a Western Union telegram: MADDIE, TURN ON WLUV CHANNEL 98.5 AT EXACTLY 8 P.M.

She couldn't get to the radio fast enough. At exactly eight o'clock she sat on the couch, hugging a pillow as the voice on the radio announced that Thursday was the night for lovers. "And our first song is dedicated to Mads. Well, I sure hope she's listening, because this one's an oldie but goodie."

As the first bars of John Denver's "Annie's Song" filtered into her living room, tears trickled from her eyes. Their song. Hers and Nick's. Even after all these years, every time she heard that melody it reminded her of him.

Friday she was bombarded with yellow roses. Dozens of them. They arrived all day long, from florists all over the county, until she lost track of how many times she'd gone to the door to accept yet another delivery.

Saturday the doorbell rang early. In a picnic basket, Maddie found everything needed for breakfast in bed. Fruit and freshly baked croissants, coffee, milk and orange juice, a morning newspaper and a single red rose, along with a note saying the champagne would be delivered after the baby was born.

Sunday morning she awoke to a delicate tinkling sound that continuously changed in pitch. She climbed out of bed, charmed by the sweet melody, and went in search of the source. She found it outside, along with a thousand particles of colored light dancing across her front porch. Wind chimes. A dozen prisms hung at various levels from a circle of blown glass, gently singing in the breeze while tossing rainbows to the wind.

Maddie thought she'd never seen anything more beautiful, and if Nick had shown up at that moment, she knew she'd be lost. As it was she could barely keep herself from calling him.

By the time she walked into the clinic on Monday morning for her five-month checkup, she thought nothing else Nick could do would surprise her. Still, she gave a start when she heard her name, spoken as soft as a caress.

"Maddie?"

Looking up from the magazine on her lap, Maddie's heart jumped at the sight of him. She should have guessed he'd ambush her here. "Hello, Nick."

He scanned her from head to toe, his gaze finally coming to rest on hers. "You look..."

"Pregnant?" she supplied.

"Yes." He grinned. "Pregnant and lovely."

Maddie's face heated and she looked away, wondering at this man's power over her. Here she was, a thirty-three-year-old woman, blushing at a simple compliment.

"Do you have a few minutes?" he asked.

Maddie glanced at the other two patients, who seemed a little too interested in their conversation. "I'm sure Dr. Sommer will be looking for me soon."

"That's okay." Nick moved up beside her and took her arm, helping her out of the chair. "We'll tell him where to find you." Maddie had little choice but to go along.

"Bette," he said, as the door to the waiting room closed behind them. "Maddie and I will be in my office for a few minutes. Let us know when Ted's ready to see her."

"Sure thing, Dr. Ryan."

Nick walked Maddie back to his office. Once inside, he closed the door and motioned toward one of the chairs on the other side of his desk.

"That was pretty smooth, Dr. Ryan," Maddie said as she took the chair he'd indicated. "Now I know how it feels to be spirited away."

Nick propped himself on the corner of his desk. "A man could grow old waiting for a woman like you to call him."

Maddie met his gaze. "And a woman could suffer a broken heart loving the wrong man."

"Is yours?" Nick crossed his arms. "Broken, that is?"

"Not anymore."

Nick studied her. He'd asked more than the words had implied. He wanted more from her than simple conversation. And she was tempted to give it to him.

"Five months, isn't it?" he said, breaking the silence.

Maddie leaned back in her chair and glanced around the cluttered office. "I have a feeling you know pretty much everything there is to know about my pregnancy, Nick."

"I keep up with Dr. Sommer's patients." Nick grinned.

Maddie shook her head, unable to stop a chuckle. He was incorrigible.

"It's hard to believe you've only been back in town for eight weeks," Nick said. "I can hardly remember when you weren't here."

It took a moment, but Maddie steeled herself against the sincerity of his words. "Enough, Nick." She started to stand, but he held up his hands in mock surrender, and she settled back into the chair.

"I'll behave," he said. Although why she should believe him was beyond her. He'd never behaved in his life. "How's the baby doing?"

Maddie sighed and shook her head. "Kicking up a storm."

Nick's gaze drifted to the swell of her stomach, and the memory of the night they'd first felt the baby kick suddenly sharpened in her mind. He lifted his gaze to hers, and she recognized the memory in his eyes as well.

She glanced away.

Nick pushed off the desk and went to sit in his chair. "Jon told me you gave him a ride the other day," he said. She thought she detected a slight tremble in his voice.

She was about to mention finding Jon at the cemetery but changed her mind. "He got a kick out of my car."

"What fifteen-year-old wouldn't? As a matter of fact, I know one thirty-five-year-old who thinks it's pretty neat."

"I told Jon he could drive it."

Nick lifted his eyebrows in surprise.

"When he's sixteen," Maddie added. "If I'm still here."

Her statement seemed to sober him. That was good. Nick needed to be reminded that she wasn't staying in Felton indefinitely.

"Nick," she said, leaning forward in her chair, "please don't send anything more to my house. It's too much." He started to say something, but she held up her hand to stop him. "I appreciate the thought behind the gifts. You made me smile and you made me cry, but..."

"Why haven't you called?"

At least they weren't dancing around the issue any longer. "I was angry."

"But not anymore."

"No. Not anymore."

He stood and came around to the front of the desk again. "Maddie, we need to talk."

She looked into his eyes and thought how easy it would be to agree. "There's nothing to say, Nick."

"There's a lot to say."

Maddie shook her head, though her heart screamed at her to let him into her life. Nick could fill all the empty places within her. He could make her forget.

"Please try and understand, Nick. There's too much going on in my life right now, too much that's unsettled. I can't continue to fight you off, but I can't accept what you're offering, either."

"I'm not asking for anything, Maddie."

"Yes, you are."

Nick glanced away, but not before she saw the turmoil in his eyes. "Please, Nick. If I ever meant any-

thing to you—'' he brought his gaze back to hers
''—let me go.''

Nick reached down to grasp her hands and pull her
to her feet. She didn't protest. She'd told him what she
wanted, what she needed. It was up to him to abide by
her wishes—or ignore them.

''Do you forgive me, Maddie?''

''Forgive you?''

''For Sarah.''

Maddie sighed and brought her hands up to his
face, rubbing her knuckles against his cheek. ''I think
maybe there's nothing to forgive.'' She saw the relief
flood his eyes. ''We were children. All of us. You did
the best you could.''

Nick brought their joined hands to his lips and
brushed her fingers with his lips. ''Thank you.''

He kept his eyes locked on hers, making her want to
fall in love with him all over again.

''I've always loved you, Maddie,'' he said. ''If you
ever need anything, I'll be here for you.'' He lowered
their hands and leaned over, brushing her mouth
lightly with his lips. Then he released her and stepped
away.

For a moment Maddie fought an overwhelming
urge to step into his arms. Then she closed her eyes
and remembered why she couldn't. Even if she *could*
bring herself to forget the past and trust Nick again,
it was too soon. She'd just put Roger behind her. She
needed time to get her life back together. She wasn't
ready to start another relationship. Especially one with
Nick, who'd already broken her heart once.

CHAPTER TEN

"ANNA!"

Lynn's voice stopped Anna's headlong flight down the stairs. Resigned to the upcoming interrogation, she sighed and took the last few steps at a slower pace before turning to face her mother. "Yeah, Mom?"

"Where are you going?"

"Over to Jon's."

"That makes the third time this week."

Anna hiked her book bag over one shoulder. "He's helping me with my algebra."

"Are you sure that's what you're doing over there?" Her mother wore her "I'm trying to be a good parent" expression. Unfortunately it usually preceded one of her "I'm doing this for your own good" speeches.

"We sit at his kitchen table and do math," Anna said with all the patience she could manage. She knew when her mom was a fraction away from telling her she couldn't do something. "He's really helping me a lot, Mom. I might even be able to pull off a *B* in the course."

Frowning, her mother crossed her arms. "Why don't the two of you come over here and work?"

"Because the little monsters make too much noise."

"Don't call your brothers names."

"Come on, Mom. It's okay. I promise. Ask Selba. She's always in the house with us."

Her mother hesitated, then sighed. "All right." Her tone indicated she was doing this against her better judgment. "But be home by seven."

"Sure thing." Anna leaned over and kissed her mom on the cheek. Her mom ate it up when Anna got mushy. "Love you."

"Yeah. Me, too."

Anna grinned and scurried out the door.

For nearly three weeks now Jon had been helping her with algebra. Not only did he understand math, but he was a surprisingly good teacher. Her grades had improved immediately. She'd actually gotten a *B* on the first test he'd helped her prepare for. It had been the first decent grade she'd gotten in math all term. Now the final was coming up, and if she could ace it, she just might squeak through with a *B* for the course.

But algebra wasn't the only reason she was going over to Jon's this afternoon. She'd heard something at school she needed to tell him. When she got to his house, she went around to the back door, knocked once and let herself in. She no longer bothered with the front door.

"Hi, Selba," she said as she dumped her bag on the kitchen table. "Where's the teach?"

"Hi, honey. He'll be down in a minute." Selba pulled something from the oven, and the room instantly filled with the aroma of freshly baked cookies. "I made you all a special treat today. Tollhouse."

Anna walked over to take a deep breath of the tempting aroma. "Oh, Selba, I'm trying to watch my weight."

Selba gave her a knowing smile but shook her head. "You're already thin enough to blow away in a strong breeze. You can afford a cookie or two." Selba took a spatula, filled a plate with the warm cookies and offered it to Anna.

"Okay. But just one." Anna took a cookie from the plate and then grabbed a second.

Selba smiled and set the plate on the table. "I'll just leave these here. I know Jon will want some when he gets down."

Jon showed up a few minutes later, and he and Anna sat down at the table and began working. But Anna's mind kept wandering. She wanted to talk about what she'd heard at school today but didn't know where to start.

She and Jon had been getting along pretty well lately, at least as long as they talked about algebra, which, to Anna's dismay, was all they did. She thought of her mother's concern about her studying with Jon every afternoon and had to smile. If only her mom knew just how safe she was with Jon Ryan.

"What's with you this afternoon?" Jon said, evidently noticing her distraction.

Anna shrugged, still hesitant to bring up what was bothering her. "Nothing."

"Well, how about paying attention here, then?"

His attitude irritated her. "You're not my teacher, Jon Ryan," she snapped. "So, lay off."

"Well, excuse me." Jon slammed the book shut. "But I thought you wanted an *A* on your final."

Anna immediately regretted her sharp words. After all, Jon was spending his own time trying to help her. "Yeah, I do." She smiled apologetically. "I'm sorry."

Jon seemed to consider her apology for a moment and then shrugged. "So, what's bugging you?"

"I saw Roc today. He's back at school."

"Yeah, I know."

Anna was silent a moment. As far as she knew, she was Jon's only friend. And from what she'd heard about the knife fight, the audience had been rooting for Roc. She couldn't imagine anybody bothering to warn Jon about Roc's return to school.

"So, what are you going to do?" she asked at last.

"What do you mean?" Jon glanced back to the math book on the table. Flipping it open, he started to look for the section they'd been working on. "I'm not going to do anything. Do you want to get back to work or what?"

"Forget the math!" Anna reached over and closed the book again. "You don't really believe Roc's going to let it go, do you?" Hadn't Jon learned anything about Roc in the past couple of months? "He thinks you told my dad about the knife. He's going to come after you."

Jon glared at her. "I didn't tell the sheriff anything."

"But Roc doesn't know that. He's been lying low for the past four weeks waiting to get back at you."

"I can't help what Roc thinks." Jon angled his chair back to rest on its hind legs.

"Jon. Talk to my dad."

Jon brought his chair down hard on all four legs. "No way."

"Then let me talk to him," Anna pleaded. "Tell him—"

"Forget it, Anna." Jon deserted his chair, his dark eyes flashing. "I'm not going to hide behind you or your father. I'm not afraid of Roc."

"Well, you should be!" Anna stood and took a step toward him, poking his chest with her finger. "You know, Jon Ryan, for a smart guy you can be pretty stupid sometimes. This isn't Atlanta, and Roc isn't some city boy. When he comes after you again, he's going to leave more than that little cut above one eye."

Anna gathered her books and stormed out of Jon's house, thinking her earlier assessment of him had been correct. He was about the dumbest boy she'd ever met.

NICK SAT on the deck nursing his second cup of coffee, wishing it was any other day of the week. The clinic was closed on Sundays, and unless there was an emergency, he had nothing to do. And that left too much time to think.

He considered going out to work on the house. It had been several weeks since he'd been there. He wondered if he could interest Jon in helping. Then he heard the glass doors open behind him and was surprised to see Jon come outside. He hadn't joined Nick for Sunday breakfast since Sarah's death.

"You're up early," Nick said as he watched the boy cross the deck, juggling a bowl, a cereal box and a large glass of milk.

Jon claimed a seat across from his father. "Couldn't sleep."

Nick nodded. Sleeplessness was something he understood. He wondered what ghosts kept Jon awake. "Exams coming up?"

"In a couple of weeks."

"Worried?"

"Nope." Jon filled his bowl with cereal and added half the glass of milk. "School's easier here."

Nick wondered if that was really true. It was hard to tell with Jon. The boy had always gotten good grades. Nick had been considering moving back to Atlanta for weeks now. Maybe this was another reason to do so.

"I was thinking about going out to work on the house today." Nick took a sip of his coffee and winced. It was tepid. "Want to come?"

"Can't," Jon answered between mouthfuls of Cheerios. "Got plans."

Nick fought down a wave of disappointment. He and Jon had made a little progress in the past few weeks. Nick had hoped they could spend the day together. "What are you doing?"

"Maddie's picking me up in a little while."

Nick sat a little straighter in his chair. "Maddie?"

Jon nodded but kept his eyes focused on the bowl in front of him. "She's been giving me a ride out to the cemetery on Sundays."

"Why didn't you tell me?"

"You've been at the hospital."

Nick had considered himself fortunate to occupy his past couple of Sundays by filling in for other doctors at the small local hospital. Now he wished he'd stayed home.

"I'd have taken you out to visit your mother's grave if I'd known that's what you wanted."

Jon shrugged and finished the last of his cereal. "It's okay, Dad. Maddie goes, anyway."

Nick sat motionless as his son finished his breakfast and then carried his dishes back into the house, closing the door behind him. How many Sundays had Nick gone with Maddie to the cemetery when they'd been Jon's age? Dozens? Maybe a hundred? Enough that he should have known that Jon would want the same thing. "Damn."

"HUNGRY?" MADDIE ASKED as Jon climbed into her car and slammed the door behind him.

"Always."

"Great." Maddie pulled away from the house. "I'm in the mood for a greasy sausage-and-egg something."

Jon grinned. "I thought adults never ate that stuff."

Maddie shot him a sideways glance. "Are you kidding?"

"Mom never did."

"Well, your mom wasn't pregnant. My figure is a lost cause right now. So I may as well enjoy myself."

Jon laughed. "You're going to regret it."

"Spoken like a true doctor's son."

Jon rested his head back against the seat. "He was acting really weird this morning."

"Your dad? How so?" She couldn't help her curiosity. She might not have seen Nick for several weeks, but that didn't mean she hadn't thought about him. Endlessly.

"I don't know. Kind of sad?"

"You know, Jon," Maddie glanced over at the teenager in her passenger seat, "your dad's been through a lot in the past couple of years."

"I guess."

"You might try cutting him a little slack."

Jon shifted sideways in his seat. "I though maybe you guys had a fight or something."

Maddie shot him a surprised look. The last thing she needed to discuss with Jon was her relationship with his father.

"How about if we eat out at the cemetery?" she said, turning into the nearest fast-food restaurant. Jon nodded his agreement and Maddie pulled up to the drive-through window, grateful for a break from the fifteen-year-old's prying.

But she only managed to stall Jon for a few minutes.

"So did you?" he asked as they left the restaurant behind and headed west.

"Did I what?"

Jon sighed loudly. "Have a fight with my dad."

"No!" She put a warning in her voice. "And it's none of your business if I did."

"I was just asking."

Maddie kept her eyes fixed on the road ahead. "Your dad and I are old friends. That's all."

"He told me you used to date."

"Did he?" That surprised her. Although maybe Nick had done the right thing. There were many peo-

ple in Felton who would be more than willing to tell
Jon the truth. "Well, it was a long time ago."

Fortunately the cemetery came into view at that
moment, its entrance marked by a monstrous set of
concrete columns supporting a stone archway. A piece
of ironwork spanned the arch, fashioned in a flower
motif.

"Here we are," she said a little too brightly.

Jon seemed to take the hint. She'd brought a blanket, and he carried everything up the hill to a tree near
his mother's grave. They sat under the tree together,
eating in silence.

Even after finishing her meal, Maddie lingered for
a few minutes, resting her back against the tree trunk.
Again the peace of the place stole over her—the only
sounds those of birds chattering overhead and an occasional insect making a pass at a patch of wildflow-
ers.

Jon, too, seemed reluctant to move. He'd stretched
out on the blanket, his hands under his head, his eyes
closed. She shifted slightly to study him. He was a
good-looking boy. Like his father in some ways, and
yet so different from Nick in others.

"What's the notebook for?" she asked quietly.
She'd considered asking him about it before, but had
always decided against it.

Jon kept his eyes closed. "Just stuff."

"Like a journal." She tried to sound matter-of-fact.

"Yeah, sort of."

"I used to write a lot when I was a girl."

Jon turned his head sideways to look at her. "What
did you write?"

Maddie pulled her knees up and wrapped her arms around them. "I started out writing 'Star Trek' stories."

Jon burst out laughing and rolled onto his side. "You're kidding!"

"Don't laugh. I absolutely loved 'Star Trek.' "

"Did you ever let anyone read them?"

"Of course. I'd write a chapter at a time and then pass it around to my friends. It was a continuing saga. And I was always the yeoman who made Spock forget his logic."

"Never happened."

"It did in my stories."

Jon laughed again and lowered his gaze. "I used to try and write fiction."

"Not 'Star Trek' I hope," Maddie teased.

"Almost as bad." Jon looked back at her, a mischievous gleam in his eye. "I'm a real Stephen King fan."

"Oh, no! You don't write the really gruesome stuff, do you?"

"Sometimes."

"How about letting me read some?"

Jon laughed nervously and shook his head. "It's not very good."

"You're just chicken." Maddie smiled temptingly. "I'll let you read my 'Star Trek' saga."

Jon scrunched his forehead into a frown. "I'll pass."

"Okay. Well, if you change your mind..." Maddie glanced at her watch. "I think it's time for me to head back down the hill. How about if we meet at the car in about an hour? Does that give you enough time?"

"Sure." Jon climbed to his feet.

Maddie reached out her hand, and Jon helped her up. "It's getting harder and harder all the time," she said, pressing her hands to her swollen belly.

Jon grinned. "Sounds like an excuse to me. You're just getting old."

Maddie punched him playfully on the shoulder and set off toward the path leading down the hill. "Just for that, you bring the stuff."

"I always end up carrying it, anyway," Jon called after her.

Maddie spent the next hour sitting peacefully next to her father's grave. Every now and then, she glanced back at Jon. She could just make him out, sitting on the grass near where she'd left him. He'd be writing in his notebook. She imagined she could see him scribbling away furiously.

When the hour had passed, she walked back to her car and found Jon waiting for her. In silent agreement, they climbed into her car and headed back toward town.

But when they reached Jon's house, he took his time getting out, searching his pockets, evidently looking for something.

"I can't seem to find my keys," he said after shoving his hands in all his pockets two or three times. "Do you mind hanging around for a minute while I make sure Dad's home?"

"Sure. Go ahead."

Jon took off up the walk, trying the door when he got there. Then he rang the bell and pounded. If Nick was home, he'd have to be comatose not to hear the racket his son was making, Maddie thought. Then, throwing her an apologetic smile, Jon headed around the side of the house.

"I'm just going to see if Dad's out back," he called.

He returned a few minutes later, looking woefully contrite. "He's not here. And the house is locked up tighter than a bank."

"Get in." Maddie motioned toward the passenger side of the car. "Where can I take you? How about your grandfather's?"

"No." Jon shook his head and climbed into the car. "Gramps is up at his cabin this weekend."

"Well," she said, trying to think what she could do with him. "You're welcome to wait at my house until your dad gets home. It's pretty torn up right now, and I have to go over to my mother's for dinner. But if *you* don't mind, *I* don't."

"Actually, would you mind taking me out to where my dad's working?"

"He's at the clinic today?"

"No." Jon gave her another apologetic smile. "He said he was going to be working on the house today. You know, the one he's building outside town. He wanted me to help, but you and I had already made plans."

Maddie was beginning to think Jon was more like his father then she'd given him credit for. "I see."

"I could help him if you'd take me out there."

"Are you sure you forgot your keys?"

Jon looked wounded, and Maddie could barely keep from laughing. "Okay, I'll take you. But I need to stop at Mother's first and tell her I'm going to be late."

"I really appreciate this, Maddie," he said a little too seriously. "I know it's a lot of trouble."

"Well, don't be too thankful yet, kiddo. You get to meet Adelia."

"Adelia?"

"Yeah. The Ice Queen."

NICK WONDERED why he'd put off coming out here for so long. One thing his old man had taught him: when the world gets you down, there's no better cure than working with your hands. The hard wood, the tools, the feel of fresh air and sun on his back, all of this eased the tension in his body. And every now and then, as he made a particularly difficult cut or worked a joint so it fit just so, he was able to forget.

Then he'd remember his disappointment that Jon hadn't come out with him. And thoughts of Jon brought thoughts of Maddie and the two of them driving off in that spunky little red car of hers. There was a certain irony to the whole thing. Sarah's son becoming close to Maddie, the woman who should have been Nick's wife. But somehow he didn't find it all that amusing.

Then he heard a car pull up outside, and he put down his tools to go investigate. He stepped onto the porch just as Jon and Maddie climbed out of her car.

"Hey, Dad," Jon called. "Boy, you sure are making a lot of progress out here. The place looks great!"

Nick eyed his son suspiciously. "Yeah?"

"I forgot my keys," Jon explained. "And Maddie agreed to bring me out here so I could give you a hand."

Nick stared at his son, his smile, the gibberish coming out of his mouth, and wondered what the boy was up to. "That was nice of her," he said as he shifted his gaze to Maddie, who shook her head, letting him know she didn't get it, either.

Then, zeroing in on Jon again, he said, "Pretty careless of you to forget your keys. Again." Jon never forgot anything. Sarah always said he'd been born the most responsible person she'd ever known. "What is this? The third time this week? Or the fourth?"

Jon shifted uncomfortably and ignored the question. "Since Maddie's already out here, why not give her a tour of the house?"

"I have to get back, Jon." Maddie took a step toward her car. "Mother's waiting."

"But she said to take your time."

"You met Adelia?" Nick asked in astonishment.

Jon smiled—an innocent smile the likes of which Nick hadn't seen on his son's face in a long time. "We stopped by to tell her Maddie was going to be late. She's cool."

"They hit it off," Maddie added, a quality of disbelief in her voice. "Perfectly."

Nick leveled another curious stare at his son. He remembered a time when Jon could charm a bird out of a tree. That, too, had been a long time ago. Nick wasn't sure what the boy was up to now, but he had an idea. And it amazed the hell out of him.

Turning back to Maddie, Nick said, "Well, I guess you do have time for a tour, then." He held out a hand to her. "Come on."

She hesitated a moment but finally nodded and took his hand. As they started for the unfinished house, Nick glanced back at Jon just in time to catch the grin on the boy's face.

It was both difficult and easy spending time with Maddie. Holding her hand. Showing her the house. Leading her from room to room. Telling her his plans. Her hand felt right in his. Natural. But he knew that when he'd finished the tour, he'd have to let go. Again.

As for the house, Nick had made little progress on it in the past few months. He'd only been out here a few times, and in truth, he'd lost interest in the project. At first he'd been building the house for Sarah, hoping it would make her happy. Then after her death he'd seen it as a way to bring him and his son back together. That had been a disaster from the beginning. Now building the house was little more than something for Nick to do, something to occasionally help work the kinks out of his muscles or take his mind off other things.

"Have you decided whether you're going to live here when it's finished?" Maddie asked as they completed the tour.

"Actually I don't think I *will* finish it."

"Too many memories?"

"No. Lack of interest."

Maddie nodded and fell silent. After a few moments, she glanced back at the partially completed structure and said, "What a waste."

"I won't just leave it. I'll sell it to someone who wants to finish it."

"Hey, Maddie!"

They watched as the boy approached from the back of the house. He'd disappeared about the time they'd first gone inside.

"How'd you like it?"

Maddie smiled. "It's great. But I think I'd better get going. Adelia's waiting. And I think your father has some work for you." She threw a glance at Nick. "Isn't that right?"

"Absolutely." Nick gave his son a smile as innocent as the one the boy had used earlier. "I've been saving up a special chore or two all afternoon."

Jon's expression became wary, and Maddie laughed and turned toward her car. "Next Sunday, Jon?" she asked over her shoulder.

Jon partially recovered his smile. "Yeah. See you."

Nick watched as she got in her car and drove away, feeling as if the sun went with her. For a brief time, he'd felt whole again as he'd led her around this place he'd built with his own hands. Now it seemed empty again.

He glanced at Jon and realized the boy had been watching him. Suddenly Nick was certain his son thought that he and Maddie belonged together. Nick couldn't begin to figure out how Jon knew this, but glancing down the road where Maddie had disappeared in her flashy red car, Nick had to agree. He and Maddie did belong together, and he wondered how long he could keep his promise to stay out of her life.

CHAPTER ELEVEN

"MADDIE!" LYNN CALLED from the front doorway. "Are you home?"

"In here," Maddie answered as she stepped around the two men tearing up carpet. She and Lynn reached the arched entry to the living room at the same time.

"What a nice surprise." Maddie gave her friend a quick hug, and then, with a sweeping gesture toward the torn-up room, she said, "Welcome to the madhouse."

Lynn glanced at the flurry of activity and smiled. "You've got that right. What's going on?"

"Oh, just a little redecorating."

"Looks like more than a little."

Maddie laughed. "Come on. Let me show you the baby's room." She grabbed Lynn's arm and led her up the stairs.

"What do you think?" Maddie stood to the side to allow Lynn to enter the nursery first.

"Wow!"

"My feelings exactly." Maddie couldn't get over how well the room had turned out. She'd had the walls and woodwork stripped and painted white, and then added a wallpaper border decorated with dancing circus animals in bright orange and yellow. The white-

and-yellow curtains fluttering at the window were the final touch. "I just finished it yesterday."

"*You* finished it?"

Maddie smiled. "Well, I didn't do the painting. I was afraid the fumes might hurt the baby. But I hung the wallpaper and curtains."

Lynn shot her a look of surprise before moving to the crib in the middle of the room. "And this?" she said, running her hands over the polished oak. "Where did you find it? It's beautiful!"

Maddie joined her friend at the crib. "It's my one big splurge. I saw it in a baby store before I left Miami. I told myself it was too expensive. But I kept the manufacturer's name and the model number." Maddie laughed softly. "Then a couple of weeks ago I said, "The hell with it," and called the store and placed the order. Isn't it great?"

"I've got to give you credit." Lynn slipped her arm around Maddie's shoulders and gave her a squeeze. "You've got style."

"The only things I still need to get for this room are the crib accessories and a throw rug." She grinned. "Want to go shopping?"

Lynn laughed. "You bet."

"Good. Now I have a favor to ask."

"How big a favor?"

Maddie shrugged. "Don't know."

"Well, out with it."

Maddie bit her bottom lip. "I need a coach."

"A coach?"

"Yeah, you know. A birthing coach. Usually it's the husband, but I don't have one. I thought about Adelia—"

"I'd love to."

"But I just couldn't see— What did you say?"

"I'd love to be your birthing coach."

"Really? It takes time. There are the natural-childbirth classes and all."

"Are you kidding, Maddie?" Lynn slipped her arm through Maddie's. "I'd be jealous if you asked anybody else. Now come on, show me what else you've been doing to this house."

They spent the next few minutes touring the rest of the upstairs, all of which was in various states of renovation. They ended up in the master bedroom, which was nearly complete.

"So what's going on?" Lynn asked. "Why are you tearing your house apart?"

Maddie plopped down on the bed. "Come here, sit down. It's not safe downstairs."

"Well?" Lynn prompted after she'd joined Maddie.

Maddie pulled her knees up to sit cross-legged, then leaned back against the headboard. "Mother was here a few weeks ago."

"That must have been interesting."

"She just showed up here one day and demanded that I eat dinner with her every Sunday. She wants to be kept informed about the baby's progress."

"Adelia?"

Maddie grinned. "Hard to believe, isn't it?"

Other than Nick, Lynn had been the only one of her childhood friends who'd known the details of her relationship with Adelia. "Maybe the Ice Queen is thawing out in her old age."

"Yeah, maybe you're right." Maddie let her thoughts drift back to the last few evenings she'd spent at her mother's house. "We've actually been getting along pretty well. Not great, but at least we're not fighting."

"Babies have that effect on people."

"Do you think that's what it is?"

Lynn shrugged. "Maybe."

"Well, anyway," Maddie said with a wave of her hand. "Getting back to the house. When mother was here, I took a good look at the place. Unfortunately I had to agree with her. A face-lift was long overdue."

"What about the furniture I saw getting hauled away downstairs?"

"It was beyond salvation. I think it was actually on its last legs when Daddy bought it." Maddie laughed lightly, remembering how she'd helped her father search through garage sales to find furnishings. "Besides, my furniture will be arriving in a couple of weeks."

Lynn looked surprised. "So the sale of your condo went through?"

"The closing is next week."

"Are you going to Miami?"

Maddie shook her head. "I sent Roger a limited power of attorney so I wouldn't have to."

"Maddie, I thought—"

"It's okay. It's over."

"Maddie, maybe if you saw him..."

"It wouldn't make any difference. Whatever I felt for him is gone, Lynn. I can't love someone who doesn't love me. Or my baby."

Lynn studied her for a moment. "And you're okay?"

Maddie thought about that for a moment before answering. "Actually I'm fine. Better than fine. I'm enjoying fixing up the house. And I've started writing again and working over at the *Finder*." She chuckled. "Carl Katz hasn't changed one whit in sixteen years. He's still a tyrant of an editor. And baby here," she rested her hand on her stomach, "has been kicking up a storm. So, yeah, I'm feeling pretty good right now."

"That's wonderful, Maddie." Lynn smiled hopefully. "So, have you ever thought of staying in Felton after the baby comes?"

"No." She had no intention of staying. Did she? "I don't think so, Lynn. What would I do here?"

Lynn shrugged. "Oh, I don't know. Work for Carl Katz?"

Maddie laughed and rolled her eyes skyward. "And what would I do for a wage I could live on?"

"I'm sure you could do something, Maddie." Lynn's smile faded. "After all, you're the one with the fancy degree."

"And the terrific job with an international consulting firm. Which, by the way, doesn't happen to have offices in greater Felton."

Lynn brushed Maddie's argument aside with a wave of her hand. "Details."

Maddie laughed again and shook her head.

"Seriously, Maddie. I'm not trying to push you or anything."

"Yes, you are."

"This is your hometown. And I thought since you were putting so much work into the house—"

"Lynn." Maddie reached over and lay a hand on her friend's arm. "I don't know what I'm going to do after the baby's born. Okay? And as far as fixing up the house goes, I'm doing it because it needs it, and I'm tired of living in dark musty rooms."

"But you're spending a lot of money."

"I'll get back whatever I've put into this house. Whether I rent it again, sell it or just hold on to it. Meanwhile I'm making it livable."

"But I thought you said you didn't like the idea of strangers living here."

Maddie thought of the peace she'd made with her father's memory. "Holding on to this house won't bring my father back."

"I guess that makes sense." But Lynn didn't look convinced.

"Come on," Maddie said. "Let's go downstairs and see what all those hardworking men are doing to my living room." Maddie pushed herself off the bed and headed for the door.

Lynn followed, but stopped before they got to the stairs. "How are things with Nick?"

Maddie stopped, too, feeling the heat staining her cheeks. "Okay."

"Maybe I shouldn't have asked?"

"No. It's nothing like that." Maddie shook her head and walked toward the stairs. For a moment she considered telling Lynn about Nick and Sarah, but decided not to. It wasn't her story to tell. "We had a disagreement a few weeks ago. But it's okay now."

"So are you spending time together?"

"No."

"Why?"

"Don't start on me, Lynn," Maddie said, her words sharper than she'd intended. Then, without looking at her friend, she added, "Sorry. It's just that Nick and I are friends. That's all." If only she could convince both herself and Nick of that. Not to mention Jon.

"That's what you told me in high school." They'd reached the bottom of the stairs, and Lynn leaned closer to Maddie so no one else could hear. "I didn't believe you then. And I don't believe you now."

Maddie crossed her arms and spun around to face her friend. "Well, it may not have been true before. But it's true now. Neither one of us is in a position for our relationship to become anything more. Nick's still mourning Sarah's death and having a hell of a time. And I," she hesitated a moment, "I'm just not ready to get involved again right now."

"Maddie, you're already involved."

"I have a baby to consider." Maddie turned and headed toward the kitchen in the back of the house. "And you forget, Nick's not exactly a saint."

"That was sixteen years ago, Maddie," Lynn said, following Maddie into the kitchen. "I know he hurt you back then. But you can bet Nick wouldn't have run off and left you alone with that baby."

Maddie froze.

"Don't you think I know?" Lynn said from behind her. "Don't you think the whole town knew why Nick married Sarah Sommer?"

Maddie turned and stared at her friend.

"Ted would never have let his only daughter marry someone like Nick Ryan if he'd had any other choice."

"Ted liked Nick," Maddie insisted.

"As a son-in-law? Wake up, Maddie." Lynn crossed her arms. "Sarah got pregnant, and Ted got Nick into med school so fast it should have been illegal. Then he spirited them both off to Atlanta."

Maddie shook her head, not wanting to believe she'd been the only one who hadn't known.

"Don't tell me you didn't know?"

"No. I mean yes. Nick just told me a few weeks ago."

Lynn took a step closer and lay a reassuring hand on Maddie's arm. "The point is, my very dear friend, Nick did the right thing by Sarah. He may have hurt you in the process, but at eighteen he had enough courage and moral fiber to take responsibility for his actions. Even though it cost him the one thing he wanted most in the world."

Maddie looked up and met her friend's gaze. "He wanted to become a doctor."

"He wanted you."

Lynn's words echoed in Maddie's head for days. It was true. Nick never would have left her alone and pregnant. He'd gone and married a woman he didn't love because she was expecting his child. Maddie wondered if she was doing the right thing keeping him at arm's length. Or even if she'd be able to do so for much longer.

THE EVENING started out normally enough—or at least as normally as things ever got with Adelia. She and Maddie sat in the dining room while Frances served an exquisitely prepared meal. More than once Maddie had thought about suggesting they give Frances the night off, order a pizza and sit in the kitchen. Somehow she didn't think Adelia would go for it.

On this particular night, however, Maddie found it harder than usual to endure the staid formality of her mother's Sunday-night dinners. She'd been thinking a lot about her father lately—probably due to the amount of time she'd spent with Jon, trying to help him adjust to his mother's death—and there were things she wanted to know. Things only Adelia could tell her.

During dinner Maddie rehearsed what she wanted to say. Several times her mother caught her mind wandering from their conversation. Finally the meal was over, and the two of them went into the sitting room.

"Frances will bring our tea in here," Adelia said, sinking gracefully into her favorite chair and motioning for Maddie to take a seat on the couch.

"Mother." For once, Maddie was going to be direct with this woman. "There's something I want to talk to you about."

"Oh?"

Frances came in with their tea, and Maddie waited until she'd left to speak. "I went out to the cemetery today. To visit Daddy's grave."

Adelia frowned but said nothing as she poured tea for the two of them.

"Actually I've been going every Sunday for weeks."

Adelia remained silent.

"Do you ever go out there?"

"Why on earth would I do that?"

"He was your husband and the father of your only child." Maddie leaned forward in her chair. "You must have loved him once."

"That was a long time ago."

"Still—"

"Why are we talking about this, Madeleine?" Maddie thought she detected a slight tremor in her mother's voice. "Let's talk about something else. How are you feeling?"

"Don't change the subject, Mother. I want to know about you and Daddy."

"Your father and I separated two years before his death."

"But you never divorced him."

Adelia sank back into her chair, forgetting the tea she'd just poured. "Divorce was never an option."

"Why?"

"It just wasn't done. Not then."

"I see. But kicking him out of your house and breaking up the family was okay?"

"There are things you don't know." Adelia lifted her chin stiffly. "Things you don't understand."

"Tell me. I'd like to understand."

"Why? Isn't it enough to know that I did what was best at the time?"

"For whom? Certainly not for me."

"Ah, yes." Adelia folded her hands in her lap. Her voice took on the quality of chipped ice. "You were always Davis's little angel. He spoiled you rotten. And in your eyes, *he* could do no wrong."

"That's not fair, Mother."

"Isn't it?" Adelia unfolded her hands and gripped the arms of the chair. "Well, let me assure you that when I asked your father to leave this house, it was for your sake."

"Please, don't give me that. I think it's a little late to play the good-mother role."

"Oh, really. And what about you, Madeleine? Do you think you were the perfect daughter?"

"I was a child. And I was alone."

Adelia shook her head. "Don't expect me to weep for you. You never wanted for a thing."

"Things. That's all you ever gave me." Years of suppressed anger boiled to the surface. "Clothes, money, cars! They were just things."

"That's all you ever wanted from me."

"That's not true. I needed more!"

"You never needed anything or anyone, Madeleine," Adelia claimed with a flick of her wrist. "You had yourself. It was always enough."

"It was never enough. I needed my father!"

An angry silence crashed down around them, and Maddie realized she'd gone too far. But there was no pulling the words back.

When Adelia spoke, her voice trembled with carefully controlled fury. "Do you really want to know why I asked Davis to leave this house?"

Maddie took a deep breath, suddenly, inexplicably, afraid of the answer. "Yes."

"Be very careful before you decide you really want to know, Madeleine." Adelia's eyes flashed, their usual cool depths becoming fiery blue flames. "You may not like what you hear."

Maddie had never seen her mother this angry. Nevertheless, she needed to know what had happened between her parents. "Tell me."

Adelia let the silence stretch for several long moments before she spoke. "Women." She met Maddie's gaze squarely. "One after another."

Maddie shook her head, refusing to believe what her mother implied, certain she'd misunderstood.

"Oh, yes," Adelia insisted. "Your father always had a way with the ladies. And I put up with it for a long time. Because of you. Because we were a family." Taking a deep breath, she drew herself up. "But when he started bringing them into this house, I knew I couldn't let it go on."

Maddie shook her head, but her mother continued. "I knew if I continued to ignore his infidelities, you would eventually find out. Sooner or later, you'd come home at the wrong time."

"Why are you saying these things?"

"I never wanted you to know. But maybe it's time you knew your father the man, not the saint you made of him."

"I don't believe you!"

"No?" Adelia shook her head, suddenly looking very tired. "I think you do."

Maddie got up from the couch and moved to the window. Outside, the late-afternoon light cast its long shadows across her mother's manicured front lawn. In the distance she could hear a lawn mower start up and children playing. Normal, happy, everyday sounds. Nothing like the angry words that had just filled this room.

"Madeleine?"

"No!" She turned to face Adelia. "That's enough, Mother."

"Madeleine—"

"I don't know why you're doing this." Moving quickly across the room, Maddie grabbed her purse and headed for the door. "But I won't listen to any more." Her mother called after her, but Maddie kept walking, slamming the front door behind her.

Within minutes she was home, curled in her rocking chair under an afghan. But even as she'd stormed out of her mother's house, she'd known she wouldn't be able to hide from her mother's words. Not this time. Not anymore. She was through running away. She didn't know if Adelia had spoken the truth. But she knew she'd have to find out.

Getting up from the chair, she headed for the attic. It was filled with boxes of her father's things: records, papers, personal belongings. If her father had done what Adelia claimed, she should be able to find proof up there somewhere.

JON FINISHED his last exam early and hurried out into the hall. The final bell of the school year would ring in about twenty minutes, and with it would go his last excuse to talk to Anna. All around him, other kids ignored the reprimands from teachers to keep quiet. Exams might have still been in progress, but everyone laughed and talked, elated that summer had begun.

"Hey, Jon," called Brad Severyn, one of the guys who'd been in Jon's gym class. "How'd you make out in math?"

Jon gave him a thumbs-up. "Okay. You?"

"I did all right." Brad gave him a quick nod and turned toward the exit. "Thanks for the help."

"Sure. No problem."

"Hey," Brad called back over his shoulder. "See you around this summer."

"Yeah." Jon was surprised. When had Brad Severyn, most likely candidate for next year's first-string quarterback position, started getting friendly? Sure, Jon had helped him with a few math problems, but the guy basically knew the stuff already. Jon had just given him a few pointers.

Shaking his head, Jon headed for his locker. He'd cleaned it out yesterday, but nonetheless now took his time gathering the couple of books he'd tossed into it this morning. Finally he closed the locker and dropped the combination lock into his book bag. Another glance at the wall clock told him he'd only used up ten minutes. Another ten to kill.

He walked around to the front exit, passing the classroom where Anna was taking her algebra final. He glanced through the glass windows as he passed and saw her near the front, head bent over her desk. Suddenly he snapped his fingers as if he'd just remembered something. Turning on his heel, he headed back in the direction he'd come, stopping at the bulletin board outside the science lab. The biology grades had been posted yesterday, so Jon already knew how he'd done, but he loitered in front of the board, reading the notices, anyway.

Finally the bell rang, and within seconds the remaining students poured out from the classrooms, filling the halls with shouts and whoops. Jon picked his way through the rowdy crowd, striding back toward the classroom where he'd seen Anna. When he spotted her, he slowed to a stroll, looking the other way as he walked by.

"Jon!"

Turning, he feigned surprise at seeing her. "Oh, hey," he said, shifting his book bag and taking a step toward her. "How'd it go?"

"I did it!" she said, bounding toward him. "I think I aced it!"

"All right!" Jon broke into a huge grin. "I knew you could do it. When will you know?"

Anna grinned back and hugged her books tight against her chest. "Mr. Dobb said he'd post the grades day after tomorrow."

"Okay! We'll walk over and check it out."

Anna fell instantly silent, and Jon realized he'd just offered to spend time with her doing something other than math. Had he meant to do that?

"That'll be great." Anna shifted her gaze away, and Jon suddenly felt stupid. After their argument a couple of weeks ago, she probably didn't want anything to do with him.

"Hey, if you have other plans," Jon said, "that's okay."

"No!" Anna gaze snapped back to his. "I mean, I'd like the company." With a nervous smile, she added, "Besides, I could be wrong, you know. I might not have done so hot on the test. And then I'll be really bummed out."

"I bet you did great," Jon said, relief flooding him.

For a few moments they just stood there, neither of them knowing how to break the awkward silence. Finally Anna said, "I'm sorry for what I said the other day. Sometimes my mouth gets away from me."

"Yeah. It does." Jon grinned again. "But I kind of like it."

"You do?"

"Yeah. And besides . . ." He reached down to take her hand. "I was being a bit of a jerk myself."

"Yeah, you were." With a glance down at their joined hands, she added, "But I've gotten kind of used to it."

"Come on." Jon gave her hand a tug. "I'll walk you home?"

Anna's eyes glowed. "Sure. That'd be great."

Heading for the main entrance, Jon thought of little else than the way Anna's hand felt in his. It was so small, and her skin was so smooth. He threw a sideways glance at her and caught her doing the same thing. She smiled shyly and looked away. Yeah, she was okay.

The moment they stepped outside, Jon spotted Roc and Fatso standing with a group of boys near the stone stairs leading down to the street. Anna's hand tensed in his, and Jon knew she'd spotted the group, as well. He and Anna had two choices he figured. They could go back inside and leave the school by a different exit, or they could try to walk by, hoping Roc wouldn't notice.

All his options disappeared when Fatso spotted them.

"Hey, it's Johnnie," Fatso said. The other boys surrounding Roc turned, and Roc stepped out from their midst.

Jon gave Anna's hand a reassuring squeeze and continued walking. "Don't worry. They're not going to cause any trouble out here in the open."

"Right," she answered sarcastically. But she didn't pull away.

"Well, now isn't that cute," Roc said as he stepped in front of Jon and Anna, stopping them. "Einstein's taken up with the sheriff's daughter. Uh-oh. I better be real careful."

Jon tightened his hold on Anna's hand. "Go to hell, Roc."

"Ohhhh. Nasty." Roc shot a glance at the group of boys standing behind him before turning back to Jon. "You're starting to scare me, Jon-boy. Look, I'm shaking."

Fatso giggled, while the rest of the group behind Roc stirred uncomfortably. Jon saw Brad Severyn standing on the edge of the group. So much for new friends.

"How's your head, Jon-boy?" Roc said after a few moments of silence. "Did your daddy fix it up all right?"

Jon fought down his temper. He knew damn well that Roc was goading him, trying to get him to take the first swing. But this time Jon wasn't going to bite. Shifting his book bag higher on his shoulder, he kept his free hand on the strap. "What do you want, Roc?"

Roc took a step closer. "I've got a score to settle with you, city-boy."

Jon laughed. "That's great, Roc. You pulled a knife on me, and now you've got a score to settle. That's about par for the brains you *haven't* got in that head of yours."

Roc took another step forward, stabbing Jon with an accusatory finger. "You squealed on me, you stupid pussy."

"Pusseee, pusseee," Fatso chanted.

Jon didn't bother to deny it. It wouldn't have done any good. "Keep your paws off me, Roc." Dropping Anna's hand, Jon knocked Roc's finger away from his chest.

"Hey, man." Brad Severyn stepped up and grabbed Roc's arm. "Forget it, Roc. You cut him. You're even."

Roc shrugged off Brad's hand. "I ain't gonna forget it."

"Yeah, we ain't gonna forget nothin'." Fatso moved up beside Roc.

"Jon-boy and Little Miss Sheriff's Daughter here got me suspended," Roc said between clenched teeth.

"Now I'm stuck in summer school if I don't want to get held back."

Anna moved forward, her eyes sparking. "We couldn't have that happen, now could we, Roc? What are you, two or three years behind now?"

"Why you little—" Roc lunged toward her, but Jon stepped between them, bringing Roc up short. Fatso moved in closer and gave Jon a shove.

"Hey, man, I said leave it." Brad grabbed Fatso's arm and pulled him away from Jon.

"Yeah, Roc. Forget it," called another boy from the group.

Roc turned on Brad. "Stay out of this, Severyn."

"I'm not staying out of it as long as it's two against one." Brad stepped between Roc and Jon. "If you want to mess Ryan up all by yourself, it ain't no skin off my back. But I'm not gonna stand here and let that monkey of yours—" he gestured at Fatso "—hold him down so you can have your shot."

Roc's face flared crimson, his eyes fixed on Brad. "You just made a big mistake, Severyn."

"Yeah, well," Brad took a step backward and shoved his hands into his pockets, "I ain't gonna cry over it."

Roc glared at him for a few more minutes before turning to Jon and Anna. "We ain't done, city-boy. So you better just watch your ass." Roc spun on his heel. "Come on, let's move. It stinks around here."

Roc and his entourage headed down the steps, while a couple of them threw glances back at Brad.

"Thanks, Brad," Jon said. "I owe you."

"I didn't like the odds."

Jon chuckled. "Me, neither."

Brad laughed. "You could have fooled me, Ryan. You sure got guts." Then with a shrug and a wink at Anna, he headed toward the parking lot. "See you around."

Jon took Anna's arm and led her down the steps. "So is it over yet?" he asked after they'd put some distance between them and the school.

"No way," Anna said. "It just got worse."

"Damn, I was afraid you'd say that."

"He's going to come after you. And he isn't going to fight fair."

"Well, I've just got to figure out a way to make it fair," Jon said, and then slowed, an idea beginning to form in his head. "Up till now it's all been his way. When he wants. Where he wants. Surrounded by his friends. Maybe it's time I take the offensive."

"What are you talking about?"

"I've got to figure out a way to get him alone without a knife, and then beat his butt."

"Or get beaten."

Jon looked down at her and grinned. "Well, that is a possibility. But, either way, it's over."

"Are you sure?"

"It can't fail."

CHAPTER TWELVE

MADDIE HAD JUST STARTED filling the bathtub when the doorbell rang. Shutting off the water, she went to peek out her bedroom window to see who was outside.

Nick's truck sat behind her car in the driveway.

Maddie groaned and pulled away from the window. She hadn't seen him in three weeks. Not since Jon had conned her into driving him out to the building site. The doorbell rang again. She wondered how long Nick would stand down there if she didn't answer. She could stay upstairs and pretend she wasn't home. Of course her car was outside, but who was to say she hadn't gone off with someone in their car? Her mother perhaps. Or Lynn. The doorbell rang a third time.

No. She knew Nick. He'd decided she was home and he'd wait out there all night ringing her doorbell until she answered. Sighing, she headed down the stairs and peered out the window next to the door. She knew she was doomed when she saw the two large pizza boxes in his hands.

Bracing herself, she opened the door.

"Hello, Maddie."

Crossing her arms, she asked, "What are you doing here, Nick?"

"I brought dinner." He lifted the pizza boxes slightly and grinned.

"I've already eaten."

"Sausage, pepperoni and extra cheese."

"I'm not hungry." Her stomach picked that exact moment to growl, making a liar of her.

Nick's grin broadened. "I can tell."

Maddie kept her arms crossed and glowered at him, fighting the temptation to give in to that grin and those dancing blue eyes.

"Are you going to make me stand out here all night?"

Maddie's resistance weakened. "It'd serve you right."

Nick glanced around. "Your neighbors might start talking."

"My neighbors already talk." What would it hurt to share a pizza with an old friend?

"Food's getting cold," Nick said, nodding toward the boxes in his hands.

It was no use. He wasn't going to go away, and if she was honest with herself, she didn't really want him to. Maddie stepped back from the door, and Nick came into the foyer, glancing around at the scrapped wallpaper and freshly sanded floor.

"Looks like you've been doing a little renovating."

Maddie closed the door behind him. "I've been keeping busy."

"I want the grand tour. But first," Nick's gaze slid over her, "you might want to change."

Maddie glanced down at her dust-covered clothes and moaned. She'd completely forgotten how grubby she was. "I've been going through stuff in the attic all day. I was just getting ready to jump in the bath when you rang."

"Don't let me stop you." He gave her a wicked smile.

"I thought the pizza was getting cold."

"We'll heat it up."

Maddie shook her head, refusing to acknowledge his outrageous innuendo, and turned toward the stairs. "Make yourself at home, Nick. This may take a while." Nick's chuckle followed her up the stairs.

Alone in her bedroom, Maddie stopped in front of her full-length mirror to take a quick inventory. She looked exactly like what she was, a pregnant woman who'd just spent the better part of the day rummaging around in an attic. She was far from a femme fatale. Still, with Nick you never knew, and she wasn't going back down there until she looked presentable.

Thirty minutes later, she returned downstairs to find Nick stretched out in the middle of her parlor floor.

"Sorry I can't offer you a chair," she said as she entered the room. "My furniture is somewhere between here and Miami." At least the new carpeting had been laid.

"I like the floor." Nick propped himself on his elbows and smiled at her. "You look terrific."

Maddie fought the wave of heat at his compliment and lowered herself onto the seat by the bay window. "Where's the pizza?"

"I put it in the oven to keep warm." Nick raised his eyebrows. "That's quite a kitchen you got there."

Maddie had forgotten about the kitchen when she'd scurried upstairs. It was the room furthest from completion. The old cabinets had been pulled out to make room for the new ones on order, and their contents were piled on every available surface.

"At least the appliances still work," she said.

Nick laughed and nodded toward the window where she sat. "I like the wind chimes in here."

Maddie glanced up at the dancing prisms above her head. "Wait'll the sun sets."

She'd hung the chimes in this window so she could enjoy them in the early evening—her favorite time of day. The plan had backfired, however. Now, every time she stepped into this room, she thought of Nick. "The room comes alive with color."

"I can't wait." Sitting up, Nick offered her his hand. "Come on down here with me."

Maddie laughed lightly and shook her head. "No way. I'll never get back up. How about that tour you wanted?" She glanced at her watch. "We have about an hour before the sun goes down."

"As long as we're back in time to see the show." Nick got to his feet.

"You do that so gracefully," Maddie said as she pushed herself off the window seat.

"Patience, Mads." Nick draped an arm around her shoulders. "You'll be able to move like a normal person again soon."

"Gee thanks, Doc." Maddie shifted out from under his arm and moved toward the door. "You know how to make a girl feel better."

"I try. So what were you hunting for in the attic?" he asked as he followed her out of the room.

"Just some old papers of my father's."

"Anything in particular?"

"I'm not sure." Maddie started up the stairs. "Adelia and I had a disagreement the other day. She said some things…about my father." She couldn't be more specific—not even with Nick. "I've been hoping to find something to prove if what she'd told me was true."

Nick seemed to hesitate before saying, "You know, Maddie, I got to know Adelia a little while Ted was laid up." He hesitated again. "She's not the person you think."

Maddie stopped at the top of the stairs and turned to look at him. "How so?"

"I'm not sure. I know we've always called her the Ice Queen, but…" He paused and ran a hand through his hair. "I don't think she's the woman we thought she was."

Maddie thought of the things her mother had said the other night. If they were true, well, maybe Nick was right. Maybe her mother was a completely different person. Maybe—

"Where shall we start?" she said, abruptly changing the subject. She'd spent the day thinking about Adelia and her father. Enough was enough.

Nick grinned. "I'd like to see the baby's room."

Maddie returned his smile. "This way." She led him down the hall.

"I knew you'd pick yellow," he said as they walked into the nursery, the sole occupant of which was the huge teddy bear sitting in one corner. When Maddie had put the final touches on the nursery, finding the perfect spot for the yellow-and-white stuffed animal had been a priority.

"Yellow and white," she explained, moving her hand to her belly. "Sunshine and purity. A new start."

Nick turned to look at her, a slow smile spreading across his face. "I think you missed your calling. You should've been a poet."

Maddie turned away, uncomfortable with Nick's evaluation.

"Have you picked out a boy's name yet?" he asked. "I remember you said a girl would be Lily."

Maddie lowered herself into the rocking chair. "Adam has a nice ring to it."

He met her gaze, and Maddie felt herself falling all over again. Maybe she should stop fighting it. Maybe she should listen to Lynn and let herself love Nick.

"Maddie." Nick moved over beside her and squatted by her chair. "Tell me about the baby's father?"

Maddie shook her head and shrugged. "There's not much to tell." Funny how she no longer felt any pain when she thought of Roger.

"Do you love him?"

For a few moments she didn't answer. A couple of months ago the word "yes" would have sprung to her lips—although she was no longer sure whether it had been true then, either. But now she knew—she didn't

love Roger. Not anymore. There was just this empti-
ness in her heart where there should have been something more. But she couldn't tell Nick that. She
couldn't tell him about Roger. Because Nick would
want to take care of her, and she wasn't sure how long
she could resist him.

Finally she gave him an answer that wasn't an answer. "He's the father of my child."

There was a flicker of emotion in Nick's eyes. Other
than that, he seemed unaffected by her simple statement. "But you never married."

"No."

Nick took her hand. "Maddie?"

He drew her to him, with nothing more than a touch
and his gentle voice. "Nick, I don't want to talk about
this."

He remained silent for a long time, and she saw the
turmoil in his eyes. But in the end he nodded, accepting her wishes.

"Come on," she said. "Let's finish up this tour
business and get on to the good stuff. I'm starving."

Nick helped Maddie up, and she showed him the
rest of the upstairs, explaining in each room what
she'd already changed and what she still had left to do.
Nick seemed genuinely interested, though he was a
little quieter than he'd been earlier. Before they headed
downstairs, Maddie grabbed an old sheet and showed
Nick where she stored the extra pillows. If they were
going to eat on the floor, they might as well be comfortable.

After they finished the tour, Nick spread the sheet
on the parlor floor while Maddie retrieved the pizza

from the oven. They sat facing the western window, propped against the wall with pillows.

"Just like a picnic," Nick said as he claimed a piece of pizza from the box.

"Without the rain or ants. This is much better."

"Knowing how you feel about stormy weather, I'd have to agree."

They sat for a long time in companionable silence, eating pizza and watching as the sun sank and the prisms cast rays of colored light around the room. As it always had been between the two of them, there didn't seem to be any need for words. They were comfortable just being together.

Nick reached over and claimed her hand. Maddie knew she shouldn't allow it. Just being with him tempted her. But the decision to pull away never went further than her thoughts.

"Nick, tell me about your marriage?"

Nick shifted to look at her. "What do you want to know?"

"Were you happy?"

Nick looked into her eyes and apparently decided she deserved to hear the truth. "We had our problems. All married people do. But we weren't unhappy. At least, not until we came back to Felton."

Maddie considered his words. Funny, she would have expected to feel jealous that he'd known some measure of happiness with Sarah, but instead, she felt the exact opposite. She was pleased that Nick had made good of a situation that had been forced.

"Tell me how it happened, Nick." Maddie shifted to lie on her side. "I need to know."

For several long moments he didn't say anything while he searched her face. When he spoke, his voice was low and hesitant. "You remember that I'd started working for Ted Sommer shortly after you left for college."

Maddie nodded. For months they'd exchanged three or four letters a week, letters filled with their hopes, dreams, love and plans for the future. Maddie still had those letters. They were upstairs, stored away somewhere in the bottom of her trunk.

"Ted needed someone to clean his offices and run occasional errands. It didn't pay much, but it was a start. I was taking classes over at the junior college, and Ted let me work whatever hours fit into my schedule.

"Well, I soon realized that the money I made wasn't enough." Nick turned and lay on his side to face her, propping his head up with one hand. "I was just barely meeting my expenses. There was no way I was going to be able to join you at the university in two years. So I warned Ted that I was looking for another job, and he started finding things for me to do at his house. Yard work, minor repairs—that sort of thing. I was pretty good with tools even back then."

Nick reached over to reclaim Maddie's hand. "Are you sure you want me to go on with this?"

Maddie wasn't sure at all. But she knew if she didn't find out the whole truth, she'd always wonder. "Yes. Please."

"Well, I was feeling pretty down, worried I'd never be able to get out of Felton. Your letters were filled with news about the university, the classes, the people you met. I felt you slipping away."

"I had no idea."

"It wasn't your fault." He pulled her hands to his lips and kissed her fingers gently. "You were just being honest."

Maddie closed her eyes, bracing herself against the feeling of his lips on her fingers and the ragged memories of their past. "Go on."

Nick lowered their joined hands to the floor. "That's when I got to know Sarah. She was very determined. And as Ted's only child, she was used to getting her own way." Nick rolled over on his back without releasing Maddie's hand and gazed at the ceiling. "I spent the first few months trying to ignore her. After a while, I had to become almost rude. But it only made her more persistent."

Nick sighed. "I must admit I was intrigued. The worse I treated her, the more she came on to me. I just didn't get it. But as I said, she'd captured my attention."

He turned his head to look at Maddie again. "Then you called to tell me about the summer job you'd gotten in Athens. The money was good. And it would save you from having to come home to Adelia's house."

Maddie pressed her lips together, realizing the part she'd played in that long-ago drama.

"I got drunk. Or more exactly, Sarah and I got drunk. And the next thing I knew we were in the back seat of her car." He paused and took a breath. "The next morning I knew I'd screwed up. I didn't know how badly yet, but I knew things would never be the same between you and I.''

''I didn't take that job.''

Nick stared at her.

''I left Athens at the end of spring term. I couldn't stay there. I couldn't bear to continue with any of the things we'd planned together.''

''When Sarah told me she was pregnant, at first I didn't believe her. Then I didn't believe the baby was mine. I fought against it every way I knew how. But in the end there was only one option open to me.''

Nick rolled back onto his side. ''I couldn't leave her and the child I'd fathered, sending them support checks from a construction worker's salary.'' He sighed and raised a hand to rub his temples. ''Ted offered me a chance to make something of myself. And I took it.''

''Did you love her?''

He met her gaze head on. ''She was my wife.''

''That's not what I asked.''

''Yes, Maddie. I loved her. Not at first. But I learned to love her.''

Maddie closed her eyes and nodded. He brushed her cheek with his fingers, and a shiver of pure delight ran through her. It felt so wonderful to be touched by him again, to feel the gentle strength in his hands.

''Maddie, I'm sorry. It should never—''

Maddie opened her eyes and pressed her fingers against his lips. ''Don't say it, Nick.'' She lowered her hand to rest it against his chest. ''You have a wonderful son.''

Nick's eyes filled with warmth. ''Yes. I do.''

Lost. She was totally and completely lost. Gazing into the depths of his eyes, she wanted to let herself drown in him. If he'd asked her at that moment what she wanted, she'd have spoken his name. Instead, he kissed her, softly, gently, almost reverently. And she couldn't have stopped him if she'd tried.

Nick lingered over the kiss, tempting, teasing himself as much as Maddie. He'd come here for this, despite Maddie's request that he stay away. He wanted this woman in his life, and he couldn't just walk away. Not without knowing if she still cared, if she still loved him.

When he lifted his lips from hers, he sought his answers in her wide gray eyes. Once they'd held more love than a man deserved. He wanted to see that again. But her eyes were bright and filled with emotions he couldn't read. And she was lovely, so lovely, with that special radiance only pregnant women seem able to obtain. He loved her so much. He'd always loved her.

"For years," he whispered, "a day never went by that I didn't think of you." She closed her eyes, and he brought his hand up to caress her cheek. "Look at me, Maddie." Her eyes fluttered open. "Tell me you don't feel the same."

"Shh." She lifted her head to touch his lips with hers, and words deserted him. He pressed her back against the pillow, and she slipped her hands around his neck, tunneling her fingers into his hair. This time he went slowly, rediscovering the taste of her and the sweet feel of her lips against his.

But it wasn't enough.

Pulling away, he framed her face with his hands, tracing the lines of her cheeks with his thumbs. "Maddie."

She opened her eyes and smiled. "It's even better than I remembered."

Nick grinned and nipped at her mouth, grateful for each moment she stayed in his arms. "I should hope so. We were pretty new at this in the old days."

Maddie laughed lightly and turned her head as he found the silky skin of her neck. She smelled of roses. He'd forgotten that about her. The way the lightest of scents clung to her skin, just enough to be detected up close.

He framed her face with his hands and feasted on the silver of her eyes. "So is it true?"

"Is what true?"

"That women never forget their first love?"

"I don't know about other women." Maddie tightened her hold on his neck and pulled him down until their lips almost touched. "But I never forgot you."

Nick let her kiss him this time, shyly at first as she brushed her lips across his before tasting him with the tip of her tongue. He moaned deep in his throat, and she got braver, exploring the shape of his mouth before plunging inside to torment him.

He buried his hands in her hair, feeling the sharp pain of longing in his groin. Maddie clung to him, her body arching into his.

It was the feel of the baby kicking that brought him to his senses. With a groan, he released her mouth. Shifting onto his back, he pulled Maddie over to rest her head on his shoulder.

"Maddie, we better stop while we still can."

Maddie giggled against his chest. "It would be a little awkward right now, wouldn't it."

Nick turned to her and lowered his hand on her stomach. "It would be beautiful anytime." Without taking his eyes off her, he pushed her onto her back and slowly moved his head down to rest lightly on her stomach. Turning his head, he kissed the silky swell of her belly while caressing her with his hands.

"We could make it beautiful, Maddie. You and I." He slipped his hands under her maternity top and pulled it up to bare her stomach.

"Nick, please, no."

"I'm just going to kiss you, Maddie." He turned his face back to her stomach, gently kissing the swell.

"Please, Nick." He heard the soft tremble in her voice. "I can't."

Nick kissed her one last time and slid back up to lie next to her, leaving his hands on her stomach.

"I'm sorry—" she began, but Nick didn't let her continue.

"There's nothing to be sorry for." He rolled onto his back again and brought her head to his shoulder. "I love you, Maddie. And I'll wait. I only wish . . ."

"What?"

Nick brought his hand down again to rest on her abdomen. "I wish this child was mine."

For the next hour, Nick lay with Maddie in his arms. A light rain began to fall outside, stirring the curtains and setting the prisms to tinkling.

They talked of inconsequential things, such as friends they'd once known and music they'd once listened to. She told him about her job and the places she'd lived. He told her about medical school and falling asleep in the doctor's lounge after twenty-four-hour shifts.

Nick caressed her arms and stroked the silky strands of her hair while Maddie rested peacefully on his chest. But he didn't kiss her again. He didn't dare start something she wasn't ready to finish. But they'd made progress tonight. She cared—despite everything she'd said, despite the ghost of her baby's father that still haunted her eyes. He knew Maddie still loved him.

It was close to midnight when Maddie let Nick out the front door. Closing it behind him, she stayed a moment, her head against the hard oak surface. It had been a night of revelations, a night she'd never forget. Nick had pushed his way in here with nothing more than his sexy eyes and an armload of pizza. But he'd left with her heart.

Or maybe he'd had it all along.

Maddie slowly climbed the stairs to her bedroom. Funny, but she felt unusually calm. As if now that she'd given up the fight, now that she admitted her feelings for Nick, everything would be all right.

MADDIE HAD STOPPED going over to her mother's for Sunday dinners. Every week she called with an excuse, and every week Adelia graciously pretended that nothing was wrong. Meanwhile, Maddie continued her search through her father's things, finding nothing that either proved or disproved her mother's claims. She knew this couldn't go on much longer. Sooner or

later she'd have to face Adelia and settle things between them.

She was in to see Ted Sommer for her seven-month
checkup when she got the idea to ask him about her
father. As usual she waited until he'd finished her
exam to talk to him.

"Dr. Sommer," she began as he made notes on her
chart, "did you know my father very well?"

"Everyone knew Davis. Why?"

"What kind of man was he?"

"A good one." Ted turned toward her and crossed
his arms, looking puzzled. "You know that."

"I only knew him as a child. What was he like with
adults?"

Ted frowned. "What are you asking me, Madeleine?"

Maddie took a deep breath. She didn't want to come
right out and ask if her father had been a philanderer,
but she wanted the truth. If anyone in town knew, it
would be Ted Sommer. "I've been trying to figure out
what happened between my parents."

He hesitated a moment and then said, "I suggest
you ask your mother."

"I did." Maddie glanced away. "She didn't want to
talk about it."

"Well, then—"

"But I kept after her, and finally... Well, the things
she told me weren't very pleasant."

Ted sighed, and Maddie looked up to meet his gaze.

"I need to know," she said.

"Why?"

"Because he was my father." Because she was tired of lies and half-truths. And because if what her mother had told her was true, it changed so much....

"I'm sorry, Maddie." Ted shook his head. "I can't help you."

"Please..."

"No," he said more firmly. "This is something you need to take up with Adelia."

Maddie nodded and looked away.

Ted seemed as if he was about to say something else and then thought better of it. Instead, he gave Maddie's shoulder a quick squeeze and left the room.

Maddie dressed quickly. Ted Sommer was right. At least about one thing. It was time she faced Adelia, and the sooner she did so the better. A half hour later she stood on her mother's front porch, wondering whether she was doing the right thing. Then, before she could change her mind, she took a deep breath and knocked.

To her surprise, Adelia herself opened the door. "Madeleine?"

"Hello, Mother."

"Is everything all right?"

"Yes, I mean, no. Can we talk?"

"Of course." Adelia moved back, and Maddie stepped into the foyer. As she closed the door, Adelia asked, "Is this about your father?"

"Yes. I need to ask you another question."

"Madeleine, please, forget what I said the other night." Adelia's voice held a note of pleading that forced Maddie to meet her mother's gaze. She looked older, almost frail, and dark circles rimmed her eyes.

Maddie fought the sudden urge to take her mother's advice. But then things would never be any different.

"One question, Mother. Please?"

Adelia hesitated and then nodded.

Maddie took a deep breath and averted her gaze. She couldn't bear to look into those tired eyes. "If what you said about Father was true, why did you let me live with him?"

"I didn't *let* you live with him. I fought it. But in the end I had no choice." Adelia sighed and motioned toward the parlor. "Can we go sit down in the other room?"

Maddie nodded and followed her mother into her sitting room, thinking she'd never seen her mother move so slowly. When Adelia sank into her favorite chair, she seemed to regain some measure of control. Maddie sat across from her on the couch.

"Since we weren't legally divorced," Adelia explained, "I had no legal means to keep you. Of course your father had no legal means to take you away, either. So we had to work it out between us. It was a difficult time." She sighed and shifted her suddenly watery eyes to stare off into the distance.

"You threw such a tantrum," Adelia continued after a few moments. "Refusing to eat or go to school. For a while I was really worried about you. I thought you'd make yourself seriously ill." She paused again, and Maddie wondered what past scenes Adelia relived in her head.

"Your father and I made a deal. You could live with him, but I held the mortgage on his house. I told him if he ever took any of his women to that house, I'd evict him and divorce him despite the scandal. And I would make sure he'd never see you again." After another moment of silence she added, "As far as I know, he kept his part of the bargain."

Maddie sighed and released the breath she hadn't realized she was holding. Her mother was telling the truth. She knew that now. Still, she couldn't reconcile all she'd learned about her father with the man she'd known.

"And the day I got lost in the storm?"

Adelia hesitated and then said, "I told you I was the one who found you."

Maddie looked at her mother and knew there was more to what had happened that day. More secrets. Things her mother wasn't saying. And then she understood that it didn't matter. It had all happened so long ago.

"Don't hate him, Maddie." Adelia's voice broke into her thoughts.

Maddie shook her head. "No, I don't. I couldn't."

"He was a good man in many ways. He was just weak." A deep sadness was evident in her voice. "And you were right. I did love him. Despite everything."

Maddie forced a smile for her mother. "I'm glad you told me." Adelia opened her mouth to speak, but Maddie stopped her. "I think Daddy would have wanted me to know."

Adelia nodded and pursed her lips.

Hesitantly Maddie reached over and took her mother's hand. It was one of the hardest things she'd ever done. "I think he would have wanted us to start over."

"Oh, Madeleine." Adelia's voice broke, and tears filled her eyes. "I would like that. I would like that very much."

Maddie drove home that afternoon feeling strangely relieved. It was as if a million questions from her childhood had been answered by her mother's revelations—her parent's arguments, her father's long absences, her mother's seeming indifference. For years Adelia had kept her secrets while Maddie put her father on a pedestal. No wonder Adelia had kept Maddie at arm's length, unable to tell her the truth, yet resenting her idolization of her father.

Maddie had been so young and so oblivious to all but the aftermath of everything happening around her. It had colored her entire life and destroyed her chance of a loving relationship with her mother. Maybe now she and Adelia could make sense of each other.

As THE WEEKS WORE ON, Maddie and her mother slowly came to terms with one another. It wasn't easy for either of them to put aside the past and forget all the pain. But they both tried. They talked and argued, laughed and cried, and Maddie grew a little closer to understanding this woman she'd always called Mother but had never really known.

At the same time Maddie gave in to the temptation to spend time with Nick. He never pushed her, never even kissed her again, except in a light carefree manner. But he was there, and she didn't ask him to stay away. It wouldn't have done any good. They both would have known she didn't mean it.

He'd started joining her and Jon on Sundays.

Sometimes they went out to the cemetery, but more and more they found other things the three of them could do together. Maddie wanted to go hiking as she'd done with her father, but Nick convinced her to wait until after the baby arrived. So they packed picnic lunches or watched movies or grilled steaks on Nick's deck.

And then there was her relationship with Jon.

Summer vacation had begun, and he spent a lot of time over at her place. At first he came to help. He mowed the lawn and washed her car. When her furniture arrived from Miami, he moved it around for her, showing a surprising amount of patience for his fifteen years. But soon he seemed to think of her house as a second home, and Maddie got used to having him around.

She often wondered what she had done before the two of them had walked into her life. And she didn't want to think about what it would be like without them.

CHAPTER THIRTEEN

NOTHING HAD FELT RIGHT to Maddie all day long. She couldn't put her finger on it, but something felt very wrong. Like dark clouds gathering on the horizon, there was an expectancy in the air of something to come.

Something turbulent.

Glancing out her kitchen window at the approaching storm, she shuddered. Maybe it was nothing more than the thunderstorm looming on the horizon. It wouldn't be long before it hit, and she wanted to be in her room safely tucked beneath the blankets before it did.

She put the last of her dinner dishes into the dishwasher and then grabbed a flashlight and a handful of small candles and matches before heading upstairs. By the time she got to her bedroom, the early-evening light had deteriorated to an eerie shade of green-yellow.

Maddie crossed to the windows to close the curtains and again caught sight of the ominous dark clouds. A shiver of apprehension slithered down her spine. Her back ached and she unconsciously rubbed it with the heel of her hand. The news on the radio earlier had said they were in for a nasty night. From the looks of the sky, the report had been right. She wished she'd had time for a long soak in the tub before the storm broke. Suppressing her odd feelings, she pulled the curtains closed.

A few minutes later she climbed into bed with a book. She propped a couple of pillows behind her, one positioned to support her aching lower back, and pulled the comforter tight around her belly and legs.

For a while she barely noticed the distant rumblings and wind brushing against her bedroom windows. She buried herself in her book, absorbed for the moment in some fictional woman's problems. Then the storm broke with a crack of thunder that shook the house. Startled, Maddie swung her gaze to the light beside her bed, wondering how long it would be before the power was out. Abandoning her book, she checked to make sure the flashlight and candles were within arm's reach and scooted beneath her blankets.

It was going to be a long night.

She must have dozed despite the wind and rain, because when the phone rang she was completely disoriented. The second ring brought her to a sitting position. Eager for anything to distract her from the maelstrom outside, Maddie reached over and picked up the receiver. "Hello?"

"Maddie, it's Nick." His voice was interrupted by static and she missed his next words.

"Nick, I can barely hear you."

"Is Jon there? Have you seen him today?" Despite the crackling line, she heard the urgency in Nick's voice.

"No. I expected him, but he never showed." Maddie cradled the receiver in both hands as Nick cursed on the other end of the line. "Nick, what's wrong?"

"He hasn't been home since early this morning."

Maddie glanced at the clock. It was after nine.

"Evidently he got into another fight today," Nick continued. "No one's seen him since."

"Was he hurt?"

"No, not that we know of. I thought maybe he'd come to you."

"Did you try Anna Banks? They've been spending a lot of time together lately."

"She was the first person I called." He hesitated briefly. "She told us about the fight. She was with him earlier, but she hasn't seen him in hours. I'm on my way over there now to talk to her. And Jack has his deputies out looking."

Maddie remembered the ominous feeling she'd had all day. "What can I do to help?"

"Nothing. Stay at home and take care of that baby. Maybe Jon will show up there. If you hear from him . . ."

"I'll let you know immediately."

"Call the sheriff's office. I'm going over to talk to Anna Banks and then I'm going out looking for him."

Maddie closed her eyes, uttering a silent prayer for Jon. "Please be careful, Nick. And let me know when you find him."

Nick hesitated and then asked, "Maddie, are you all right? With the storm and all . . ."

"I'm fine, Nick. Go find your son."

Maddie hung up the phone, her mind sorting through the last few weeks for some clue as to where Jon might have gone. The two of them had spent a lot of time together lately. He'd become comfortable with her, telling her things she suspected he hadn't told anyone else. She went over their conversations in her mind, but nothing jumped out at her. Where would he have gone? Or was he lying hurt somewhere? Possibly by the same boy who'd pulled a knife on him the last time.

Then it hit her, and she couldn't believe no one else had thought of it earlier. Sarah's grave.

The first time she and Jon had really talked had been at the cemetery. What had he said about the place? "I feel close to her here." And Sarah had died during a storm such as the one raging outside now.

Maddie threw a nervous glance toward her windows and grabbed the phone, punching in the numbers for the sheriff's office before she even had the receiver to her ear. But nothing happened. She stabbed the receiver button several times without success. There was no dial tone.

For a moment Maddie remained perfectly still, while lightning flashed behind the closed curtains and thunder rolled over her house. Then the lights flickered, jarring her, and she put her hand on the flashlight.

Jon was out there in the middle of this storm, sitting next to his mother's grave. She knew it. Again she glanced toward the closed curtains, fear for Jon warring with her fear of the storm. Before she could change her mind, she threw off the comforter and hurried to pull on the last pair of maternity jeans that still fit and a large bulky sweater.

Downstairs she found her umbrella and pulled on a bright yellow rain poncho. She made it all the way to the back door without hesitating. Then, with her hand on the doorknob, she froze.

Outside the storm raged.

The last thing she wanted to do was be out in it. She just needed to get over to the sheriff's office, she argued with herself. She would tell Jack where they could find Jon. Then she could come right back home.

Taking a deep breath, she plunged into the wet darkness.

NICK PARKED his truck in front of the Banks house. Jack had beat him here. He wondered if this was going to be a waste of time. Anna had told him on the phone that she hadn't seen Jon for hours. Nick thought his time would be better spent driving around looking for Jon, but Jack Banks had insisted Nick come over. He'd assured Nick that talking to Anna would shed some light on their search.

Pulling up the collar of his all-weather coat, Nick got out of the truck and made a dash for the front porch. As he knocked, he shook the moisture from his coat.

Lynn opened the door, her expression grim. "Come in, Nick. Anna and Jack are in the living room."

"Thanks." Nick stepped through the door, and Lynn reached for his coat. "I'm really sorry about all this," he said.

Lynn shook her head. "Don't be sorry for our sake, Nick. You need to find Jon. If Anna can help, she will."

Nick nodded, grateful for her understanding, and followed her into the living room. Anna sat on the edge of the couch, her small hands balled tightly in her lap and her tear-streaked face the picture of distress. Jack stood across the room, near an old brick fireplace, looking formidable. Lynn sat down next to her daughter and wrapped a protective arm around her.

"Anna was just telling me about the fight this afternoon," Jack said. "Evidently Jon, Anna here and a boy named Brad Severyn planned it."

Nick turned to look at Jack. "Jon planned it?"

"He didn't have a choice," Anna interjected.

"He should have come to me," Jack stated, folding his arms and glaring at his daughter. "*You* should have come to me."

"Daddy, can't you understand? That would've only made things worse."

"Wait a minute," Nick said, going to sit in an armchair across from Anna. "Back up. What do you mean he didn't have a choice?"

Anna took a deep breath and met his gaze head on. "Roc, that is, Rick Moran, was out to get Jon."

"The boy who attacked him with a knife?"

"Yes." Anna nodded. "I wasn't there that day, but I was around earlier when Roc was being his usual bullying self. Jon stood up to him. And Roc's not used to that. He pushes everyone around and gets away with it."

"Roc's eighteen," Jack clarified for Nick. "He's bigger and stronger than most of the other kids."

Nick swiveled back to Anna. "Okay. So what happened?"

"As I said, I wasn't there the first time they really got into it, but from what I was told, Jon wouldn't back down. Not even when Roc pulled the knife. Between him and Fatso—"

"Fatso?" Nick glanced at Jack, and then back to Anna.

Anna rolled her eyes. "Evan Bradley. But everyone calls him Fatso. He's Roc's main sidekick and general pain in the—"

"We get the idea, Anna," her father interrupted. "Go on with the story."

"Roc would've hurt Jon a lot worse that day, but once he pulled the knife and cut Jon, a couple of the other boys stepped in and stopped it."

"One of them told me about Roc's knife," Jack added.

"Okay," Nick said, turning back to Anna. "So what happened today?"

"Roc wouldn't let things alone. He's been baiting Jon for weeks. He thought it was Jon who told Daddy about the knife."

Nick nodded. He'd grown up on the wrong side of Felton and understood how these things worked. The biggest and meanest boys ran things, and everyone else stayed out of their way. He'd hoped by raising Jon in a better environment, he would never have to face any of this. He'd been an idiot.

"Jon came up with this great idea to end it all," Anna said, breaking into his thoughts.

Jack snorted in disgust, and Anna's gaze swung to her father, then back to Nick. "Jon figured if he could face Roc in a fair fight, without Fatso or a knife, he could settle things."

"Yeah, and get his butt kicked," Jack said.

"Jack, please," Lynn said. "Let her finish."

"Jon was willing to take that risk, if that's what it took to get Roc to leave him alone."

Nick shook his head and ran a hand through his hair. Had he been asleep? He thought things were getting better between him and Jon. How could all this have been going on without his knowledge?

"It's not your fault, Nick," Lynn said as if reading his thoughts.

Nick gave her a tight smile and returned his attention to Anna. "Okay. Go on."

"We got Brad Severyn to help. And he enlisted a few of his football buddies. It was their job to make sure Fatso was out of the way, and it was my job to make sure Roc didn't have a knife on him."

"Your job?" Jack blurted. "What the hell—"

"Jack." Lynn leveled a warning glare at her husband.

"It's okay, Daddy," Anna said. "I had an easy part. I just waited until Roc was swimming in the river. Then I snuck up and stole his knife out of his pocket."

"You stole his knife?" Jack looked ready to come unraveled.

"Borrowed it?"

"Can we please get on with the story?" Lynn said, glaring at her husband again. "We need to find that boy. Go on, Anna."

"We set the whole thing up for this afternoon," Anna continued. "There's a swimming hole about half a mile north of town that a lot of the kids use in the summer."

Nick nodded. He knew the place. When he was growing up, only kids from the wrong side of the river frequented the spot. Had things changed?

"It's one of Roc's favorite haunts," Anna said. "And it was probably the last place he expected to see Jon."

"So I take it the two of you just sauntered on down there?" Jack said. Nick realized that things hadn't really changed at the swimming hole.

"Brad was with us," Anna said to her father. "And a couple of other guys from the team." Turning back to Nick, she said, "It worked just the way Jon planned it." She smiled shyly. "He's really smart, Dr. Ryan."

"Anna..." her mother warned.

Anna blushed and carried on with her story. "So I got Roc's knife like we planned. Then when he and Fatso got out of the water, they spotted Jon. It was great! Roc's so stupid he played right into our hands. As usual he started shoving Jon around, eager for a fight. But when Fatso moved in, Brad and his friends stopped him. And then Roc went for his knife, but it had disappeared. So it was just Roc and Jon."

Anna stopped. Nick waited. "And?" he prodded at last.

"That's pretty much it." Anna shrugged. "Jon held his own pretty well. Everybody declared it a draw. Roc's obviously not used to fighting without Fatso on his side. But what could he do? He'd started things, and by that time the place was crawling with kids. Roc couldn't back out."

"Was Jon hurt?"

"I don't think so. He had a cut lip and a couple of bruises. I told him he should go see you at the clinic."

Nick shook his head. "He didn't show up."

"He said he had something else to take care of today."

"What was that?"

"He wouldn't tell me. He walked me home and then took off."

"But now Jon's missing," Jack said. "And Roc might have had something to do with it." He glanced at Nick. "I've already sent someone out to pick up Roc and Fatso and bring them in. If either of them had anything to do with Jon's disappearance, we'll know within the hour."

"Okay." Nick rose from his chair and nodded at Anna. "Thanks. I appreciate your telling me all this." He paused and then added, "You've been a good friend to my son."

THE DRIVE to the sheriff's office normally took five minutes. With the torrential rain and fierce winds, it took Maddie nearly fifteen. And she'd never been more grateful to see the bright streetlamps in front of the building. Pulling her hood over her head, she hurried inside as quickly as her awkward bulk would allow.

"What are you doing out in this mess?" asked Helen Webb, the night radio dispatcher, when Maddie blew into the office, along with a rush of wind and rain.

"I need to talk to Sheriff Banks." Maddie shoved back her hood and shook some of the water off her poncho. "And the phones are out."

"He's not here."

"Is anyone?"

"Just me." Helen smiled apologetically. "They're all out looking for Jon Ryan. He's been missing since this afternoon."

"That's what I need to talk to Jack about," Maddie said, lowering herself into a chair next to Helen. "I think I know where Jon is. Can you get Jack on the radio?"

"I can try." Helen swung back to the radio. "With the storm, there's been a lot of interference. Sometimes I can get him. Sometimes not."

Helen worked the radio for a few minutes, while Maddie tapped her fingers nervously against the table. Helen tried calling Jack and the two other deputies on duty. Either she couldn't get through due to the storm's interference, or the men weren't in their cars.

Finally Maddie couldn't wait any longer. "Helen, keep trying to get hold of someone," she said as she pushed herself to her feet. "I'm going after Jon."

"Maddie, you shouldn't be out there in your condition." Helen eyed Maddie's protruding stomach.

"There have been tornadoes sighted all over the county."

"All the more reason I can't leave Jon out there alone." Maddie moved to the door and pulled the hood back over her head. "One of us has to go after him. You need to stay here and try to reach Jack. That leaves me."

"But, Maddie—"

"When you get hold of Jack," Maddie interrupted. "Tell him I'm on my way out to the cemetery. I think that's where Jon is."

Helen's face whitened. "The cemetery?"

"At his mother's grave." Maddie headed out the door before Helen could say anything else. She feared that if she stayed any longer, Helen would talk her out of going.

Outside, Maddie immediately wished she had any other option than going after Jon herself. If possible the storm had worsened. The wind blew the rain in horizontal sheets that tore at Maddie's heavy plastic coat. With her balance already off, it was all she could do to keep from falling. She wondered how she'd manage in the hilly cemetery, but quickly pushed the thought aside. She'd deal with that when she got there.

Closed inside her car, she felt a little safer. Then another bolt of lightning split the sky, and she wished to God she was home tucked beneath her blankets. She thought of the massive number of old trees out at the cemetery and, pushing her own fear aside, started the car.

Driving was a nightmare. After living three years in South Florida with its tropical rains, she'd believed there wasn't a storm she couldn't drive through. She'd been wrong. The problem here was the utter and complete darkness, pierced momentarily by blinding flashes of lightning. Several times she almost pulled over. But that, too, held risks. She could barely make out the sides of the road.

Finally the old gates marking the entrance to the cemetery loomed before her, and Maddie breathed a sigh of relief. At least she'd made it this far. Now she needed to negotiate the hills and hairpin curves within the grounds. She'd never been here at night, and there were no lights.

Years of traveling these roads helped, however. She seemed instinctively to know where she was at each intersection and which turns to take. When she found the spot below Sarah's grave where she usually left her car, she thanked whatever powers were watching out for her.

She parked her car but hesitated before getting out. All around her, huge trees shielded the grounds from the worst of the storm. But the trees also drew danger. Only the thought of Jon sitting under one of these ancient sentinels gave her the courage to get out of the car.

This time she took the umbrella and flashlight. Running the light over the hill above her, she tried to see if Jon was up there. But the night was too dark, and the beam of light too limited.

"Jon," she called, but the wind ripped at her voice and she knew he couldn't possibly have heard her. She tried again. Louder. "Jon!" Her only answer was the howl of the wind and the hammering of the rain.

She started walking up the hill, carefully picking her way among the gravestones, using the trees to support her along the way. As she got closer, a streak of lightning blazed across the sky, momentarily transforming the night to day. That was when she saw him, a dark, barely distinguishable lump huddling next to Sarah's grave.

Maddie moved up beside him, holding the umbrella over his head. Jon glanced up, but didn't really seem to see her.

"Jon, your father's worried about you."

He nodded and looked back at the grave. "She died two years ago today."

Maddie felt his pain constrict around her heart. "Is that why you're here?"

"I had to come. It was time."

Maddie sighed and used the headstone to lower herself to the ground next to him. "I understand."

She remembered spending the entire day next to her father's grave on the anniversary of his death. But it hadn't been storming, and the whole town hadn't been out looking for her.

"Jon, it's late and there are tornado warnings. Everyone's worried about you. *I* was worried about you."

He looked at her again, his eyes like bottomless black holes in the dark night. "I didn't mean for anyone to worry. I just had to say goodbye. I'm letting her go, Maddie."

"Come on, Jon." Maddie offered him her hand, and he silently took it but didn't make any move to stand. Another flash of lightning forked through the sky, followed by a crash of thunder. Maddie shuddered, barely holding on to her courage.

"You're in danger here," Maddie pleaded. "'We're both in danger."

He looked at her and suddenly his eyes lost their glazed expression. It was as if he was seeing her for the first time. "Maddie, what are doing out here?" Climbing to his feet, he helped her stand. "The ground's slippery. You could've hurt yourself."

Maddie glanced back down the muddy hill she'd just climbed and winced. "I came after a friend."

"Yeah, well, it wasn't the smartest thing you've ever done."

Maddie looked at him and grinned. "No, I guess not. But then, what are friends for?" She shot another uncertain glance at the hill. "How about a little help getting back down?"

"Come on." Jon took her hand and slipped his other arm around her ample waist. "We'll take it slow."

The trip down the hill took an eternity. Around them the storm raged, but Maddie knew they'd be okay. Jon reminded her more of his father at that moment than ever before. Calm. Patient. Strong. He held her firmly but gently as they made their way down the slippery slope.

They'd just reached the road when a police cruiser pulled up behind Maddie's car. Jack Banks jumped out of the vehicle and raced to their side.

"Are you two okay?" he asked, taking in Jon's hold on Maddie's hand and waist.

"We're fine," she assured him, taking a step away from Jon but giving his hand one final squeeze before releasing it. "Jon helped me down the hill."

"Down the hill? What in the hell were you doing up there?"

"I'm okay, Jack."

He took a moment longer, looking her up and down as if assuring himself she was telling the truth. Then he turned his attention to Jon. "And you, young man. Where the hell have you been? You've scared us all half to death."

Jon met the older man's gaze and nodded. "I know. I'm sorry. I didn't mean to worry everybody."

Jack seemed a little taken aback by Jon's acceptance of blame.

"It's okay," Maddie started. "He's . . ." Her voice trailed off as another set of headlights lit the night.

"That'll be your father," Jack said to Jon. "I expect you'll have a little explaining to do. And when he gets done with you, there's a little matter of a fight you and I need to discuss."

"Yes, sir." But Jon's attention was now focused on the truck as it came to a screeching halt behind Jack's police cruiser.

Nick leapt out of the cab, covering the distance between them in seconds. Without a word he pulled Jon into his arms. "Don't ever do that again," Nick said, his voice ragged. "I thought . . ." He pulled the boy closer, leaving the rest of the thought unspoken.

Jon buried his head against his father's chest. "I'm sorry, Dad."

Maddie took hold of Jack's arm and motioned toward her car, wanting to give Nick and Jon a little space. Jack nodded and took her elbow.

When they'd moved out of earshot from the others, he asked, "What was he doing out here?"

Maddie looked up at the big man. "Saying goodbye."

Jack looked confused, but he let it go. "Come on," he said, motioning toward the police cruiser parked behind her car. "I'll drive you home. You shouldn't be out here in this weather."

"I can drive."

"Lynn will have my hide if she finds out I let you drive home alone."

"How about if we don't tell her?"

Jack gave her the same glowering look he'd given Jon a few minutes earlier.

Maddie relented. "Okay, but what about my car?"

"I'll have one of my deputies come get it in the morning." He grinned. "Or maybe I'll come get it myself."

Maddie was too tired to argue further, and she didn't really have any desire to drive, anyway. Getting out here had been enough of an adventure. It had been a heck of a night, and her back hurt. She just wanted to get home and curl up beneath a pile of blankets.

She'd started walking with Jack toward his cruiser when the first pain hit her. Starting low in her belly, it snuck up on her until it filled her lower body, doubling her over on the spot.

"Jack," she moaned, leaning hard against his arm.

"Maddie, are you all right?"

She couldn't answer.

"Nick, get over here," Jack called as he shifted his arm around her back to give her more support. "I think Maddie's having labor pains."

Maddie shook her head, barely able to get the words past her sudden fear. "Too early."

Suddenly Nick was by her side, taking her weight against him, and her fear subsided. Nick would take care of her.

"Let's get her into the car," Nick said.

"Nick, it's too early," Maddie repeated, but the men weren't listening. Jack opened the back door of the car, and Nick lowered her onto the seat.

"Okay, Maddie," Nick said, leaning over her. "Just take it easy. It's been a rough night. We're going to get you to the hospital and check you out."

"I'm fine, Nick, it was just—" The rest of her sentence got lost as another wave of pain hit her.

"It's okay, Maddie. Breathe." Nick's voice reached her through the onslaught of pain, pulling her back, reminding her to take air into her lungs. "That's it, Mads. Breathe deep."

"Jack, let's see how fast you can get us to the hospital." Then to Jon, he called, "Come on, Jon. Get in."

As soon as the wave of pain eased, Nick closed the door and circled around to climb in the other. "It's going to be okay, Mads. I'll take care of you."

Maddie leaned her head against his shoulder. "It's too early, Nick."

"Nonsense. Babies come when they're ready." To Jack he said, "Get on the radio. Warn the hospital we're on the way. And see if anyone can get hold of Ted."

Jack didn't need to be told twice. "Banks to Central. Come in, Helen."

The radio crackled and popped, but finally Helen's voice filtered through. "I hear you, Sheriff. Did you find Maddie and the boy?"

"Yes. We're taking Maddie to the hospital now. Send someone out to Doc Sommer's place. Then get someone over to pick up my wife and bring her in, too."

"Your wife?"

"You heard me. Maddie may be in labor. And Lynn's her coach."

CHAPTER FOURTEEN

JON SAT SIDEWAYS in the front of the police car unable to take his eyes off his dad and Maddie in the back seat. His dad had managed to get Maddie out of her rain slicker and he sat with one arm wrapped around her shoulders, while pressing the other hand against her stomach.

"It's okay," he said to Maddie. "We've got plenty of time."

"Easy for you to say," Maddie replied with a grin just before another contraction hit. Jon bit back his own moan. Even though she didn't make a sound, he could tell when the pains came. It tore him apart.

"Just relax and go with it. Remember to breathe deep."

Maddie's hands gripped the seat while her eyes never left his dad's face. She took several deep breaths.

"That's right. A little slower, Maddie. Good."

Jon swore he'd never have kids. No way was he ever going to put someone he loved through this.

"We're almost there," Sheriff Banks said. "Another five minutes. Can you hold on five more minutes, Maddie?"

"Yeah, we're doing fine back here."

Jon had to agree with Maddie's earlier statement. It was easy for his dad to say—he wasn't the one being tortured back there.

They pulled up to the emergency entrance and things happened so fast Jon could hardly follow. A nurse brought a wheelchair out to the car and helped his dad get Maddie into it.

"Has Dr. Sommer showed up?" he asked the nurse.

"No, sir. Not yet."

"Okay. Take Maddie into labor room four and stay with her. I'll scrub up and be with you in a minute." Then he squatted down next to Maddie and took her hand. "I'll be with you in just a few minutes, Mads."

Maddie nodded, and the nurse pushed her inside with his dad close behind. Jon started to follow, but his dad stopped him.

"Jon, go with Sheriff Banks. He'll take you home."

"I want to stay." For a moment they locked gazes, and Jon thought his dad was going to make him leave. "Please," he said. "She's my friend, too."

Just then the emergency doors slid open behind them and Mrs. Banks rushed in. "Where is she?"

"There's no rush, Lynn. It's going to be a long night. She's in labor room four. Go get cleaned up and I'll meet you there."

"Anything I can do?" Jack asked, nodding at Jon.

Jon turned to his father, willing him to understand how much he wanted to stay. "Dad." He put all his feelings into that one word.

"Okay, see if one of the nurses can find you some dry clothes."

Jon smiled his thanks, but his dad had already turned back to the sheriff. "Find out what you can about Ted. Maybe Bette knows something."

"Sure thing."

Everyone rushed off, Sheriff Banks out into the stormy night, and his dad and Mrs. Banks down the same hallway where Maddie had been taken moments earlier.

Jon found his way to a hard plastic chair in the waiting room, feeling more than a little stunned. Maddie's baby wasn't due for three weeks yet, but here she was in labor—right after coming out in the middle of a storm to look for him. If anything happened to either her or the baby, Jon didn't know if he could ever forgive himself.

Suddenly Maddie's mother rushed through the emergency doors with a gust of wind, pulling Jon from his thoughts. After a moment's discussion with the nurse on duty, she descended on Jon.

"What are you doing here?" she asked.

"I was with Maddie when she went into labor."

"Why are you all wet? Come on, we'll find you something dry to wear."

Taking Jon under her wing, Mrs. Aims headed back to the nurses' station. Within a few minutes Jon was dressed in a pair of green scrubs one of the nurses had found for him, and they both settled down to wait.

Time stretched forever.

Jon had never known waiting could be this difficult. Of course he could never remember having to wait like this before, either. Maddie's mom paced more than she sat, going up to the nurses' station every ten minutes or so to ask if there was any news. The nurses were patient, but Jon figured they had to be ready to tear their hair. But maybe they were used to people bugging them.

He just sat. There was a TV in the room, but he couldn't seem to concentrate on any of the programs. For a while, he flipped through some magazines, but even that seemed too much trouble. One of the nurses offered to bring them something to drink, and Mrs. Aims paid for it. That took a whole five minutes out of the waiting process.

Suddenly his dad stepped into the waiting room, and they both jumped to their feet in unison. Mrs. Aims, who'd been sitting closest to the door, got to him first.

"Dr. Ryan?"

His dad took her hands. "You have a beautiful healthy granddaughter, Mrs. Aims."

"All right!" Jon said.

Mrs. Aims burst into tears. "When can I see her?"

"Right now. In fact, Maddie's been asking for you." His dad slipped an arm around her shoulders. "But it's been a long night, and she's tired. So, let's keep it short."

His dad started to lead Mrs. Aims down the hall, then stopped and turned. "You, too," he said, motioning for Jon to follow. "Come on."

"All right!" Jon said again, and followed his dad.

As MADDIE LOOKED down at her brand-new daughter sleeping in her arms, she knew it had all been worth it. Nothing that had gone before mattered now. Not all those months of awkwardness and swollen feet. Not the pain of the delivery. Not even Roger.

"She's beautiful, isn't she?"

Lynn brushed a strand of hair away from Maddie's forehead. "Yes, she is."

"I don't think I've ever seen a prettier baby." Maddie touched the tiny, tightly curled fingers. "So perfect."

"Thank you, Maddie."

Maddie looked up at her friend and saw moisture in her eyes. "For what?"

"For letting me be here."

Maddie took Lynn's hand. "I wouldn't have had anyone else."

Just then Nick pushed open the door and stood aside. "I brought company."

"Madeleine."

Tears sprang to Maddie's eyes as her mother crossed the room to the bed and dropped a kiss on her forehead. Then Adelia caught sight of Lily. "Oh, my, look at her. She's beautiful!"

Maddie smiled through her tears. "Isn't she?"

"Just like an angel." Adelia stroked the baby's cheek, cooing like only a grandmother could. Maddie's heart leapt. Lily would be good for them. For both of them. Maddie and her mother. And for the new relationship they were struggling to form.

Maddie glanced behind her mother and saw Jon hovering near the door.

"Come over here, Jon," she said. "Come meet Lily." Jon moved toward the bed. "You look a little drier than the last time I saw you," she teased.

"You, too."

Maddie laughed, and Jon moved closer to peer down at the sleeping infant. His gaze immediately snapped back to Maddie. "She's so little."

Maddie nodded. "Yeah."

"Can I touch her?"

"Sure."

Jon reached down and traced the baby's fingers with his own. Lily gave a tiny sigh of contentment.

"See," Maddie said. "She already likes your touch." Jon beamed. Lily had just made her first male conquest.

Fifteen minutes later, Nick ushered the group out of the room and closed the door behind them. With a warm smile, he crossed to sit on the edge of her bed.

"You did good, Mads."

"You didn't do too bad yourself, Doc."

Nick grinned and took her free hand. "Yeah, but I had the easy part."

"No doubt about it."

Nick's gaze shifted to Lily, his expression turning suddenly wistful. Maddie's heart melted. This man already loved her daughter, a child who wasn't even his.

"Nick, I've decided to stay in Felton a while longer."

His gaze slid back to her and his hold on her hand tightened a fraction, but he didn't say anything.

"I called my boss in Miami last week and told him I wasn't coming back."

Still Nick remained silent.

"He wouldn't let me quit. Instead, he extended my leave for another twelve months."

Finally Nick asked, "And Lily's father?"

"That's over."

"Where does that leave us?"

"I'm not sure." Maddie looked down at her daughter. "But I don't want to miss this time with Lily. And..." she brought her gaze back to Nick, "I think you and I need some time, as well."

Nick leaned over and brushed her lips with his. "That's all I ask, Maddie. For now."

Maddie sighed and melted into his kiss.

"Excuse me." Nick pulled away slowly at the sound of the woman's voice at the door. "Maddie, Dr. Ryan, I need to take the baby now." The nurse moved into the room and Maddie reluctantly handed Lily over.

"Oh, by the way," the nurse said, stopping at the door before leaving. "Dr. Sommer just called. He said to tell you he got stuck out at his cabin. You know, with the storm and all. And he hopes you two managed without him."

After the nurse left, Nick shook his head and laughed lightly. "The old coot. He probably got stuck out there on purpose."

Maddie squeezed his hand and stifled a yawn.

"Get some rest." Nick kissed her on the cheek. "I imagine the whole gang will be back tomorrow."

Maddie smiled and let the fatigue she'd been fighting take over. She fell asleep feeling confident everything was going to work out.

THE SUN WAS no more than a whisper of gray on the horizon when Nick pulled into the driveway in front of his house. Shutting off the engine, he looked over at Jon, who'd fallen asleep on the way home from the hospital. Nick hated waking him. The boy'd had one hell of a night. They'd all had a hell of a night.

"Jon." Nick reached over and gently shook his son. "Wake up. We're home."

Jon stirred and rubbed his eyes. "Man, so soon?"

Nick chuckled and climbed out of the truck. "Your bed's within walking distance."

Once inside, Jon headed upstairs, but Nick was too wired to sleep. He needed to think. Grabbing a beer from the refrigerator, he went outside onto the deck and collapsed into a chair.

He'd delivered hundreds of babies. And only once before had he looked into eyes that were only a few minutes old and lost his heart. Lily had captured him as surely as his own son had, as surely as her mother had.

"Dad."

Nick looked around to see Jon standing in the doorway behind him. Funny, he hadn't even heard the door open. He must be more tired than he thought. "Come on out, Jon. We've got some talking to do."

He heard the door close, and Jon crossed the deck to sit in the chair next to him. "Awesome morning."

For the first time Nick noticed the glorious reds and pinks edging over the horizon. "Yeah," he agreed. "Awesome."

They sat in silence for a while, neither one of them eager to break the spell of the sunrise.

"Maybe we should save this discussion until after we've both had some sleep," Nick suggested.

"I don't think I can."

Nick glanced at his son.

"Sleep, that is," Jon clarified. "I tried. But I've just never seen anything like it."

Nick knew exactly what the boy meant. "Yeah, newborn babies are pretty... awesome."

Jon chuckled and Nick smiled. Again, silence fell between them.

"Dad," Jon said after a few minutes, "was it my fault?"

Confused, Nick swiveled in his chair to face Jon. "Your fault?"

"You know." Jon glanced away nervously. "The baby coming early."

Nick sighed and reached over to take Jon's hand. The boy stiffened, but Nick held on. "Look at me, Jon. You've got a lot of things to account for last night. But that baby isn't one of them."

"But—"

"No buts." Nick raised a hand to silence him. "Maddie had been in labor all day long. Back labor. It feels just like a backache, and if they don't expect it, a lot of first-time mothers miss it."

"No kidding?"

"Ask her yourself." Nick let go of Jon's hand. "Besides, Lily's birth weight was within normal range. I'm not so sure she was all that early."

After a few minutes, Nick said, "Now, maybe you can explain a few other things to me. Like fighting with this joker Roc and then disappearing."

"Roc's been pushing me around all year."

"Why didn't you ask for help?"

Jon just looked at his father, as if he'd just asked the dumbest question in the world. Nick realized the boy had a point. He knew damn well why Jon hadn't asked for help.

"Okay, you needed to settle it yourself. I understand that. But you could have been seriously hurt."

"But I wasn't."

Nick started to protest but stopped himself. Still, as a parent, he couldn't help worrying.

"So is this thing with Roc over now?"

Jon shrugged. "I messed up his face pretty good."

Nick reached over and tilted Jon's head back to get a better look at the cut on his lip and the bruised cheekbone. "Looks like he did a little damage himself."

"It's not so bad."

"Okay. I understand about the fight. I don't like it. And next time, I want you to come to me. But that doesn't explain your going off on your own in the middle of a storm."

"It wasn't raining when I headed out there."

"Jon."

"You're right. I should have let someone know. It's just..." Jon hesitated, "I had to go out there."

"Why tonight?"

"Mom died two years ago yesterday."

Regret tightened in Nick's stomach. "I'm sorry. I didn't...realize."

"It's okay, Dad. Maddie told me there comes a time when you have to let go. It doesn't mean you stop loving or missing the person you've lost, but you have to get on with your own life." Jon paused a moment. "I said goodbye to Mom last night."

Nick looked at his son, love and pride welling in him. Jon was growing up, facing the difficult things in life and coming out ahead. "Jon, I've been doing a lot of thinking lately. What do you say about you and I moving back to Atlanta?"

Jon fell silent.

"Well?"

"Gee, Dad. I don't know."

Nick wasn't sure he'd heard right. "You don't know? You've been giving me hell about this place for the past three years, and now you don't know?"

Jon grinned and shrugged. "I guess I've gotten used to it here."

Nick was unable to believe his ears. Of course he wanted to stay in Felton. But who could possibly understand the capricious moods of teenagers?

"Besides," Jon added, "Maddie and Lily are here now. We can't just leave them."

Nick looked into his son's eyes and saw his own feelings reflected there. Maddie and Lily had caught Jon's heart just as they'd captured his own. The realization scared him. With Jon's heart on the line, the stakes just got a whole lot higher.

"Get some sleep, Jon. We'll go over to the hospital again this afternoon."

Jon rose from his chair and headed toward the house, but stopped and turned just before going inside. "Dad?"

"Yes?"

"I know it wasn't your fault."

Nick turned to look at him.

"I mean, Mom was drinking pretty heavy that night." Jon shifted his gaze to the floorboards. "Anyway, I know it wasn't your fault."

For several long moments, Nick couldn't speak. All the pain and guilt he'd felt over the last two years lodged somewhere in his chest. Then suddenly, it vanished, like a gigantic burden lifted from his shoulders. "Thank you, Son."

Jon shrugged and disappeared into the house.

Nick leaned back in his chair. Jon's words had released him, and now Nick believed he could forgive himself for Sarah's death.

THE WEEKS PASSED quickly once Maddie brought Lily home. Between her mother, Nick and Jon, the house always seemed full of people. Maddie loved it. Of course other well-wishers stopped in at first, neighbors, friends of her mother's. Those visits slacked off after the first week. But Nick and Jon did everything but sleep there.

Adelia, too, became adept at stopping in.

"Just dropped by to check on my angel," she'd say as she breezed in and scooped Lily into her arms.

Maddie had never known her mother to be so unconcerned about herself. She always seemed to have endless time to cuddle her granddaughter. It didn't matter where she was headed or what she wore, being late or the baby's drooling on her collar didn't seem to bother her. It was a different side of Adelia. One Maddie was growing to like.

Lily had been home about seven weeks when Adelia showed up early one evening.

"Mother," Maddie said, as she opened the door. "It's a little late for you, isn't it?"

"Nonsense, Madeleine. It's not late at all." Adelia swooped into the foyer and plucked Lily from Maddie's arms. "Come here, Angel. Come to Grandma."

Maddie rolled her eyes and headed for the parlor.

"Oh, no, you don't, Madeleine."

Maddie stopped midstride. "Excuse me?"

"You need to go upstairs and get ready."

"For what?"

"Did I forget to tell you?"

"Mother." Maddie rested her hands on her hips, waiting for Adelia to explain.

"Oh, I guess I did forget to tell you. Nick and I have decided you need a night out of the house."

"You and Nick decided?"

"Jon and I will take care of Lily."

"I appreciate the offer, Mother." Maddie shook her head and crossed her arms. "But I don't want to leave Lily."

Adelia pinned Maddie with an icy stare. "You don't trust me to watch my own granddaughter?"

"Of course. It's not that—"

"Then go get cleaned up." When Maddie still didn't move, Adelia gave her daughter a gentle push toward the stairs. "Go on, Madeleine. Nick and Jon will be here any minute."

Maddie inched toward the stairs, not quite sure what to make of this. Adelia and Nick conspiring to get her out of the house.

What were they up to?

But she finally went upstairs and took a quick shower. Afterward she stood staring at her closet, wondering what to wear. She really didn't have anything that fit since she'd had the baby. The past seven weeks she'd been living in stretch leggings and sweats. Pulling out a pair of navy linen slacks, she wondered if she dared try them on. What the heck, she told herself, and stepped into the slacks.

To her surprise, they slipped on easily and zipped without a hitch. She couldn't believe it. Turning sideways, she studied her belly. It was gone. Well, almost gone—there was still a slight swell that the pants easily hid. Maddie started laughing and dug in her closet for her favorite gray silk blouse. Okay, maybe getting out of the house wasn't such a bad idea, after all.

A few minutes later she walked down the stairs feeling like a new woman.

"Whoa! Hey Dad, get a load of Maddie."

Maddie felt her face turn crimson as Nick stepped out of the parlor and stopped at the bottom of the stairs. His eyes slid over her, inspecting her from head to toe.

"I don't think I know this woman."

"Me, neither."

Maddie took the last few steps in a hurry. "Come on, guys. Give me a break." Though in truth, Maddie loved their reaction.

"So what's this about you and my mother forcing me out of the house tonight?" she asked, feigning displeasure.

Nick grinned. "Doctor's orders."

"You're not my doctor."

Nick snapped his fingers. "I forgot. Maybe we should give Ted a call."

"Never mind." Turning to Jon, she said, "Are you sure you and Adelia will be okay?"

Jon rolled his eyes and didn't bother to answer as he disappeared into the parlor. Maddie followed and found her mother tickling Lily on a blanket on the floor.

"We'll be fine, Madeleine." Adelia didn't even look up. "Won't we, Angel?"

Maddie looked at Nick, who had nothing to offer but a smile.

"Okay, Ted's number is by the phone. And if you need me ..." She turned to Nick. "Where are we going?"

"We'll call when we get there."

"Is that okay, Mother?"

"That's fine, Madeleine. Now, have a good time."

Maddie knelt down on the floor to give Lily a kiss goodbye. When she didn't get up right away, Nick took her arm and pulled her to her feet.

"Come on, Maddie. Your mother is perfectly capable of looking after Lily."

Maddie nodded and reluctantly let Nick lead her to the door. A few minutes later they were in Nick's truck, heading away from town.

"First off," he said, "stop worrying. Lily will be fine."

Maddie smiled a little guiltily. "How did you know what I was thinking?"

"Because you're a new mom. I figure they must teach you all how to worry in new-mom school or something."

Maddie laughed and leaned back against the seat. Nick was right. Lily would be just fine with Jon and Adelia. "Where are we going?"

"Well, you have a couple of choices. We could see a movie, or there's a nice little lounge on the edge of town. Music. Dancing. A couple of drinks."

"I don't know if I'm up to drinking and dancing."

"Then how about a little time alone with an old friend?"

Maddie turned her head to look at him. "I think I can handle that."

"Good. Because I know just the place."

Maddie knew where they were heading. And she couldn't think of anywhere else she'd rather be.

"You know," he said as they pulled into the clearing at the top of the hill, "we really should give this spot a name."

"Did you have something in mind?"

Nick grinned and climbed out of the cab. "I'm working on it." Reaching into the back of the truck, he pulled out a blanket.

"You came prepared."

"I always wanted to be a Boy Scout." Nick held out his hand. "Come on."

They walked to the edge of the steep hill. Nick spread the blanket. Then, with a flourish and a bow, he motioned for her to sit. Maddie giggled, feeling like a schoolgirl.

"I'll be right back," he said.

She watched as he returned to the truck, wondering what he was up to. He returned a few minutes later carrying a basket and a small cooler.

"What if I'd wanted to go dancing?" she asked, trying to decide what amazed her more, his absolute self-confidence or how well he knew her.

"But you didn't."

Nick sat down next to her and opened the cooler. He pulled out a bottle of champagne and held it for her inspection. "As I recall, I owe you this."

She was puzzled for a moment, then she remembered. "It was missing from my breakfast basket!"

"I saved it."

He removed the cork, then took a towel from the basket, wrapped it around the bottle and handed it her. "Hold this a minute." Then he retrieved two more napkin-wrapped objects from the basket.

Crystal champagne flutes.

"You're an incurable romantic, Nick Ryan."

"Yes, ma'am." Nick smiled at her, tempting her with his dark blue gaze. Suddenly Maddie couldn't breathe. It was as if the fire in his eyes had used up all the available oxygen.

"Hold steady." He reached up with his free hand and wrapped it around hers to hold her glass as he filled it with champagne. Then he released her hand, and she felt the absence of his warmth like a chilling breeze.

"Shall we make a toast?" Nick asked.

Maddie raised her glass, her hand trembling.

"To Lily," he whispered, and touched her glass with his. He took a sip, never taking his eyes off her, and

Maddie followed his lead, letting the first taste of champagne slip past her lips.

"Your turn," he said.

"To Jon."

They clicked their glasses together again and took another drink.

"Now it's my turn," Nick said. Dipping a finger into his flute, he brought it up to Maddie's mouth, gently teasing the curve of her lips. "To us."

Maddie froze, unable to move. His eyes held her and his finger stroked her mouth until she closed her lips around it, gently tasting the last of the champagne.

"Your turn," Nick said, his voice a husky whisper.

Without speaking, Maddie imitated Nick's actions, dipping her finger into the champagne, bringing it to his mouth, tracing his lips.

Nick groaned and took both their glasses and set them down on top of the cooler. Then he gently stroked her cheek with his fingers before sliding his hand to the back of her head, drawing her forward until their lips touched.

Maddie sighed, aware she'd been waiting sixteen years for this. "You planned this," she whispered.

"Yes." He kissed her again, harder, deeper, and she felt her response in the deepest part of her. She opened to him, winding her fingers into his hair, drawing him closer until kisses were no longer enough for either of them.

Nick pulled away slightly, searching her eyes for the passion he'd felt in her kiss. He saw it, warm and glittering like a million diamonds sparkling in the silver of her eyes.

"I brought you out here to make you mine," he said as he gently lowered her to the blanket.

Maddie wrapped her arms around his neck, drawing him down on top of her. "I've always been yours."

He sought her kiss like a starving man seeks food—the sweet honey of her lips, the warm dusky taste of her mouth and the soft smell of roses on her skin. She was sweetness and passion, and the essence of love, all rolled into one. He'd wanted her before he'd known other women existed. And he still wanted her.

Raising himself on one arm, he locked his gaze with hers as he sought the buttons of her blouse and slowly unfastened them, one by one. Then he opened first one side, then the other, to reveal the creamy mounds of her breasts, barely covered by a bra of frothy gray lace. With the back of his knuckles he caressed the soft flesh, hardening her nipples beneath the fine fabric.

"Beautiful," he whispered, as he dipped one finger beneath the lace. With a twist of his fingers he unfastened the front closure and moved the fabric out of his way.

Slowly he lowered himself to one breast and kissed her lightly, then moved to the other, barely touching her with his lips. She moaned and longing surged through him, nearly drowning him in its intensity.

Maddie thought she might shatter in a million pieces as Nick caressed her. Her body answered his, deep in the pit of her stomach, at the core of her femininity, tightening, yearning, aching for more.

"Nick," she moaned, winding her fingers into his hair, pulling him up to cover her.

He moved easily, his mouth seeking hers. She grabbed his shirt, dragging it from the waistband of his jeans until her fingers could touch the warm skin of his back and trace the muscles rippling across his shoulders.

God, how she wanted this man!

He rose up on one elbow and helped her yank his shirt over his head. And then he was above her again, flesh to flesh, heart to heart, the soft hair of his chest teasing the tender skin of her nipples.

His mouth found the sensitive skin of her neck and the shell of her ear. He slipped a leg between hers, and she arched into him, seeking to relieve the pressure between her thighs. She wanted to feel him, all of him, without the layers of clothing between them. Running her fingers down his back, she tried to show him how much she wanted him. How much she needed him.

Barely able to breathe, Nick shifted away from her just enough to slip a hand between them to the belt of her slacks. He fumbled with the catch until Maddie reached down to help him, holding her slacks steady as he unfastened the belt and lowered the zipper. Then he slid his hand inside, seeking the warm, wet heat of her, both of them moaning as he found her throbbing center.

She was perfect. Hot and ready. Wanting him. He could take her all the way now, stroking her until she exploded in his arms. And he was tempted. But he wanted more. He wanted to see her, to feel her sheathed around him again.

Maddie grappled with his jeans, and he rolled away to rid himself of the heavy denim. He turned back to her, and she, too, had shed her remaining clothing. Then he stopped, stunned at the sight of her lying beside him. She'd been reed thin as a teenager, all angles and bones. Now she was a woman, soft and rounded.

"God, Maddie, you're beautiful!"

Blushing, she reached for him, and he moved over her, loving the feel of her soft skin beneath him.

"Maddie," he said as he moved between her thighs, "you may be a little tender. I'll try not to hurt you."

She wrapped her hands around his neck and arched against him. "Love me, Nick. Just love me."

He lowered himself slowly, gently seeking her soft opening. "I do love you, Maddie," he said, as he sank slowly into her. "I've always loved you."

CHAPTER FIFTEEN

NOTHING WAS QUITE the same after Maddie and Nick made love. Yet nothing really changed, either. Nick still spent all his free time with Maddie and the baby, and a new closeness developed between them. They laughed and teased and kissed, as if they'd never been anything but best friends and lovers. But they didn't talk about their future together.

Maddie wouldn't allow it.

Once Nick tried to bring it up, but she silenced him. He didn't push, and she was grateful. Though she knew that, sooner or later, it was something they'd have to discuss. She loved Nick with all her heart and couldn't imagine a future without him. But there were a number of things still unsettled.

Things such as Roger and her career.

She harbored no illusions about her feelings toward Roger. Whatever she'd once felt for him had died when he'd turned his back on her. But he was Lily's father, and she needed to face him and learn his intentions, if any, regarding his daughter.

As for her career, she knew she could never be content without some kind of professional work. Yet the idea of returning to Miami held no appeal. Living in Felton, reading her old journals and working with

Carl Katz had awakened an old dream. She wanted to write. But had she waited too long and lost whatever talent she might have once possessed?

So she put Nick off, even though she fell a little more in love with him every day.

SUMMER WAS NEARLY OVER when Maddie took Carl her first real attempt at fiction in nearly seventeen years. Waiting for him to finish reading, she tapped her fingers against the ink-stained counter.

"If you don't stop that," Carl snapped, "you're going to wake the baby, and then you'll have to wait outside."

Maddie snatched her hand away from the counter. "Sorry."

Carl grunted and returned to his reading.

Maddie moved to the window facing the street and folded her arms around the sleeping baby in the sling-carrier on her chest. Late summer. A lazy time of the year. The days stretched forever, long and hot, achingly the same.

She turned away from the window and walked back over to the counter, careful to keep her hands against Lily's back. Carl sat hunched over the typed manuscript she'd given him. She chewed on her bottom lip, waiting.

"Is it any good?" she blurted at last.

"If you'd let me finish it, I could tell you."

"Sorry."

Again the grunt. Maddie moved back to the window and stared out at the nearly deserted street. Forever. He was taking forever just to torment her.

"Interesting."

Carl's voice brought her around and she moved to sit in the chair next to his desk. "Interesting?"

Carl nodded.

"What does that mean?" Maddie had the strongest urge to strangle him.

"It means you haven't lost your touch. Only," he peered at her over the rims of his glasses, "it looks like now you finally have something to say."

Maddie broke into a huge grin and, remembering the sleeping baby, just barely stopped herself letting out a whoop. "Is there anything you can do with it?"

"Well I could print it in the *Finder* . . ."

"But?"

"It would be a waste." Carl tapped the manuscript. "If you're willing to do a little work, clean it up some, I might get somebody with better circulation to look at it. I still have a connection or two."

"Anything." Maddie inched forward in her chair. "I'll do anything you say."

Carl let out a short laugh. "That'll be a first. When you're through with it, I'll edit it."

"Thanks Carl." Maddie rose from her chair and leaned over to give him a kiss on the cheek. "You're the best."

Carl turned crimson and waved her away. "Go on, get out of here before that baby wakes up."

Maddie left, grinning from ear to ear.

It was only a short story—a small piece about a mother and daughter coming together after years of hostility. The idea had come to her right after Lily's birth. She'd written it in two days while her child napped, but it had taken her weeks to get up the nerve to show it to Carl. Now she couldn't believe she'd waited so long. Carl's approval had given her hope. True, it was only one small story, but it was a start. It gave her direction and a new dream for her future.

IT WAS A RARE AFTERNOON of quiet. Nick had gone out to his unfinished house north of town. He had a builder interested in buying the property and completing the house. Jon was off somewhere with Anna, and Maddie's mother was playing bridge.

Maddie found she liked the solitude, as long as it was short-lived. Usually she had to compete with three other people to do things for her daughter.

Lily had just drifted off to sleep in her arms when the doorbell rang. The baby stirred, but Maddie held her close, rocking her gently and murmuring soothing words.

"There you go, sweetheart." Maddie lay the sleeping infant in her crib, taking another moment to rub the baby's back. The doorbell rang again, and Maddie swore she was going to have the damn thing disconnected. "Sleep tight."

Tiptoeing out of the room, she pulled the door partially closed behind her and hurried down the stairs before whoever was ringing the bell could do it again. Out of habit, she glanced out the side window and came to a dead stop. It was a few moments before she could breathe again. She slowly opened the front door.

"Hello, Maddie."

At first she couldn't say anything. Nothing had prepared her to see Roger standing on her front porch, his arms laden with boxes wrapped in pink paper and bright pink bows.

"How are you?" he asked.

Maddie found her voice. "Fine. I'm fine."

"May I come in?" He lifted his arms a little to imply the packages were heavy.

Maddie stepped aside, wishing to God she had the nerve to tell him to get lost. "Yes."

Roger stepped through the door. "Where can I put these?"

"On the table will be fine."

He set the gifts on the hall table, and Maddie closed the door behind him. He looked out of place in her small foyer, despite the new paint and freshly finished floors. He looked too...polished. Yes, that was it. Then she brushed the thought off as ridiculous. Roger looked exactly as he'd always looked. Handsome. Well-groomed. Dressed impeccably in perfectly pressed khaki trousers and a polo shirt.

"Quaint," he said after taking a moment to glance around.

"Yes, isn't it." Folding her arms, Maddie leaned against the staircase railing. "What are you doing here, Roger?"

He looked embarrassed, glancing away while sliding his hands into his pockets. "I, uh, got your announcement."

"Oh, yes. That." Maddie had sent out birth announcements. And although a vindictive streak within her considered not sending one to Roger, in the end, she'd relented.

"You could have called and told me you were coming."

"I wanted to surprise you."

"You succeeded."

Maddie moved away from him, into the parlor. She needed a little space and a place to sit down. Roger followed but remained standing.

"Where is she?" he asked, after a few minutes of silence.

"I just put her down for a nap."

"Can I see her?"

"Why the sudden interest?"

"Look, Maddie," Roger spread his hands and sat on the couch across from her, "I know I haven't been the most supportive—"

Maddie burst out laughing.

"Look, I'm here to make amends." Roger abandoned his seat on the couch, his posture rigid with indignation. "If we can't talk about this civilly, I'll leave and have my lawyer give you a call in the morning."

"Your lawyer!" It was one of the things she feared most—that he might try to claim their daughter. She came forward in her chair, months of suppressed anger flaring to the surface. "Is that some kind of threat?"

Roger held up his hands and took a step back. "No. I didn't mean that. I just want to talk. Please, Maddie."

For a moment she glared at him, wanting nothing more than to tell him to get the hell out of her house. Then she sank back in the love seat, her anger dissolving as quickly as it had flared.

Roger had given her Lily.

Despite all the pain he'd caused her, he'd given her something wonderful, something perfect. How could she hate him?

"Okay," she said finally. "Let's talk."

"Good." Roger visibly relaxed and settled back onto the couch. He took a few minutes, studying his hands, as if trying to decide the best way to begin the conversation. When at last he looked up at her, he wore an expression of warmth and humility. Carefully constructed, Maddie thought. "Things have been going very well for me since you left," he said. "I've been offered the directorship of the Berlin office."

"That's quite a coup. Congratulations."

"Of course it means more money. More prestige."

"What does this have to do with me?"

Roger looked a little taken aback. "I want you to come with me. Both of you."

Nothing could have shocked her more. Even his showing up on her doorstep hadn't prepared her for the possibility that Roger might want to marry her after all this time.

"Why?"

Roger's face registered shock. "Why what?"

"Why do you want us to come to Berlin with you?"

"Isn't it what you want? I ran into Tom Brando the other day. He said they can't wait for you to come back to work."

"Brando wants me back so I can cover his mistakes."

Roger stared at her blankly, obviously at a loss for words. Maddie had never spoken ill of Tom Brando.

He was her boss, and one of Roger's strongest supporters in the company. But sometime during the past few months, corporate politics had lost its importance to her. As had Roger.

"I'm not going with you to Berlin."

Her words brought him out of his stunned state. "Now, Maddie, I know things have been a little strained between us. But we can work it out."

She shook her head. "No. I don't think so."

Just then she heard the low rumble of a truck pulling up outside. Nick had promised to stop over after his meeting with the builder. Maddie closed her eyes and took a deep breath. For once she wished Nick hadn't kept his word. She imagined him climbing out of his truck, barely noticing the strange car parked out front, and making his way up her walk. She heard him take the steps two at a time and cross the porch, then the quick single knock on her front door before it swung open.

"Hey, Mads." Nick stepped into the foyer and caught sight of her on the couch. With a huge smile he headed into the room. "Just wait'll—" He came to an abrupt stop as Roger rose from the couch and turned.

Silence.

The only sound in the room was the pounding of her heart as the two men faced each other. Maddie focused on Nick, though he hadn't so much as blinked an eye in her direction since spotting Roger. She registered his initial shock, and then both were gone. Hidden. He stood immobile, his face a picture of stoic calm.

"Roger," she said, breaking the silence. Still, neither man moved. "This is Dr. Nick Ryan. He's an old friend and the doctor who delivered Lily. Nick. This is Roger Day." She hesitated, wishing she didn't have to say the last two words. "Lily's father."

Nick moved first, extending his hand while dread settled in the pit of his stomach. "Roger." His tone sounded civil enough, despite the spark of anger stirring within him. "You have a beautiful daughter." Roger took his hand. "Too bad you weren't around for the delivery."

Roger's smile faded. "I don't plan to miss much else."

Nick kept his gaze locked on the other man, unwilling to be the first to break the handshake. Maddie cleared her throat, breaking the tension, and Roger pulled his hand from Nick's.

"Please, Dr. Ryan," Roger said, motioning toward the couch as he sat next to Maddie on the love seat. "Sit down."

Nick nodded, fighting the urge to grab hold of this guy and ask him where the hell he'd been for the past six months. Instead, he asked, "Did you drive up from Miami?"

"Heavens, no." Roger smiled broadly. "I flew into Atlanta. And then drove up."

Nick had seen this guy before. Or at least a dozen others like him. Slick. Polished. And as phony as a three-dollar bill. "So when are you going back?"

Roger lost any pretense of a smile. "That depends."

"You still have time before dark."

"I don't think so." His mouth curled up at the corners. "You see, Maddie and I were just making wedding plans."

Nick's gaze snapped to Maddie, but all her attention was on the man sitting next to her. She looked stunned.

"Well, we haven't exactly set a date yet." Roger smiled and reached down to put a possessive hand on Maddie's thigh. "We were just getting around to that."

Maddie shifted away from his hand, her gaze sliding to Nick. "I don't think this is the time to discuss this."

"I tell you what." Nick rose from his chair, feeling his world crumbling around him. "How about if I take off. Then the two of you can go ahead with your plans."

"There's no reason to rush off, Doctor."

"Nonsense. There's every reason."

Roger stood and shoved his hands into his pockets. "Well, Maddie and I do have a lot to discuss."

Nick looked at Maddie. "Yes. I suppose you do."

"Nick, I..." He heard the plea in Maddie's voice. He would have liked to ignore it, but couldn't. "Roger's right. We have a lot to discuss."

Nick stood for a moment, searching her face for something that would make him stay. All it would take was one word, one flicker of emotion in those gray eyes, and he'd toss this guy out on his ear. But there was nothing. Just a dark cloud of determination that ripped at his heart.

"Yeah. Later." Nodding to Roger, he headed for the door.

Maddie closed her eyes as the door slammed behind him.

"Who the hell was that?" Roger demanded.

She couldn't look at him. "I told you. An old friend."

"Come on, Maddie. Who are you kidding? The minute I turn my back you take up with some hometown boy."

Her anger boiled over. "What right did you have to tell him we were getting married?"

"Well, aren't we?"

"No!"

"Look, Maddie," Roger said, sitting back down next to her and slipping an arm around her waist. "I'm sorry if I've been a little distant—"

"A little distant!" Maddie deserted the love seat. "Roger, you were absent. Utterly and totally absent. And I'm *not* going to marry you!"

"Now, Maddie." Roger stood and moved toward her. "You're angry, and I understand how you feel, but—"

"You don't have the faintest idea how I feel." Maddie backed away from him. "I don't love you. I wonder now if I ever did. And I don't want you in my life."

"Please, Maddie. You're upset." Roger made another attempt to close the distance between them, but again she stepped out of reach.

"The only reason you're suddenly interested in Lily and me is because of your new job."

"That's ridiculous!"

"Is it? Don't forget, I know the business as well as you do. Directors have wives and families. What did you have to tell the big boys in New York to get your offer?"

"Nothing. Everyone knows I'm engaged."

Maddie leaned down to pick up a baby toy from the floor and drop it into the playpen. "Well, then, I guess you'd better find yourself another fiancée."

Roger stood rigidly still for several minutes while Maddie continued picking up Lily's things. Finally she sat on the couch and looked at him, waiting for his next attack. She knew him too well to think this was over. Roger didn't like to lose.

"This is because of him, isn't it?"

Maddie arched an eyebrow. "Him?"

"This is your petty way of getting back at me. Taking up with some country doctor."

Maddie fought down the anger. It would only get in her way when dealing with Roger. "This has nothing to do with Nick."

"Oh, no?" She recognized the glint in his eyes, the streak of ruthlessness that had gotten him through the corporate jungle and won him a director's chair. "As the baby's father, I'm sure I'm entitled to certain privileges. Extended visitation rights, that sort of thing. Who knows, I may even be granted custody."

"I don't think so," Maddie stated, still struggling with her anger, as well as the panic inching its way into her thoughts. "You're not interested in Lily."

He remained quiet, an intimidation strategy she'd seen him use often, and forced herself to remain calm.

"In fact, I think you should give up your rights to her."

"Why should I?"

"Because you don't want to spend the next six months in court." Maddie rose from the couch to face him. "Custody battles take time. And I suspect you need to get to Berlin."

Roger laughed harshly. "Don't try and bluff me, Maddie. You can't afford a custody battle."

"Oh, didn't I ever tell you about my mother? She's from an old Southern family, with lots of old Southern money." Maddie shrugged and crossed her arms. "I hate taking anything from her, but if it's for Lily..."

Roger stood still for a very long time, and Maddie thought she could almost see the wheels working inside his head. Above all else, Roger was ambitious. And practical. She was counting on those attributes.

"Keep the kid," he said with a sneer. "I don't need the headaches."

"That's what I thought." Maddie held his gaze. "I'll have the papers drawn up and sent to Miami by the end of the week." Turning her back to him, she moved to the window. "Goodbye Roger.

After a few minutes of silence, she heard him leave the room and close the front door behind him. She watched through the window as he climbed into his rental car and drove away. Only then did she allow herself to surrender to the emotions that overwhelmed her. She stumbled to the couch and sat, trembling, her head in her hands. The tears that fell between her fingers were not tears of sadness. They were tears of relief.

It was over.

Roger wouldn't come back. She knew that as certainly as she knew she'd never regret her time with him because it had given her Lily. He'd sign away his rights to her daughter, and Maddie would be free to build a home for Lily based on love, not of convenience.

Now she needed to find Nick.

An hour later she drove into the clearing on top of the hill overlooking Felton. She knew he'd be here. She saw him the minute she pulled in. He sat on a rock at the edge of the cliff, looking out at the hills and valleys below.

He didn't turn when she got out of the car or even when she walked up behind him—though she had no doubt he knew she was there. The muscles along his shoulders tensed, and she stilled the urge to massage away the strain.

"Jon and Anna are watching Lily."

Nick remained silent.

She moved to sit next to him. "They were on their way to a movie. But I bribed them."

"Say what you've come here to say and be done with it."

"Are you so sure you know why I'm here, Nick?"

He met her gaze, his eyes dark and hurt.

She could no longer resist the urge to touch him. She reached up and ran her fingers along the tense muscles of his cheek. "Don't you know how I feel about you?"

His eyes softened. "I've always known."

"Then why are you so sure I'd marry Roger?"

"I know how much you want a family." He pulled her hand away from his face and held it tight against his thigh. "How much it means to you to give Lily what you never had."

"Isn't that what we're doing? You and I? Giving both of our children the home we never knew?"

He searched her face, and she saw the despair giving way to hope. "And Lily's father?"

"You're Lily's father. In every way that counts." She leaned forward and brushed her lips against his. "As for Roger, he's on his way to Berlin."

She teased his lips again, hearing his groan as he deepened the kiss, pulling her hard against his chest. "I was so sure I'd lost you," he said a few moments later.

"Never." Maddie nipped at his mouth. "Marry me."

He pulled away just enough to look into her eyes. "Are you sure, Maddie? Really sure?"

Maddie reached up between them and pressed her open hand to his chest. "This is where I belong, Nick. Where I've always belonged. This is where my heart is."

EPILOGUE

"COME ON, Lily-pooh." Jon reached into the passenger side of the van and unfastened the harness of Lily's seat. "Let's go see Mom."

"Mom, Mom, Mom," echoed the two-year old.

"You got it, Lily-pooh. Mom, Mom, Mom." Jon lifted her from the seat and slammed the door, hoping none of his friends would see him driving Maddie's car.

Her Porsche had been traded in long ago for the latest in family vehicles, the minivan. But Jon didn't mind too much. Because Maddie had bought him his own Jeep Wrangler in the process. His dad had hemmed and hawed about that for a while, but Maddie had insisted that as long as Jon maintained his grades, the car was his. Well, grades were never a problem.

With Lily resting on his hip, Jon headed across the hospital parking lot, listening to the little girl's singsong. "Mom, Mom, Mom."

"How about saying something else? Say Jon."

"Shon, Shon, Shon."

"That's right. Shon." Jon laughed and pushed his way through the hospital doors.

"Who have you got there, Jon?" asked the nurse at the reception desk as she came around to take Lily's hand. Lily pulled away and turned to bury her head against her brother's shoulder.

"Maddie says she's going through a shy phase," he said to the nurse. "Personally," he slid one hand up to tickle the little girl in his arms, "I think she's just being a stinker."

The nurse laughed and gestured down the hall. "Maddie's in room 105. Go on back."

Lily giggled all the way down the hall as Jon continued to tickle her. "Stinker, stinker," he whispered in her ear. Maddie would love it when Lily came out with that one.

"Here we go, Lily-pooh," he said as he stepped into Maddie's room. "Mom, Mom, Mom."

Maddie looked up from the bundle in her arms and smiled. "Hi, you two. Come on in."

"Mom, Mom, Mom," Lily chanted, seeing her mother.

Jon moved up beside the bed and bent over to allow Lily to hug Maddie, while he checked out the small bundle in Maddie's arms.

"Look here, Lily," he said, straightening. "We've got a new baby brother." He couldn't remember Lily being so tiny or so fragile. But Lily didn't look too pleased when she caught sight of the infant in her mother's arms. "Can you say 'baby'?" Jon asked.

Lily shook her head sternly.

"Uh-oh," his dad said from the door. "It looks like our little princess is jealous already."

"Da, da." Lily reached out her arms, and Nick crossed the room and took Lily from Jon.

"What's the matter, Princess? Feeling a little insecure?"

"Right," Maddie said. "Between the two of you, she's spoiled rotten. She could use a little competition."

"Well, she's got some." Jon sat down on the edge of the bed, looking at the new baby. "Can I hold him?"

Maddie smiled and shifted so he could take the sleeping infant. A brother. He couldn't believe it. "How ya doing, Adam?" He slipped his finger into the tiny fists.

His dad had legally adopted Lily right after marrying Maddie, and Lily would always be his first love. But a brother! He'd always wanted a brother.

"So, when are you coming home?" he asked, not taking his eyes off the infant.

"Miss my cooking already?" Maddie teased.

"Please." Jon grinned. "I think we should have Selba move in with us permanently. We've got plenty of room now."

They'd lived at Maddie's while his dad had built their new house. Her place had been okay, and Jon had been glad they'd decided to rent it instead of selling it, but it had been a little crowded. The new house was really big and was in a clearing on the west side of town, overlooking Felton. Maddie said it was one of their favorite places when they were kids. "Selba could help you with Lily and Adam."

"And cook," added his dad.

"And maybe then we wouldn't all starve to death."

Maddie laughed. "Yeah, we'd all turn into little butterballs. Say, Jon, did you get that manuscript printed off for me and over to Carl?"

"Yes, boss," Jon said, though his attention was back on the tiny bundle in his arms. "I took it over this morning."

Maddie had taken over as business manager for the *Felton Finder.* Not much of a job for an MBA from Northwestern, his dad would tease. But Maddie claimed her job was the three of them—now four— and that she was just helping out at the newspaper. She could have fooled Jon. Besides working for the *Finder* she was beginning to make a name for herself as a short-fiction writer in a couple of national magazines.

"And what about that article you wrote for Carl last week?" she asked. "Did you get it finished?"

"Maddie," his father interrupted, moving to sit on the other side of the bed with Lily on his lap. "Can we forget about the *Finder* for a day or two?"

Maddie smiled and nodded, taking his dad's hand in hers. "Yeah. I guess you're right." Then turning to Jon, she reached out and took his free hand, as well. "Sorry."

Jon returned her smile, his chest tightening with emotion. No one could replace his mother, but Maddie held a special place in his heart.

"It's okay," he said with a grin. "I'm used to working for a slave driver. Besides," he said, nodding toward the baby in his arms, "you can bug me all you want as long as I've got Adam here."

Maddie's eyes glistened and she squeezed his hand. "We've all been very lucky, haven't we?"

Jon smiled and looked back down at his new baby brother. Yeah, he thought. Who'd have thought he'd end up with Lily, a new baby brother and a stepmom like Maddie? Yeah, he'd been pretty lucky.

HARLEQUIN®

Deceit, betrayal, murder

Join Harlequin's intrepid heroines, India Leigh
and Mary Hadfield, as they ferret out the truth
behind the mysterious goings-on in their
neighborhood. These two women are no milk-
and-water misses. In fact, they thrive on

MISCHIEF & MAYHEM

Watch for their incredible adventures in this
special two-book collection. Available in March,
wherever Harlequin books are sold.

The Wrong Twin
by Rebecca Winters

Abby Clarke is unmarried, unemployed and pregnant—but she's not *really* on her own. Not while she's got her twin sister, Kellie.

Kellie insists that Abby go to her husband's ranch in Montana for a few weeks' rest—but she insists that Abby go *in Kellie's place.* Despite Abby's reluctance, Kellie manages to convince her.

Then Kellie disappears. And Abby is left trying to explain to Max Sutherland why he's come home to find the wrong twin in his bed—a woman who looks exactly like his estranged wife. A woman who's pregnant with another man's child...

Rebecca Winters is an award-winning romance author known for her dramatic and highly emotional stories. The Wrong Twin will be available in March, wherever Harlequin books are sold.

NML-3

HARLEQUIN SUPERROMANCE®

ADAM THEN AND NOW
by
Vicki Lewis Thompson

It's been twenty years since Loren Montgomery last saw Adam Riordan, and a lot has happened since. For one thing, Adam now has an eighteen-year-old daughter named Daphne—the name Adam and she once dreamed would belong to *their* daughter. And Loren has a son, Joshua—the name they'd chosen for the son they'd hoped to have.

Is history about to repeat itself? There's no doubt that the kids are attracted to each other—a development Loren isn't entirely happy about. There's also no doubt that the chemistry between Adam and Loren is just as strong as it was when *they* were teens. All Adam has to do is convince Loren that sometimes dreams are simply put on hold....

REUNITED!
First Love...Last Love

Available in March, wherever Harlequin books are sold.

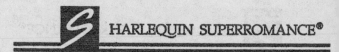

HARLEQUIN SUPERROMANCE®

WELCOME BACK TO ETERNITY!

For generations, couples have been coming to Eternity, Massachusetts, to exchange wedding vows. Legend has it that those married in Eternity's chapel are destined for a lifetime of happiness. And the townsfolk are more than willing to help keep the legend intact.

ETERNITY...*where dreams can come true.*

MARRY ME TONIGHT
by
Marisa Carroll

Everyone in Eternity is really excited. Weddings, Inc. bridal consultant Bronwyn Powell—after planning weddings for countless other people—is about to become a bride herself. The townsfolk have braced themselves for a wedding to end all weddings. The only thing Bronwyn and her fiancé, Ryan Mears, have to do is set the date—and stick to it. Nobody understands why they're finding that so hard....

Available in March, wherever Harlequin books are sold.